For Gerard

The wind beneath my wings

CHAPTER 1

Of course she'd known it wouldn't be easy, not with all those eyes trained on her every move. But this was unbearable. The heat now lay trapped under a sultry August haze that hung like a pall over the churchyard. Her throat was as parched as the Lakeland fells and her high-heeled shoes were gripping her feet in a clammy embrace. Liberty Westerman was convinced that now even the weather was conspiring against her.

Wedged between Ben and Ruth, all she could do was stare in a kind of stunned fascination at the coffin that dangled precariously across two ropes. But not daring to think about what it contained, she concentrated instead on the grave-diggers, their grey uniforms dark with dust and sweat, as they lowered the casket into the parched earth. Perspiration trickled in grimy streams down their faces and dripped from the ends of their noses.

Suddenly a snipe swooped overhead, its high-pitched, frantic scream shattering the silence. Grateful for the distraction, Liberty lifted her head to watch it, envying its carefree existence and longing for the ritual to end.

'It has pleased Almighty God to call our brother from this life to Himself. Accordingly we commit his body to the earth whence it came...'

Father O'Malley's lilting, sombre tones came to her as if from a great distance as a buzzing in her ears drowned out his words. The crazed bird faded into a distant blur and she felt herself swaying - not noticeably, she hoped. She mustn't give these people another excuse to analyse her. What would they say this time? That she was under the influence? Maybe she was. She wouldn't be the first – or last - widow to find consolation in the bottle.

According to Millie, they'd already been saying she wouldn't be able to cope alone in that big house. And at times over the last ten days she'd feared that *they*, whoever they were, would be proved right.

Her head was swimming now but she clenched her jaw and dug her tongue hard into the gap between her front teeth. Why did she let them get to her? All these people who pretended they knew her so well, who'd crawled over every inch of her life since Joe's murder and claimed her as public property.

Gradually the dizziness began to fade and she became aware of Ruth's slender body vibrating softly against her. She screwed her eyes shut, painfully aware that at this moment she was incapable of offering her daughter even the slightest comfort. On her other side, Ben shifted uncomfortably, then stiffened. How like his father. Joe never gave way to any show of emotion either.

Moments later, she opened her eyes warily and saw that the tiny churchyard, like a voracious animal, had swallowed up her husband's body. But now, instead of the persistent feeling that she was just a hollowed-out shell, she was surprised to find some scrap of comfort. At least Joe now rested side by with his family and other brave men, some of whom had defended their country against Norman invaders and marauding Scots. But how many of them, she wondered, had been as prepared as Joe to meet their maker?

She took a slow, laboured breath and shifted her gaze to the lake where a white-sailed dinghy sat becalmed. On the opposite shore, the shadowy outline of Skiddaw paled, like her future, into a hazy nothingness.

Once, this view had been one of her favourites. In happier times it had given her the comfort of knowing that a greater force than herself was in charge. But all that had changed. She could no longer make out a heavenly presence in the silk-smooth lake and murky fells.

It struck her now that maybe *He* had never been there at all. Had His existence been merely an hallucination brought on by a diet of natural beauty and flavoured by her simple beliefs? The swathe of heather across the face of the mountain suddenly seemed like a disfigurement, a gigantic port-wine stain masking its former glory.

'Keep us ever mindful of the shortness of life and the uncertainty of the moment of our death . . .'

Father O'Malley's words hung for a moment in the leaden atmosphere before sinking in. How true that was for Joe.

She blinked hard but her eyes pricked with tears. Then, with a sickening realisation, she saw that the clergyman was beckoning.

A moment of panic seized her and her feet clung to the spot. *Must* she go? She tried to shake her head. But she knew they'd be watching her. Again. Almost blindly she reached for her daughter's arm. But Ruth's face lay buried in her husband's shoulder, the mass of strawberry blonde hair shielding her eyes.

Liberty turned and swivelled – a little too quickly - towards Ben. Her head started to spin and she clutched at his arm, fighting to regain her balance. At the same moment, as if on cue, Ruth turned, pressing a single red rose into her palm. Liberty steadied herself against Ben's firm body and tried to focus on Father O'Malley's outstretched hand.

But as she reached the hessian matting covering the sides of the open grave, Ben's arm slipped away. She would have to take the last few steps alone. But the heat seemed to have sapped her will as well as her strength.

She hesitated, pushing down the urge to turn and run. That really would give them something to gossip about. Instead she forced herself to ignore the rasping sounds coming from her mouth and pressed the bud to her lips. But as she planted a kiss on its velvety crown there was no hint of its delicate perfume.

'Rest in peace, Joe,' she whispered and stepped forward.

But at that moment her stiletto caught in the rough edge of the matting. Arms flailing, she felt herself propelled forward. A gasp escaped from her throat as her bag dropped from her shoulder and the rose floated down onto the coffin as if in slow motion. The newly-inscribed brass plate flashed and the gaping hole, like the devil's mouth, seemed poised to devour her.

With a wide sweep of his surplice, Father O'Malley snatched at her bare arm. But the searing heat of his grip made her shriek and he let go as if he too had felt the burning sensation.

She pulled back, mortified but thankful that the incident had ended without further mishap.

It was then that she felt the familiar, unnatural heat-surge through her body like a volcano ready to erupt. A second later it burned into her neck and face. Not here, she wanted to shout, instinctively clasping a hand across the tell-tale signs. A pulse pounded under the wet skin.

She couldn't miss Ben's look of stoical resignation as he picked up the bag and handed it to her. But she sensed rather than saw Ruth's delicate features twisted in embarrassment. Liberty pushed a stray piece of blonde hair from her face and straightened herself up, tugging at her figure-hugging dress.

But the sound of low whispers behind left her in no doubt that once again she was public property, to analyse and criticise. She clutched at the bag, wondering what else could go wrong. Soon they'd be saying it was Joe who had kept her together and prevented her from making such a fool of herself.

She sighed. Perhaps they'd be right. He'd certainly have pointed out how ridiculous those shoes were. 'You'll never change the way God made you,' he used to say. But that had never stopped her trying. Sister Monica too had voiced similar misgivings about Liberty's fondness for unsuitable footwear.

So the shoes had been a mistake. But they gave her a couple of inches. And they made her legs look good. Surely even Joe wouldn't expect her to mope round in sensible shoes and shapeless black dresses?

For a 48-year-old she was still quite attractive. Her skin was clear with few lines round the eyes and throat. And she had a figure many 20-year-olds would envy. So why did she feel so guilty about making the most of herself?

Slowly and carefully she leaned forward to take a last look at the coffin but suddenly, and as clearly as if the lid had been lifted, she felt the glare of Joe's eyes. Distorted and bulging, they cut through her with an icy precision as a sinewy finger wagged accusingly from within an ill-fashioned shroud. The ugly gash on the side of his head, like a gaping mouth, seemed to mock her.

Liberty blinked furiously, then looked away. Father O'Malley was sprinkling holy water and concluding the burial prayers: 'Eternal rest grant to him, O Lord.'

'And let perpetual light shine upon him,' Liberty murmured quickly and crossed herself.

A hand touched her shoulder and she jumped, startled. Then she saw it was Ben's and felt herself relax. Her son's quiet strength had been a great comfort to her over the past few days but she was well aware that to press him into the role of a surrogate husband would be neither fair to him nor healthy for herself. And no doubt the local gossips would feel justified. She'd not been able to cope so she'd played the guilt card of the clinging, widowed mother. That would please them. She patted the hand and, after a few moments, removed it.

A gentle touch on her other shoulder told her that Ruth had once again copied her brother's lead. How like Ruth, never one to be left out. Liberty clasped the long delicate fingers but she couldn't look her in the eye. It wouldn't do to break down now. It was nearly over.

As Ruth took a step towards the grave, Liberty stayed back scarcely able to watch. With damp strands of hair clinging to the side of her waif-like, ashen face she looked more like one of her pupils than the ambitious young woman she was.

But Ruth was suffering more than the grief of her loss. She was feeling guilty. Her last hurtful, angry words to her father could never be unspoken now. And the memory would haunt her forever. It didn't matter that Joe had caused the row by being so uncompromising, so insulting. But that was Joe. And Ruth had sprung loyally to Crispin's defence.

Liberty sighed wishing with all her heart that she could turn the clock back, for all their sakes. But she knew her daughter well enough to realise that nothing she could ever say or do would wipe away her guilt.

As Ben joined his sister at the graveside, Liberty caught Father O'Malley's eye, mouthed her thanks and turned to go. She'd get away now, before anyone else. But as she picked her way over mounds of rough grass, she found she couldn't look at the wreathes that sweated in their cellophane covers. She couldn't face reading those little cards with their sympathy and raw sentiment. It was too soon.

At that moment she caught sight of Chief Inspector Leatheringham, half-hidden behind a tall headstone like a naughty boy hiding from his mother. Surely he didn't expect Joe's killer to turn up here? She looked away. Who knew *what* that man expected? He probably didn't even know himself.

But before she had time to dwell on it, Bob Brock stepped into her path. He had the look of a troubled man and for a moment she thought he was the bearer of more bad news. But then he leaned over, bending his dripping face close to hers. His stale breath, smelling faintly of last night's garlic, hovered between them. His words sounded forced and a little too loud.

'Liberty. . .' he said uncertainly, laying a firm hand on her arm. 'Are you all right?'

'I'm fine, Bob. Really.' She glanced round. People were watching.

'It's just that . . . you seem . . .well . . .it's not surprising. But I want you to know you can count on me . . .Susan and me. If there's anything . . . anything at all.' A strange smile, sympathetic yet smug, trembled on his lips and his intense blue eyes gazed into hers. He squeezed her arm then added, 'You only have to ask. And if you're worried about the business...'

Liberty shook her head. 'No,' she said more forcefully than she'd intended. 'No.' Why was he talking about the business at a time like this? She tried to move on but he still held her.

'Because if you are. . . I've got it all under control. You don't need to. . .' Then, realising that his words were inappropriate and unwelcome at this moment, he trailed off, his smile fading.

Liberty could only stare in stunned silence, wondering at his sense of timing. He wasn't usually so insensitive.

For a brief moment he seemed dazed. Then he slid his hand down her wrist and grabbed at her clasped hands, wrapping both of his damp palms round them.

Instinctively, Liberty pulled back. But the strong, sinuous hands tightened their grip.

While Joe was alive, Bob's admiring glances and persistent touching had been a bit of fun to relieve the tedium of office life. He was a touchy-feely person and she hadn't taken offence. Besides, while the haulage business depended on them all working together in harmony, there was little probability that Bob would be so stupid as to risk his long partnership with Joe. His mildly flirtatious comments she'd interpreted as no more than the easy banter of a close friend.

But his fond gaze at this moment was an unwelcome intrusion and she snatched her hands away roughly.

A quick glance in his wife's direction told her that Susan Brock had noticed nothing untoward in her husband's behaviour. Clearly wrapped up in a verbal assault on Crispin, she'd attached herself like a leech to his side. With her black felt hat slightly askew over limp, mousy hair, she was totally absorbed in her usual non-stop gossip, always ready to find fault with something or somebody.

Liberty noted Crispin's tortured expression as he shifted from one foot to the other in his fashionably heavy boots. But *he* was lucky. Soon he'd be free to escape with his water-colours to some isolated corner of the Lakes. If only she could escape too.

'I'm sorry, Bob. I . . . I'll catch up with you later.' Out of the corner of her eye she could see the Chief Inspector watching her.

The boughs of a gnarled yew tree shaded her as she teetered towards the old stone church. It seemed forlorn and forgotten now, the stained-glass windows lifeless in contrast to the display of colours they'd showered onto Joe's coffin during the Requiem Mass. Each pane had sent a shaft of multi-coloured light cascading into the crowded church, clothing the walls in a splendour rivalled only by the natural beauty of the surrounding countryside. She felt calmer now but it wasn't over yet.

Outside the south entrance, two men with cameras chatted to some of the regular church-goers and other locals. As Liberty approached, one by one they ceased their whispered conversations. It was obvious what were they discussing. Their silent gaze, a mixture of awkwardness and sorrow, made her feel like a freak and she passed them with her head bowed, not caring that a camera clicked close to her face.

But when she came to a small group huddled by the path, she knew she would have to stop. These were the people who had shown her nothing but kindness.

John Waggoner, his stooped figure hovering over the others, screwed up his deep-set, myopic eyes. No other church in the northern fells had such a gifted organist, but Liberty had long since realised that his wary, morose nature was better suited to funerals than weddings.

In front of him Millie Albright rubbed at her eyes with a soggy handkerchief in a rare display of emotion. The cleaner's usual sturdiness, not just of body but of will, was not always appreciated by more mild-mannered villagers. But to Liberty she was a godsend, a rough diamond who had lightened her load considerably at Lowthwaite House.

Jacob Newington stood dwarf-like by Millie's side, his two-tone grey beard and collar-length hair giving him more than a passing resemblance to one of the little people. But, far from being a source of amusement, he cut a tragic figure, dressed as always in greys and blacks. Liberty wondered how long it would be before he was back in this church presiding over the funeral of his own dead spouse.

Standing slightly apart from them, even though only moments before he'd been one of their most vociferous members, Giles Tranter eyed Liberty with his blood-shot, piggy eyes. Not one normally lost for words, he now seemed distinctly ill-at-ease, his bulging face and neck giving the impression that his shirt collar was choking him. But, although he and his common-law wife had for a long-time been her nearest neighbours, Liberty had had few reasons to visit Bagley Hall, preferring instead to leave any discussions about shooting rights and boundaries to Joe.

Other parishioners were gathering now and she hesitated, not wanting to offer any invitations but knowing she must. She swallowed and in the lightest tone she could muster said, 'Thank you for coming. I'd be very pleased if you'd . . . you'd be very welcome to come back to the house for some lunch. All of you.' How easily the lie slipped out. 'Maybe a drink or two.'

Some looked embarrassed and she could tell what they were thinking. No-one spoke for a moment. Then Millie glanced round, her face puffed and indignant.

'What's the matter with you all? Not going to let all that food go to waste, are you? Me and Mrs Westerman here, we've been working like blacks all morning.'

Mary Monkton, who was emerging from the church which that morning she'd decorated with discreet displays of white rosebuds, intermingled with ivy and laurel leaves, bent her gaze towards the gravel path. A look of dismay, bordering on panic, flickered across the faces of the rest.

She recognised fear now in their blank stares. They preferred not to get involved. To accept her invitation to visit the scene of the murder, for what was ultimately a social gathering, must seem to them at the least disconcerting and at worst threatening. Whatever their reservations, the murderer was still at large and, until he was caught, all of them were under suspicion and none of them was safe.

She pressed her lips into a thin smile and moved on towards Bretherton who waited by the gate, tears welling in his eyes. Another man, whom she didn't recall ever having seen before but presumed was a new employee at Westerman and Brock's, stood beside him.

Big-hearted Bretherton as he was sometimes called - she never knew his first name - was one of that rare breed who had the dubious capacity to soak up tragedy on a massive scale, while remaining deeply sensitive. Those who didn't know him well had no idea that, both in his private life and in his career he had overcome the kinds of nightmare situations only vaguely imagined by those fortunate enough to escape them. She'd assumed that these were the qualities that Joe had admired when he'd taken on the ex-policeman as a security man. But then again, Bretherton's eye for anyone on the take, together with his contacts in the police, would probably have been the deciding factor.

'*You'll* come back to Lowthwaite, won't you? Both of you,' she asked, suddenly jaded.

Bretherton glanced at his companion before they nodded and murmured their thanks.

Liberty turned her back on the lichen-covered gravestones but, as she approached the wooden crucifix outside the gate, she became aware of a woman reclining on the steps, under the life-sized bronze Christ. Almost like an apparition, the scene mirrored a picture she'd once seen in Joe's prayer book.

Liberty stared at the olive-skinned beauty draped in a flowing black, lace-edged dress. Jet-black locks framed her delicate features. Liberty couldn't be sure exactly what it was that held her attention but she sensed that the woman was waiting for her.

The letter appeared as if by magic, thrust towards her in a self-assured but pleading gesture as Liberty drew near. Presuming it to be a message of condolence, she took the envelope from between the heavily-ringed fingers.

But before she could utter even a word of thanks, the woman had turned, lifting her trailing skirt off the grass and was disappearing into the trees between the church grounds and the Keswick to Cockermouth road.

Liberty shook her head and glanced at the confident handwriting on the envelope. It was addressed to herself, the words Private and Confidential printed in the top left-hand corner. Why all the mystery? And who the hell *was* this woman? Liberty was irritated that, after all that had happened to her, she could be intrigued so easily. But intrigued she was.

Suddenly aware of her son and daughter by her side, she gestured towards the black limousines waiting in the shade of a nearby copse.

'You go on. I'll be with you in a minute,' she said, tearing at the envelope with her forefinger. But the implications of the short note were too far-reaching for her to comprehend in one brief moment.

CHAPTER 2

Lowthwaite House provided a welcome refuge for the few mourners who gathered there after the funeral. While its thick stone-walls kept the early afternoon heat at bay, its position on the north shore of Bassenthwaite meant that, even on such an oppressive day, a faint breath of air channelled between the fells on either side of the lake and seeped through the open windows.

Liberty watched them through the kitchen doorway as she ripped cling-film off the dishes she and Millie had prepared that morning. They stood in a small group in the dining room, each seeking the security of companionship in a situation of which only Bretherton had any previous experience. The usual platitudes and expressions of regret had dried up, leaving embarrassed silences that became impossible to fill with idle chit-chat. So they shuffled and coughed in obvious discomfort.

No-one, it seemed, wished to be reminded of the circumstances of Joe's death now that the burial was complete. The subject was avoided. Only Millie, darting in and out with plates of food for the buffet, insisted on mentioning his name.

'He was a good man was Mr Joe. Didn't deserve to die like that,' she announced, carefully laying down a whole dressed salmon and ignoring the fact that no-one had suggested otherwise.

Liberty reached for one of the bottles of Beaujolais which Ben had uncorked and left to chambray. She wished more than anything that she didn't have to go through with this charade. But conditioned by a lifetime of putting the best face on things, she didn't know what else to do.

Filling a large glass to the top, she checked that Millie was still occupied in the dining room before taking three long gulps. The smooth, slightly fruity liquid had an immediate calming effect. She started to relax, to believe she could cope, but a second later the guilt kicked in. She quickly swallowed the rest of the wine and rinsed out the glass before picking up a baguette and cutting it roughly into thick slices. It was stupid to feel like an alcoholic just because she fancied a drink, she told herself, throwing the bread into a basket.

She could hear voices now and moved closer to the door. It sounded like the conversation had turned to everyday concerns. But some unspoken code, which dictated that it was insensitive to do so, was causing a mood of uncertainty. Simple questions and monosyllabic answers were punctuated only by nervous laughter. It was obvious they were hoping they wouldn't have to endure the situation much longer.

When Liberty finally emerged from the kitchen with the bottle of wine and basket of bread, the low hum of voices ceased altogether.

'I hope you're going to eat all this,' she said impatiently, 'or maybe we should go and drag in all those nosy parkers who were hanging round Holy Cross.' She noticed the glances then, the nervous smiles that said more than words. She placed the bottle behind a large bowl of green salad and hoped that no-one would notice the missing wine.

It was Bob who broke the silence. 'Liberty, I really am worried about you living alone in this house,' he began, twisting his six-foot, two-inch frame away from his wife as they reached the table. 'I don't want to alarm you but there's a murderer still at large out there. Who knows . . . he's killed once.'

Susan grunted and dropped a handful of crisps on her plate. She had a natural optimism that Liberty envied. 'Aren't you the cheerful one? What are you trying to do, scare her half to death?'

'Of course not. Don't be so ridiculous,' Bob snapped with an impatient snort. 'I was merely stating the obvious.' He turned back to Liberty. 'I'm sorry to be so blunt but I think you should seriously think about moving.'

For a moment, Liberty was lost for words. She thrust a plate at Bretherton wondering why everyone thought they knew what was best for her.

'Lovely buffet.' Susan's words gave Liberty a moment to reconsider her reply.

'Thanks,' she said before facing Bob. 'And where do you suggest I move to?'

'You're more than welcome to stay with Susan and me . . . until you find somewhere more suitable. Isn't she, Susan?'

So he was taking the fatherly approach now, thought Liberty, relieved that his earlier, enamoured mood had subsided. But his sentiments were nonetheless unwelcome.

'I can't think why she'd want to do that,' replied Susan, taking the words out of Liberty's mouth.

'I appreciate your concern, Bob, but I have no intention whatsoever of moving from Lowthwaite House, either now or in the future.' Her forthrightness surprised her and, by the stunned look on Bob's face, had produced the desired effect. Bretherton and his companion, their heads bowed, hovered uncomfortably at the far end of the table.

Ben, who was sitting on a low seat under the window, leaned forward. Looking uncannily like his father, in a grey waistcoat and white shirt, he screwed up his narrow eyes in exasperation.

'It's no use. I've tried talking to her about moving,' he said, his lips betraying just a hint of a pout. 'But for once it looks as though she's made up her mind.' He pushed himself to his feet and sidled up to the table.

'And what does that mean?' she asked, handing him a plate and accepting, not for the first time, that he was more his father's son than hers.

He shrugged and stuffed a piece of quiche into his mouth.

Liberty knew he was right. She was rarely decisive. But she wasn't in the mood for letting the implied criticism go. 'I don't understand why you of all people can't see it would be a mistake to give up Lowthwaite. I seem to remember when you first went to live in Sheffield, you couldn't wait to come back home at weekends.' Recognising the chastened look he used to put on as a child whenever she'd scolded him, she forced a smile and added, 'And I don't kid myself it was because you were missing me - or your father for that matter.'

'Yeah, I suppose so,' he agreed, loosening his black tie. 'But it wasn't just that. The job was stressing me out.'

'Exactly,' said Liberty, wondering where the note of triumph in her voice had come from. 'That's just what I mean. This is the ideal place to relax. Where else could I find that was so peaceful?' He opened his mouth to interrupt but she answered him, 'I know. I know. How can it be peaceful when your father was murdered here? But where else would I go? It's pointless to try to run away. And you know as well as I do that I could never sell Lowthwaite.'

Ben twisted his mouth, dropped a piece of Cumberland ham on his plate but said nothing. His natural inclination was not to argue but to hold back from situations which threatened to embroil him. Typically, his father had interpreted this reluctance as a sign of weakness, an inability to hold his own, whereas Liberty had always seen it as Ben's way of protecting his sensitive nature from attack. Whatever the truth, this method of personal survival had served him well so far.

Bob gave her a side-ways look and turned away from the cheese-board to face Ben. 'But I thought you'd want to follow in your father's footsteps. Then you could live at home and look after your mother.'

Liberty could feel her anger boiling. Why did everybody want to plan her life for her? Intercepting her son's reply she tried to keep her voice even. 'I'm sorry, Bob, but Ben is perfectly happy doing what he's doing. You can't seriously expect him to pack in a real vocation to work in the haulage business - or to look after me.'

'Well he could do a lot worse,' Bob replied, taking a bite out of a sausage roll.

Liberty took a deep breath. 'He's already taken enough time off. Now I've got to get used to being on my own.'

'And what about Liberty?' Susan asked, pushing past Bob and almost knocking his plate out of his hand. 'Doesn't *she* get the chance to follow in Joe's footsteps?'

Bob almost choked. His face turned a deep red and his eyes bulged. He coughed loudly then retorted, 'Don't be so ridiculous. Liberty has no ambitions to run a haulage company.'

'Why not?' Susan persisted. 'It's half hers now.' She grinned mischievously. 'What do *you* say, Liberty?'

It wasn't something that had ever occurred to her. She hadn't the intelligence or the business acumen. A bit of typing and sorting out the wages was all she'd ever done.

'Oh, I . . . I wouldn't know where to start,' she said.

Bob looked relieved. 'Well I still think Ben would be better off at Westerman and Brock's. He could start in the traffic office. Anything's got to be better than chasing round after a load of loonies.'

Liberty knew what was coming.

Ben's voice was cold and clear. 'I think you'll find that psychiatric patients is the more politically correct term, Bob.'

Bob stared as if he'd been slapped in the face. For a moment, the silence was broken only by the sound of metal scraping on glass as Ruth, with a deliberately provocative clatter of cutlery, helped herself from the salad bowl.

Liberty handed a knife and fork wrapped in a paper napkin to Bretherton and struggled to find the right words. But the thought that she, recently bereaved, should be expected to reassure the other mourners struck her as vaguely ludicrous. She picked up the bottle.

'Wine, anyone?' she enquired, emptying the bottle into four glasses.

But only Susan took one.

At that moment Millie dragged her plump hands across her apron and snatched up the empty bottle. 'Mr Joe would turn in his grave if this house was sold off to some stranger,' she said thoughtfully, as if loath to drop the subject. 'The Westermans built this place and they belong here,' she said, before trundling into the kitchen. A low murmur seemed to add weight to her words.

Liberty picked up one of the glasses and took a mouthful of wine. But then her eyes met her daughter's across the table. Their reproach was quite clear even at a distance. Liberty thought for a moment that she was going to say something. Ruth had never let anything stop her from making her opinions known. But today, to Liberty's relief, she held back.

Whether Crispin's calming influence in the few months of their marriage was having an effect or whether teaching a class of impressionable 7 and 8 year-olds had curbed her urge to interfere in other people's lives, Liberty could only guess. But she was glad not to have to enter into a war of words with her daughter at this moment.

Behind Ruth, Crispin paced up and down, both hands gripping an empty plate, his gaze fixed on the buffet. Liberty realised that he hadn't spoken yet. But he wasn't comfortable with any kind of disagreement. He would probably be more relieved than her to avoid any unpleasantness.

It was a pity Joe had never appreciated Crispin's finer qualities. He'd found it incomprehensible that his daughter should fall for a lad whose unconventional appearance was a constant source of irritation. Joe preferred men to be clean-shaven, with Army-style haircuts and to dress traditionally in suit and tie. Crispin was probably as different to this ideal as it was possible to be. He preferred more casual clothes, like the outfit he was wearing today - an open-neck, checked shirt and black jeans. But it wasn't just his appearance. Joe's cryptic comments about Crispin's inability to secure a regular job or to take up employment-training had further widened the gap between father-in-law and son-in-law, as well as between father and daughter.

Liberty had tried to see beyond the ginger pony-tail, gold studs and tattered jeans. And her effort had been repaid a hundred times. In his ready smile and appealing, emerald green eyes, she'd recognised a kindred spirit, an insecure, lonely individual who was desperate for peace at any price. And her son-in-law had come to enjoy her company.

With a defiant glance in her daughter's direction, she drained her glass. Then she reached for another bottle of red wine and filled her own and Susan's glass.

No-one spoke. But Susan, who had been unusually quiet, was unable to contain herself any longer. Taking a long gulp, she exploded in a torrent of words.

'I don't know how you do it, Liberty. You're so calm. It must be really difficult on your own. I couldn't imagine life without Bob. Not that I can't bear to be parted from the old goat but it's the little things. . . Don't you find that? Like having no-one to sort out the car, or bank statements. . . Things like that can really drive you mad if you're not used to them, don't you think?' She nodded as if in satisfaction at her sentiments.

Liberty wondered why it was that Susan's crass insensitivity should still surprise her after more than 20 years. 'I've worked out that I have three choices,' Liberty began with relish. 'I can play the grieving widow, the plucky little woman or the spitting cat. I chose the spitting cat.' She glanced round at the horrified expressions and felt suddenly impatient to conclude the day's proceedings.

Shortly after three o'clock only Ben, Ruth and an increasingly fidgety Crispin remained. Obviously reluctant to leave her, they hung around the kitchen pleading for some little job to do, even though Millie had already packed the fridge and freezer with mounds of left-over food and cleared every dirty plate into the dishwasher. Liberty left them in no doubt that she needed to be alone.

As Crispin's ten-year-old Volkswagen and Ben's only-slightly-newer Ford Escort reversed at full throttle onto the road, she turned back towards the house. The sprawling lakeland-stone property had changed little since Joe's grandfather, John Westerman, had built it in the mid 1890's. John, a Cumbrian sheep farmer, and his Irish immigrant wife, Alice, had been given the land as part payment of a debt by the owner of Bagley Hall. Liberty never knew the details, only that their children, George and Cecilia - Joe's father and aunt - had both been born and brought up there in the early nineteen hundreds.

With a backward glance up the long drive, Liberty felt reassured that, although the manner of Joe's death might be public property, her privacy from prying eyes was protected here. A natural garden of ash, oak, sycamore and wild flowers acted as a natural screen between the house and the road.

She discarded her troublesome shoes in the hallway, savouring the cooling tiles on the soles of her feet. As she paused, reluctant to move on, a memory, locked away in her subconscious until this moment, stirred. So long ago that it almost seemed to have happened to someone else, she could see the young bridegroom scoop his bride into his arms and carry her across this very threshold. The sensation on that day, when her stockinged feet had met the floor, had been remarkably similar. So too had her feelings. A sense of relief that all the ceremony was over, anxiety as a new life beckoned and hope for the future were all suffused with sadness at the loss of a loved one.

She padded through to the kitchen and took an unopened bottle of Chardonnay from the fridge, remembering that the end for Joe's Aunt Cecilia had also come suddenly - only three weeks before their wedding. But it had been a more peaceful and less premature death than Joe's, the 69-year-old passing away in her sleep. Dr. Firth had confirmed that her weak heart had finally packed up, although previously he'd given them hope that she would be fit enough to see Joe take his vows. But the doctor had been newly-qualified and had obviously underestimated the severity of her illness.

Liberty had wanted to postpone the nuptials, but Joe had persuaded her that Cecilia would have wanted them to go ahead. Reluctantly, she'd agreed. After all, Joe had known his aunt better than anyone. She had nurtured and loved him from the moment his mother had died giving birth to him. And, in spite of his shaky start and the absence of his father, Joe had grown into the self-assured, up-and-coming young businessman Liberty had instantly been attracted to on her first holiday in the Lakes.

She managed a smile now, remembering that no matter how often Cecilia had tried to reassure her, Liberty had felt completely out of her depth. But what had changed? She ripped the cork out of the bottle and tipped wine into a tumbler. The chilled liquid felt good on her tongue.

But she knew what the difference was. Then she'd been a naïve teenager with few practical skills other than typing. Her nervousness had been understandable. Joe, the talented son of a former Major in the British Army, had a right to high expectations. But Liberty had been filled with self-doubt. The thought that one day she might be elevated to the role of mistress of Lowthwaite House had given her many a sleepless night. With Cecilia's death she'd been forced to confront her nightmare sooner than expected. She and Joe had cancelled their plans to rent a flat near Cockermouth and had moved into his childhood home on their wedding day.

But the house wasn't the problem. As if inhabited by a benign spirit, it had actually become a powerful source of comfort.

Liberty took her bag from the dresser and pulled out the torn envelope. It was time to face her fears. She took another gulp of wine and went through to the patio. She'd read somewhere that, in the eighteenth century, nature was the medium through which man had explored his spiritual being. She understood that better than most, the ever-changing scene from the back of the house rarely failing to either inspire or overawe her. At that moment her thoughts were overtaken by the brooding power which surged through the fells, threatening to erupt.

Hazy peaks blended with a heavy, white-grey sky, and the heat, almost tropical in its intensity and humidity, made her think of less troubled times. On clear summer days she'd sat here and gazed at the lake, like a huge mirror, duplicating the mountains which kept a watchful eye from every side. And in the winter, they'd been covered with a dusting of snow, so fine and powdery it looked as if it had been sprinkled through a giant sieve.

But whatever the weather, Liberty never doubted nature's capacity to seal the fate of anyone who may be tempted to treat it with anything less than the greatest respect.

The sweet scent of honeysuckle drifted across the patio as she placed her glass carefully on the ornamental iron table and dropped wearily into a chair. Perspiration glistened on her fingers as she lifted the cream vellum out of its matching envelope. There was no address, no greeting and, more disappointingly, no signature. She placed the page on the table and, aware of a tightness in her throat, sipped from the glass as she read the text for the second time that day.

The few words, written in a bold sweep across the middle of the page, were not difficult to understand, yet she struggled to comprehend their message. She read them again, this time aloud: '*Joe had many enemies. One of them killed him. Believe me, his murder was premeditated.*'

She placed a trembling hand over the words and dribbled the last of the wine into her mouth. She was having trouble taking it in and her head felt as if it were floating. It was all so melodramatic and unreal. But the words, stark and unambiguous, seemed to leap out from the page to assault her. She couldn't ignore them.

She slumped back against the chair and put a finger on the small, painful pulse that throbbed in her temple. What was she supposed to do now? Go to the police? But Chief Inspector Leatheringham was convinced Joe had been killed by a burglar who'd panicked. He'd no doubt dismiss the note as a hoax.

She gazed at it again. Her initial observation, that the writer must be fairly well-educated - not only because of the use of the word *premeditated* but also because of its correct spelling - gave her little satisfaction. But no other clue presented itself. Whether the woman outside the cemetery was the author, or someone else, she had no idea. She folded the paper and returned it to its envelope. She must have some time to think.

Not since the morning of Joe's death had she ridden Merry, the mare she'd inherited when Ruth had swapped horses for boys. She'd lost her confidence, imagining that Merry would sense her uncertainty and throw her off. But now the familiar urge to feel the air on her face and enjoy the freedom of the fells became too strong to resist.

She changed quickly into jodhpurs and T-shirt and hurried down to the paddock. She could see Merry standing by the gate flicking flies away with her tail and shaking her mane. But as Liberty approached, the horse bolted, kicking her back legs high into the air. So that was how it was going to be. Uncurling the head collar from the fence, Liberty made up her mind not to be put off, either by this unwelcome rejection or by the knowledge that she must retrieve the bridle and saddle from the stables.

Jacob had assured her over a week ago that he'd bleached the floor after Detective Chief Inspector Leatheringham and his scenes-of-crime officers had finished their fingertip search. But, as she lifted the bar off the heavy wooden doors she braced herself. For a moment she blinked, trying to adjust to the dim light, then her eyes sought the spot, in the second stall. But a thin layer of wood-shavings was all she could see. She twisted her face away and stumbled past, towards the tack on the far wall. The muted tread of her riding boots was only faintly louder than the pounding of her heart.

A vague awareness that she had at last begun to surface from a living death accompanied her as she let Merry take her along the edge of the lake. The warm body between her legs felt strangely soothing and liberating but she couldn't remember ever having ridden in such exhausting weather. Kicking the 14-year-old chestnut into a trot, she felt light-headed yet, at the same time, heavy-limbed. Perspiration seeped from under her riding hat and ran down the side of her face.

The bridal [*bridle*] paths across land belonging to Bagley Hall were familiar territory but now the shade of the wooded area beyond was too inviting to resist. She slowed Merry down and with a gentle pull on the bit turned the sweating horse onto the soft earth where pools of sunlight dotted the ground between the firs. There was no path here and she was well aware that it was only a matter of time before the way would be blocked, but she pressed on, not caring. As she trekked deeper into the forest a thick carpet of pine needles cushioned the sound of the horse's hooves. All she could hear was Merry's regular, almost melodic breathing and the cracking of twigs.

Leaving the mare to find her own way through, she leaned forward in the saddle to avoid bushes and branches which were bound together in a strangle-hold by suffocating creepers and briars. The effect was of a denseness, like a thick, pine-scented blanket, which cocooned her. It blotted out not just the heat and light but the horror of the last few days.

Suddenly she imagined she was a baby once again, held safe in her mother's womb. But now the tangled branches fused into a solid mass, bringing the horse to a halt. In an exhausted daze, Liberty buried her face in the mane and wrapped her arms round the wet, silky neck. As if sensing her mistress's need, Merry stood still and waited.

It took Liberty a few minutes before she could rouse herself. But when she did, her head felt clearer and her thoughts once again fixed on the note. But what if it *was* a hoax? One of those vicious poison-pen letters that mentally unbalanced individuals send to people in the news. Local and national newspapers had been full of the story. Most had even included a photo – the one of Joe standing behind her, his hands on her shoulders. It hadn't been a particularly good one of either of them. A strong wind had been blowing, revealing a darker re-growth under her blonde highlights, and strands of wispy hair had lain, as if frozen, across her face. Her smile, too, had been fixed, the gap between her two front teeth seeming more pronounced than ever. Joe, whilst looking his usual immaculate self, with not a dark wavy hair out of place, seemed tense, his eyes reduced to slits and his thin lips twisted under his moustache as if he were in pain. She thought the photo must have been taken at a church fete some years back but she couldn't recall who'd taken it. Or how it had fallen into the hands of the press.

Liberty ran her fingers through the ruffled mane. Maybe this mystery woman had seen the coverage and decided, for reasons best known to herself, to cast doubt on the police investigation? But then, if she were up to no good, surely she wouldn't have brought the letter in person. Maybe she was just the courier? Liberty wondered, struggling to get to grips with the letter-writer's motives. Had he or she some firsthand knowledge? Had Joe pushed one small business too many into liquidation? Or made the fatal mistake of sacking a driver who had his own way of settling a score? But if that were the case, why hadn't this informant gone to the police? And what about the woman herself? Where did *she* come into it? Gripping the reins tightly Liberty gritted her teeth. At this moment she didn't want to think about that.

Only one thing was certain, she decided, turning Merry round and heading for home. Whatever her reservations, she must take this new piece of evidence to the police.

CHAPTER 3

It was later that evening, after she'd showered and changed into navy silk pyjamas, when Liberty decided that if Joe really did know his killer, it might be helpful to the investigation if she could come up with, at the least, a list of associates and acquaintances. She poured herself a large vodka and tonic and made up her mind to look in his study.

No-one had been in the small upstairs room since the police had given it a cursory glance the day after Joe's death. Liberty hadn't felt up to facing the inevitable clear-out of his personal effects and had left the study locked, concentrating her attention instead on packing up Joe's clothes for the charity shop in Cockermouth. A dusty, airless smell greeted her as soon as she unlocked the door but, instead of finding it overpoweringly stuffy after being closed up for so long, Liberty became immediately aware of an almost unnatural chill. She shivered and glanced about her.

Joe's prized collection of stuffed fish still dominated the room. The glass cases, each one displaying a glistening specimen, some with rows of needle-sharp teeth, covered every available wall-space. Their eyes, cold and staring, seemed to be watching her now from their artificial reed beds. Pike and perch had been among Joe's favourites but salmon, trout and freshwater eels made up the rest of the collection, most of which he'd caught himself in nearby streams and lakes.

Joe had never trusted anyone to dust his trophies. She recalled the time some years ago when she'd suggested that Millie should spring-clean the room and he'd snapped: 'And give that woman a chance to go tittle-tattling round the village with all my business? Not likely.' That was when he'd taken to locking the door.

The cleaner's little habit of reading any letters left lying around, although annoying and at times intrusive, hadn't at first posed an insurmountable problem for Liberty, who'd felt that Millie's value lay in her capacity for hard work rather than in her diplomacy and social graces. Of course Joe had seen it differently. Joe always seemed to see everything differently. But when he'd urged Liberty to find a replacement, for once she'd managed to get her own way.

It was a strange sensation standing in this room without Joe. Never before had she been here alone. It had crossed her mind on more than one occasion that perhaps Millie wasn't the only one he'd wanted to keep out. But she'd accepted that Joe liked his space and privacy. And she'd not been offended when he'd suggested she give the room 'a quick going-over' while he was there. On the contrary, in the early days she'd seen it as a rare opportunity to spend some time alone with him.

So it was with the eye of a relative stranger that she now viewed the room. The curtainless, north-facing window let in little of the fading light, casting a gloom over the frayed carpet and scuffed furniture. She'd never realised how shabby and neglected it all was. The roll-top desk in particular, a legacy from Joe's father, had been almost vandalised. The top had been left rolled-up and, in the half-light, its gouged and pitted surface was clearly visible. The tarnished knobs and brass label-holders on the drawers she noticed as if for the first time. It struck her as odd that he'd never shown any interest in maintaining the 19th Century heirloom, while the cases of stuffed fish were polished to perfection. With a glance at the dark cracks in the leather swivel chair, she wondered what it was that had made him so reluctant to modernise this room.

Seating herself at the desk, she took a sip of vodka and decided to tackle the two large drawers on either side. As she'd expected, everything was meticulously organised. The chequebook stubs and bank statements reminded her that sooner or later she'd have to face the task of sorting out Joe's finances. But, for the time being, she could manage on the small amount in her own bank account. A gold pen that Ruth had given Joe for his last birthday, his fifty-fourth, caught her eye. But she couldn't afford to get bogged down in empty sentimentality and turned her attention quickly to a pile of insurance forms and bills. Nothing there of much use, she concluded, taking a long drink and pulling an assortment of papers from one of the cubby-holes at the back of the desk. She hoped these would be more useful.

A number of letters headed Joyce, James and Jackson (Solicitors) dealt with an alleged breech of contract with a brewery in Blackburn. She hadn't heard any mention at the depot of an impending court case but then she didn't know everything that went on. Other correspondence, from a stockbroker named Gillibrand and Turner who had offices in London, referred to various shares which Joe had bought and sold over the past six months. She couldn't recall him ever mentioning any share deals. And yet some of them involved substantial amounts. She flicked through them again, noting one particular reference to a cheque for £20,000.

For reasons best known to himself, Joe had obviously decided not to tell her about his investments. Of course, he wasn't in the habit of discussing every little detail of their finances with her, but £20,000 was hardly a small amount. She bit her lip and drained the glass. Why had Joe kept her in the dark about so much? She replaced the letters in the cubby-hole with a feeling that she'd had enough for one day. But what was more important? To nurse her wounded pride or to find the names of all those Joe had dealings with?

She'd worked at Westerman and Brock's for a few hours a week ever since Ben's first day at St. Margaret's Catholic Comprehensive in Cockermouth. But she'd rarely dealt with Joe's correspondence except when one of his ever-changing secretaries had been either sick or on holiday. Or, as had happened the day before his death, when the latest one had left without warning.

Liberty calculated that Joe must have dealt with hundreds of people she'd never even heard of: customers, suppliers, bankers, insurers, civil servants, the list was endless. Most of those names and addresses would be in Joe's office at the depot, but he must have kept *some* here. She drummed her fingers on the desk reluctant to give up just yet. He'd often had to sort out one crisis or another, even in the middle of the night. So where would he ...?

Of course, his briefcase. How stupid of her to forget that. She bent down and pulled the black leather case from under the desk. But it contained only the basics: keys, assorted pens and pencils, a calculator and a mobile phone. No letters and no diary or address book. And there'd been nothing of that nature in the personal effects the police had returned to her. She'd have to wait and search his office when she returned to work. But what now? Another drink seemed the obvious answer.

But when she returned with a glass of red wine she was beginning to feel the pointlessness of it all. Nowhere was there even a scrap of paper which had outlived its usefulness. Everything was consigned to a drawer or compartment in the same compulsive way that the rest of his life – including her – had been compartmentalised.

It was almost as if Joe had deliberately eliminated everything that might have provided any clues and she was left with the distinct impression of being a stranger in her own home.

Through glazed eyes she stared at the slimy-looking skin of a stuffed eel above the desk. It seemed unbelievable that the man she'd been married to for 29 years could be so clinical and calculating in his quest for secrecy. She'd always thought she understood him, even if, at times, she'd felt left out of his plans. There'd been occasions - especially after Ben and Ruth had reached an age when they were able to be left on their own - when she would have liked to go with him on one of his weekend fishing trips. But he'd never suggested it and she'd never asked.

She'd always assumed that his difficult childhood had moulded an independent spirit. He'd needed to be alone and she'd never begrudged him the space.

But it wasn't just a little peace and quiet to pursue his own interests which Joe had sought. He'd systematically blotted her out of his life - in the same way he'd so painstakingly wiped out any trace of his past or present. She thought of some of the things she'd accumulated over the years: childish drawings and cards lovingly made by Ben and Ruth; memorial cards of friends and relatives; a reference written by Sister Monica 32 years ago; newspaper clippings of family announcements; and the bill for £12 2s 6d from the Lakeside Hotel for their two-day honeymoon.

Where were Joe's mementoes? Had he kept *nothing* of their life together? But not one photograph adorned the room. Obviously, she and the children had meant less to him than his precious fish.

A sudden and unnerving anger gripped her and she clenched her teeth, banging the desk-top shut and almost trapping her thumbs. But *who* was she angry with? Joe because he'd stopped loving her? Or herself because she'd let him? She downed the wine, not caring to savour the taste. A second later, the feeling had passed, replaced by a familiar lethargy and an all-consuming guilt.

She sank forward, her arms splayed out across the lid and a long, low groan, somewhere between a sigh and a sob, broke from the back of her throat. She pressed her face into the ridged top, gaining some slight satisfaction from the dull pain across her nose and forehead. How could it have gone so wrong? How *could* she be left with such hateful thoughts about the only man she'd ever loved?

'Why, Joe? *Why*? she whispered, squeezing her eyes shut in an effort to pinpoint just when it had all started to go wrong. But it was impossible to know. She lifted her head up and wiped her eyes roughly. It was then that the nightmare returned, more vivid and terrifying than ever. But this time it was different.

This time Joe's eyes were closed as he lay, bloodless and rigid in his coffin. This time his old school tie wound itself like a serpent round his neck and body, the blue and red stripes twisting in a deformed spiral. His thick wavy hair and moustache, jet black against the pallor of his skin, quivered frenziedly as if caught in a storm. But it was the starkness of the deep red stain, thick and clotted on the satin pillow beneath his head, that made her blood run cold.

Throwing herself back so violently that the chair threatened to topple, she tried to erase the image by concentrating her gaze on the dead pike which grinned down at her. Moments later, her head flopped onto her arms. Exhausted, she collapsed in a fit of sobbing.

But between the fitful gasps, her admittance of defeat gave her no sense of release. The truth about Joe's death still remained a mystery. And, in all likelihood, would remain so. The police were on the wrong track. That much was clear. They were no nearer now to solving the case than they were ten days ago. But what could she do about it?

A quotation, used by Sister Monica to spur on her charges at St. Hilda's, came unexpectedly to mind: 'By perseverance the snail reached the Ark.' She gave a dry laugh. The simple quotation, linked with a fond memory of the strict but fair headmistress, had a sobering effect.

She pushed herself up onto her elbows, pulled a tissue out of the pocket of her pyjamas and blew her nose with a vigour and energy that surprised her. Her head held high, she swivelled the chair round and studied the room with renewed hope.

The bookcase caught her eye first. Perhaps Joe's address book was tucked away on one of its shelves? She fell to her knees, her eyes quickly scanning the titles and her fingers flicking along the spines of the books. It was only when she came to the Douay version of the Bible that she stopped.

The words of this holy book had been a source of inspiration for her on other occasions. Could it have anything to offer her now? But then why should it? God's words were empty and meaningless, hadn't she found that out to her cost? She'd always done her best to live a good life and help other people. Now look at her. Alone and tormented.

But something - whether some inborn compulsion, years of indoctrination or just plain superstition - prevented her from leaving it unopened. With an irritated grunt, she dragged the leather-bound volume from its place.

The newspaper cutting, which had been tucked between the Bible and the Oxford Dictionary, fluttered to the floor. For a brief moment she stared at the yellowed scrap, then picked it up, carefully unwrapping its worn edges. The front page of the Cumbria Post gradually revealed itself and she saw the headline, in a larger and bolder type than usual: TWO DIE AS BOMB RIPS THROUGH HOTEL.

She glanced at the date and was surprised to discover that it had been four years since terrorists had attacked the Fellside Hotel at Blenhurst. Liberty recalled some of the details of the case which had received a vast amount of publicity nationally as well as throughout Cumbria. At the time, it had seemed incredible and quite unnerving that a hotel not 20 miles away should be chosen as a terrorist target.

The IRA had come under suspicion, she recalled, but had never claimed responsibility. As far as she could remember, the blame had initially been put on a breakaway group which, it was thought, had set up in the northern fells. But after a thorough search by police and security forces, the group responsible for the massive 1000 pound device had been no more easily detected than the reason behind the bombing. It had been concluded by most commentators that the aim could only have been to sabotage the peace process. She shook her head and wondered whether some things would ever change.

Scanning the details more closely, she became intrigued to know why Joe had kept this particular cutting for so long. Surely he must have seen it every time he took out either his Bible or the dictionary?

The dead woman, Vera Dougherty, a 42-year-old shop assistant from Liverpool, had been on holiday with her 17-year-old daughter Sarah. The bomb, which had been hidden under a chair in the foyer, had killed the mother outright, but her daughter - according to the report, a bright, lively student at 6th Form College - had died several hours later from extensive injuries. Liberty felt a pang of motherly anguish for the lost years of the girl who, if she'd lived, would have been Ben's age.

The clipping gave further, brief details of the tragic family's background. Recently divorced, the mother was taking a few days' break with the eldest of her three children. Two boys aged 12 and 15 had been staying with grandparents at the time. Were they still being looked after by those same grandparents, she wondered, lovingly shielded from a violent world? Or had they grown into hardened young men, psychologically scarred and intent on revenge for a family torn apart?

But that was nothing to do with Joe. Gazing up into the lifeless, glazed eye of a conga eel she hoped that, whatever had happened to them, they would find some happiness in their young lives. She folded the page along the well-defined lines and replaced it between the two volumes.

The rest of the bookcase revealed little. Joe's collection of novels took up most of the space on the shelves. James Joyce was a favourite, along with Graham Greene, G.K. Chesterton and Hilaire Belloc. His reference collection was more varied: books on fishing, the history of Ireland, the Lake District and church architecture mingled with volumes on law, accountancy, economics and transport.

Then she noticed it. The crumpled red card stuck out only a fraction from between the pages of 'A Fisherman's Guide to the Lake District.'

She opened the book where the bookmark lay and searched the pages. But it soon became clear that the information about trout fishing on the Derwent, bore no relation to her present search. The book-mark, however, proved more interesting. Crudely cut into the shape of a 3-leaf clover, the thin card was inscribed, in black ink, with the words, Irish Rebellion Force. It meant nothing to her.

She turned the card over and noted the rusty mark left by a small safety pin. Fragments of sticky tape, which had probably kept the pin in place, were still visible. As a badge it was a childish attempt, not the kind of thing Joe would ever have worn. And yet its presence, in a book that she had given him only last Christmas, was surely significant.

His interest in Ireland, its culture and its writers was not a new revelation to her but now she wondered vaguely whether this preoccupation with the birthplace of his grandfather might have some connection with his death, although precisely what she couldn't imagine.

As she pondered the badge's significance, her eyes pricked with fatigue and her neck and shoulders ached. For the first time since Joe's death, the attraction of bed was irresistible. She'd done all she could here. Tomorrow she would pay a visit to DCI Leatheringham.

CHAPTER 4

She awoke at dawn with a start. Her first thought was relief that nighttime, with all its dark spirits and troubled dreams, had passed in comparative peace. She didn't linger, quickly putting on her dressing gown and throwing back the heavy brocade curtains to reveal a fresher-looking day. A faint breeze from the south was blowing between the fells, swaying the branches of the oak trees which formed a guard of honour down the right side of the garden almost to the edge of the lake. But the early morning sun, rising behind Skiddaw, gave no hint of a break in the heat wave.

Liberty hurried downstairs to make some breakfast, but as she dropped the slice of whole-grain toast onto the plate in front of her she knew she couldn't eat it. She poured steaming tea and glanced at the clock over the Aga.

It was still only 7 o'clock, too early to ring the police station. Or was it? The incident room would be manned all night, surely. But, as much as she wanted to get this visit out of the way she still couldn't bring herself to ring yet.

Her long-held fear of being a nuisance niggled at her as she filled her time over the next two hours rummaging through drawers and cupboards in a last concerted effort to find anything that might lead to Joe's murderer. All the time she was conscious that today she must get a grip on herself, to try to keep her wits about her. But, as she'd expected, the search revealed nothing.

At nine o'clock prompt she rang the police station. Her call was answered immediately but her request to see DCI Leatheringham was greeted with a mixture of caution and indifference by the female voice at the other end.

'We're not expecting him in today, Mrs Westerman.'

Liberty hadn't expected that. But her information was too important to trust to anyone of a lower rank. She decided to insist. 'I have some important new evidence about my husband's murder. It's essential that I speak to him today, or to someone else in authority. Can you arrange that?'

'I'll have to see. You'd better hang on.'

Several minutes later the voice confirmed that the Detective Chief Inspector had been located and would be able to see her at four o'clock.

Her first reaction was disappointment and frustration that precious time might be wasted. But then she could always call in at Westerman & Brock's to see Bob earlier than she'd planned. The visit would help to break her in gently before she returned to her desk.

But, for the next couple of hours, it seemed like half the parishioners of Holy Cross had conspired to ensure she had little time for feeling lonely. Either that, or they were curious to discover whether she'd gone over the edge yet. She was on her third phone call, assuring Mary Monkton that she would think about coming back to the church flower-arranging group next Tuesday evening, when Jacob arrived. As usual, he gave a short, sharp tap on the French windows which she'd already flung open to allow the stale, warm air in the kitchen to circulate.

She noticed straight away the dark semi-circles magnified behind his thick-rimmed glasses. The tic too was more noticeable. Normally a faint, intermittent trembling of his top lip, it had developed into a constant twitching which pulled up one side of his mouth under the thick stubbly beard and made him look like a snarling though not vicious dog.

'How's Ellen?' she asked, vaguely wondering what she would say if he answered truthfully: 'She's dying.'

'As well as can be expected, thank you, Mrs Westerman.'

Liberty was used to the understatement which characterised his replies, but she would have preferred it if sometimes he would confide more in her. The whole parish knew that Ellen Newington had only days to live but Jacob never spoke voluntarily about her illness either to Liberty or, as far as she was aware, to anyone else.

The news had first been conveyed to her in early June by Millie who lived next door to the eldest of Jacob's four sons. Since then Liberty had maintained a kind of charade in which she admitted to knowing that Ellen was sick without ever mentioning the stomach cancer itself or its consequences.

She nodded absentmindedly. He'd been tending the gardens at Lowthwaite since before her marriage and she looked on him as a friend of the family. But Jacob, always mindful of the employer/employee relationship, insisted on maintaining a strictly formal code of conduct.

'Is there anything particular you want me to do today, Mrs Westerman?' He always asked the question no matter how many times she told him she was happy to leave the garden to him.

'No, nothing Jacob, thank you.'

'I thought I'd sort the orchard out, like. The damsons need picking sharpish and the apples aren't far off. The lawn's in need of a mow too. If that's all right with you?'

'Yes, that's fine, Jacob,' she replied. 'Whatever you think.'

She stood for a moment watching the small, pitiful figure shuffle across the patio in the Jesus sandals he preferred in hot weather. But she could never tell him that, for safety reasons, she would prefer him to wear his heavy brogues.

His grey hair, which fell from a central parting into a thin, uneven fringe at the front, hung thick and limp over the collar of his sweat-stained black shirt. She'd never known him be so careless about his appearance and wondered whether he was coping. But, according to Millie, he'd refused all offers of help from neighbours and parishioners, preferring instead to soldier on alone. Even his sons and their wives, if Millie was to be believed, had been kept at bay.

Through a blur of Russian vine she caught sight of the crimson and canary yellow dahlias he'd planted by the meadow in the spring, when life had seemed to promise so much, not only for him and Ellen but for herself and Joe. She decided to cut some for the dining room table.

Picking her way along the gravel footpath overgrown with withered lavender, she wondered how much longer he could keep going without becoming ill himself. It wasn't just his wife's condition that was dragging him down. The garden too seemed to be taking its toll on him.

Only a few months ago, in spite of being not far off his sixtieth birthday, he'd still shown some of the sprightliness of his youth, mowing and trimming the large lawn in not much more than an hour. Now it took almost half a day of pushing and pulling the heavy petrol mower, his face set in a painful grimace.

Pausing to admire the deep purple cones of a buddleia which hung over a bed of delphiniums, she took in the sweet, reviving scents which once were so familiar yet now seemed alien, as if she were smelling them for the first time. At least this part of the garden didn't need much looking-after at this time of year, she thought, with a grim foreboding that Jacob might not be with her much longer.

At half past ten Ruth rang, an obligation she'd fulfilled every morning since her father's death. 'I thought I'd pop round later this afternoon,' she said, the tension in her high voice unmistakable. 'Only term starts tomorrow so I might not be able to get to see you as often. I wish I didn't have to go back so soon.'

In previous years, Liberty would have made some remark about seven weeks' summer holiday being quite sufficient for anybody. But today neither she nor Ruth was in any mood for teasing. She chose her words with care, omitting any mention of her forthcoming visit to the police. 'I'm sure you've got better things to do with the last day of your holidays than keep me company. Besides, I have to go out later. Bob's desperate for me to return to work so I thought I'd call in at the depot this afternoon.'

'Oh!' Ruth sounded put out.

'Yes, he's mowed under with work.'

'Well maybe he should consider taking on a new partner. Why don't you go for it?'

'Oh, it would be very tying. I don't think. . .'

'Don't be so negative,' Ruth interrupted. 'You'll have plenty of time on your hands now. You need to keep busy.'

For a moment Liberty said nothing. Whether she had more time or not she had no intention of taking on something that was beyond her capabilities. She had enough problems just getting through each day without a business to worry about. But it was easier not to disagree.

'I'll think about it,' was all she said.

The thought occurred to her as she put the phone down that she might sell her share of the business - or, more accurately, Joe's share.

But after four more visitors from Holy Cross, bringing with them an assortment of home-grown fruit, flowers and good wishes she decided she must take more time before she committed herself to a decision which would shape the rest of her life. Did she really want to be stuck at home for the rest of her life, the object of pity and gossip?

It was fast approaching lunch-time and she made up her mind to forego the visit to Westerman and Brock's until another day. Instead she'd have a leisurely lunch and a glass of wine. Then she'd use the afternoon to take down the cards of condolence which still littered the house and reply to some of the letters she'd received.

It took only three minutes to reach the police station, a white, pebble-dashed detached house separated from the Keswick to Carlisle road by a small paved area. DCI Leatheringham was waiting for her in front of the duty desk.

Liberty had forgotten what a strange-looking man he was, with a shock of black hair and thick eyebrows which joined in the middle and hung over his eyes like an awning over a shop window. His nose was long and bony but a kink in the middle made her think that it might, at one time, have been broken, possibly in the line of duty.

'Come with me, please, Mrs Westerman,' he said, leading the way into a small interview room.

She followed, keenly aware that Joe would always have insisted on her going first. But perhaps police protocol didn't allow for social niceties.

From behind she could see that the Chief Inspector's lanky frame was bent and angled, his round shoulders pulling the hem of his badly-fitting jacket out of shape. The smell of body-odour combined with cheap after-shave overpowered her and she had to turn her head to one side to avoid its full force. Hopefully a man's attractiveness was no indication of his efficiency, she told herself. But when he turned and smiled, pointing to a chair on the near side of a rickety table, she noticed a white foam spilling out from behind uneven, yellowing teeth.

Barely managing a nod, she fought to suppress an untimely and overwhelming feeling of revulsion. She couldn't recall the same reaction when he'd spoken to her in the days after Joe's death. But then she could recall very little of that time.

She perched on the end of the chair, running damp palms nervously up and down her earth-coloured jeans and wishing that the room were not so warm. The smell was really quite nauseous. The Chief Inspector settled himself comfortably, an elbow across the wooden back of the chair and the other hand poised over a ball-point pen and a clean sheet of paper. Liberty was surprised that there was no tape recorder. Then she reminded herself that she was not a suspect.

She waited for him to speak, well aware that his appearance of relaxed unconcern had been cultivated over many years of dealing with the devious and demented. But she had nothing to hide.

'The sergeant tells me you have some new evidence?'

Why did she have the feeling that he didn't believe that? She placed the envelope containing the note on the table and slid it across to him.

'A woman - I'd never seen her before - gave me this outside the churchyard after my husband's funeral.' She paused and waited, watching him pull out the folded paper with nicotine-stained fingers. Her eyes drifted towards the shiny sleeve of his suit and wished with growing unease that she could have more confidence in his ability.

'You can't take much notice of anonymous notes,' he said at last, fixing her with a cold stare. 'Besides which, there'd be little hope of finding the person who wrote this.' He tossed the paper onto the table.

'But I saw the woman quite clearly. I can give you a description if you like.' Liberty had the distinct feeling that she was creating the pace. What was wrong with the man?

'If you think it might be useful,' he said grudgingly. 'But I have to warn you that it's probably a hoax. We get this sort of thing all the time, especially when there's been a lot of publicity.'

His lethargy was really irritating her now. 'Well, if you'd like my opinion I don't think it is a hoax. I can't believe that someone would hand me a note in person if they were only out for some sick amusement. And she seemed so . . well, so plausible.' Whether he wanted a description or not he was going to get one, she decided and launched into as full a description as she could, trying to stick to the facts.

He scribbled a few notes but she was quite sure he had no intention of ever using the information. He leaned across the desk, squeezing the hooded eyes into a near squint. 'Do you know of anyone with a grudge against either you or your husband, Mrs Westerman?'

The question took her by surprise but she answered without hesitation.

'No, I don't. But I still think someone with a grudge may have killed Joe.'

He pressed his lips together in an irritable scowl and his voice was brusque. 'I was trying to establish whether someone with a grudge might have written the note.'

'Oh! I'm sorry, I thought....' she muttered, wondering why she was apologising. But his unexpected antagonism had thrown her.

For a moment his unwavering eyes held hers. She knew he was weighing her up. 'You were married for 29 years, is that right?' he asked. Liberty squeezed her hands together on her lap and nodded. Why did he want to know that? 'And would you say you were happily married, Mrs Westerman?'

Liberty vaguely remembered a similar query, though not as forthright, in the interview after Joe's death, but she hadn't expected their relationship to come under scrutiny now. What was he after?

She shifted on her chair trying to subdue the feeling that she was in the dock. She must protest her innocence and point out that she was the one bringing fresh evidence. But then it hit her. Of course, how stupid of her not to see it before. She closed her eyes and almost groaned aloud.

If she'd had any involvement in the murder, either directly or through a third party, an anonymous note would be a simple and effective way of diverting suspicion. She took a deep breath and held his gaze as confidently as she could. But it was no use. She could feel her neck and face beginning to glow, while bile rose from her stomach to the back of her mouth. He showed no sign of noticing her discomfort but she knew the patchy red blotches would be painfully obvious by now. She resolved not to protest her innocence before any accusation had been made.

His forehead was wrinkling now and his eyes had narrowed almost to slits. Liberty shifted uncomfortably. He was right to suspect that their marriage had been less than successful. Certainly in the first flush of married life they'd been besotted with each other, desperate to spend as much time as possible in each other's company. But after that?

After the arrival of Ruth - which had roughly coincided with Joe's ambitions to run his own company being fulfilled - after that, they'd gradually, though amicably, settled into their separate roles. She'd had the children to look after. He'd had the business.

She tried to clear her throat but her voice sounded strangely high-pitched. 'Yes, of course we were happy,' she began, 'We had our ups and downs like every other married couple, but after nearly 30 years together I think I can safely say that we had a good marriage.' She noted with a sinking feeling the mixture of surprise and suspicion on his face. 'My husband led a very busy life, Chief Inspector,' she continued, breathlessly. 'He had to travel a lot. It was difficult to find time together. But we were both happy with the way things were.'

She paused, hearing the defensiveness in her answer and wondered why she was telling him all this. Surely none of it was relevant. But the Chief Inspector nodded for her to continue.

'I think I've answered your question,' she answered curtly. 'I loved my husband and I'm sure he loved me. And if you think I might have murdered him you're wrong.' But she hadn't meant to say that. Her hands sprang together in an involuntary clench and she waited for a reaction.

His expression didn't falter but he sounded pleased. 'You must realise, Mrs Westerman, that we must pursue all lines of enquiry.' He smiled then and the froth which had covered his teeth began to ooze out of the corners of his mouth. Liberty forced herself not to avert her eyes. Speaking softly, he continued, 'Of course we have the statement you made at the station on the eighth of August, the day after your husband's death. But it might be helpful if you could go over the details again.'

She knew he was checking to make sure her story was consistent and for a moment she panicked. What *had* she said? Either then or immediately after she'd found Joe's body. Her memories were no more than a blur. But she judged that if she told the truth there would be no inconsistencies.

'As I probably told you, Joe had been at Holy Cross since about six o'clock. He always helped Fr. O'Malley on Saturday evenings - to keep the church's accounts in order, print the bulletins, pay the bills, that sort of thing. After half past seven Mass he would count the collection and deal with any other matters Father O'Malley hadn't got round to. So I was never quite sure what time to expect him. Although it was rarely before nine o'clock. Anyway, some time after nine - about ten past or just after - I heard his car on the path. I was watching the news and when Joe didn't come in I just presumed he was doing something outside . . . he'd sometimes walk round the house to check that all the security lights were working or . . .' She shrugged. Was she gabbling? She took a breath. 'Anyway, a few minutes later I decided to go and look for him. His evening meal was in the oven, lamb chops, and I didn't want them to dry up.'

'How could you be sure it was your husband's car you heard?' the Chief Inspector asked with a frown which seemed to give life to his thick brows.

'It was a diesel engine. They're not very common round here except in HGVs. So I just presumed it was Joe's.'

'And you couldn't see the garage - or stable, as you call it - from the house?'

'Well, no. I mean you can see it from the hall window. But I was in the sitting room.'

He scribbled something on the piece of paper and nodded for her to continue.

She swallowed. Why did she feel so defensive?

'Anyway, I decided to go and look for him. I wasn't worried or anything. I've never had reason to feel unsafe at Lowthwaite, even though it's quite cut-off. But as I opened the door I heard footsteps. Someone running away down the path. I couldn't see anyone. The trees were blocking my view. But I started to get worried then. So I ran round to the courtyard and saw Joe's car half in and half out of the stable doors as if something - or someone - had stopped him parking.' She paused trying to blot out the image, then tried to finish. 'The headlights were shining across the floor and I could see Joe just lying there . . .' But she couldn't go on.

The terror she'd felt then came flooding back. Her throat seemed to close up and her lips trembled. But the thought of breaking down in front of the Chief Inspector's sceptical gaze gave her the will not to give him the satisfaction. She tried to concentrate on the thin rays of light seeping through the vertical blinds behind his head and continued: 'I knew straight away he was dead . . .there was blood everywhere . . .but I still had to check . . .it must only have been a couple of minutes later when I dialled 999 on the car phone.'

He leaned forward on his elbow, supporting his chin with a thumb and forefinger and setting her with a quizzical look. 'And what did you do during those two minutes, Mrs Westerman? And the following minutes before a squad car arrived?'

She clenched her jaws tightly, wondering how far he would go before accusing her of something. What the hell did he think she was doing? Hiding evidence that might incriminate her? She stroked the throbbing in her neck and said, 'I was in shock, I suppose, I just knelt down next to him and felt for a pulse. I didn't move anything if that's what you mean. I just held his hand, put my head on his chest, I don't know. I was in a daze.' She shook her head, reluctant to delve too deeply into the painful memory. 'I can't tell you any more. It was all just a blur.'

'It was quite dark in the stalls, as I remember, Mrs Westerman. And considering the state you were in, the shock you'd just had, could you say for sure that the murderer was nowhere on the premises?'

She hesitated. The thought had never occurred to her. 'No, I couldn't. I'd just heard someone running away. So I presumed, I suppose . . . Of course, there could have been two of them . . . I hadn't thought of that.' He nodded, unconvinced.

'Tell me, Mrs Westerman.' He paused and sank back in his chair, the pen between his teeth. 'Tell me, who stands to benefit financially from your husband's death?'

Liberty wasn't prepared for that but she understood the implication instantly. Her neck felt as though it were on fire. 'I . . . I suppose I do.' She gulped, trying to release the knot in her throat. 'I don't remember Joe ever making a will. So I suppose . . . I don't know . . . I think it must all come to me.'

'By *all* I presume you mean the house and his share of the business, together with any bank accounts and insurance policies?'

'Well, yes. Although I don't know how much that would come to. For all I know he might have mortgaged us to the hilt if he'd had a cash flow problem.'

His eyebrows curled up like furry caterpillars over his surprised eyes. 'And is that likely, Mrs Westerman? Would your husband do such a thing without consulting you first?'

If he'd asked her that question last week she'd have said No. Now she wasn't so sure. 'Probably not,' she replied. 'But it's possible.'

'Thank you, Mrs Westerman,' he said, pushing his chair back and stretching his gangly legs under the table. 'I don't think I have any more questions for you at present. But I may need to speak to you again soon.'

Liberty watched the self-satisfied flicker of a smile and felt her shoulders, which had risen to a level somewhere above her chin and below her ears, stiffen even more. But he hadn't finished yet. 'I'm afraid,' he continued, stubbing the blunt end of his pen on the table and gazing at something over the top of her head, 'that in an investigation such as this, when there is very little forensic evidence, every avenue must be explored. As I informed you a few days ago, our main line of enquiry centres on the burglary of two houses in the area the previous week. All the evidence we have so far points to the probability that the thief was about to break into your property when he was disturbed by your husband and panicked.'

He bent forward, almost confidingly, and the tobacco-laden breath felt warm on her face. Her stomach lurched. She must get out of here. 'But rest assured, Mrs Westerman, whoever murdered your husband will not escape justice. I'll make sure of that.' It sounded too much like a threat. She shook her head, desperate to divert his suspicion.

'What about the note?' she asked, hating the high-pitch of her voice. 'I should have thought that was your biggest lead.'

The Chief Inspector scribbled on the sheet of paper again, then threw his pen onto the table and said: 'We've already received a number of letters - and phone calls - from the public about this case. All of them will be checked thoroughly of course, but most, if not all, will prove useless. From what you've told me, Mrs Westerman, I can only conclude at this time that this note will be no different. We will, of course, look into these latest developments and the items will be sent to forensics to be checked out for fingerprints etcetera. But until I receive the results, I am unable to comment further. I'm sure you understand.'

Liberty nodded. She understood perfectly.

The intense heat of the afternoon met her as she hurried out of the police station, but she didn't care. She was out of that place. And when a wall of hot air met her from inside her Sierra she leaned on the roof and waited, a hand pressed against her burning cheek. The Chief Inspector had made it quite plain that she was under suspicion. The suggestion had seemed unbelievable at first. But not any longer. Now, she realised, she was frightened. Another wave of nausea passed over her and she steadied herself against the car door, aware only of a deep distrust of DCI Leatheringham's ability.

A minute later she jumped in the car and gripped the hot steering wheel, but she knew it was pointless going home in this mood. What she needed was the chance to vent her feelings, not just of fear, frustration and anger but of her own inadequacy. Instead of heading back up the lakeside to Lowthwaite House, she steered the car towards Keswick where she stopped at a pub she'd never been in before.

As she drove off again, after downing a long vodka and tonic, cooler air rushed in through the open window but she still felt hot and clammy. The Chief Inspector was a fool. What other explanation was there for thinking her capable of murdering Joe? She shook her head, taking a right-hand bend faster than she'd intended. Her only consolation was in assuming that if he'd known her better he could never have considered it.

She drove on through the bustling market town where fell walkers in shorts and hiking boots mingled with families making the most of the last few days of the school holidays and locals in a last-minute dash to the shops before closing-time. As she left the town behind, Derwentwater to her right sparkled in an uplifting display. She slowed to take in the view.

A few minutes later she stopped the car between a nineteenth century chapel and the riverbank where more than one bride had posed for wedding photos, a pristine gown trailing along the sheep-grazed turf, her dreams still intact.

Almost as soon as the engine was switched off, the temperature began to rise but Liberty felt no urge to move. Her neck ached and she let her head fall back against the headrest while she gazed at the artists whose easels dotted a stony islet in midstream. They seemed so remote, removed from the worries of the world as they dabbed at their canvasses, and she envied them.

She sighed, closing her eyes and struggling to make some sense of the day's developments. She couldn't get it out of her mind that the mysterious note was a genuine attempt to help track down Joe's killer. Yet if Chief Inspector Leatheringham had his way it would soon be consigned to a file with Joe's name on it, a file across which she now imagined the word UNSOLVED in thick red lettering.

If the Chief Inspector could suspect *her*, he must be desperate. She wondered whether grasping at straws was his usual way of solving a case. Was he even interested in finding out the truth or was he happy to charge any plausible suspect? She found herself remembering one of Sister Monica's quotations. What was it now? Something about truth being the cement of society. At that moment she couldn't shake off the suspicion that the truth about Joe's death would never be known. But worse still, she could end up being wrongly accused or even found guilty of murder. Now that really *would* set the tongues wagging. If they weren't already accusing her.

She shuddered, wrapping her arms tightly round her body and wondering how life had suddenly become so complicated. Not two weeks ago she'd had hardly a care in the world. Now she could find no consolation - except in the bottle. Certainly there was none in praying. Since Joe's death the words she'd chanted since childhood had seemed just that, words, empty and pointless words.

She watched the water trickle through beds of stone and tried to make sense of the thoughts which swirled around in the mire inside her head. What could she, a pre-menopausal widow with an infuriatingly mediocre brain and a knack of making a mess of things, do to rectify the situation?

Beads of sweat began to trickle down her cheeks. There was nothing she could do that would make the slightest difference. And yet...

Her peace of mind - and perhaps even her freedom - depended on her doing something. Anything. All she knew was that she couldn't trust Chief Inspector Leatheringham to find Joe's murderer.

She flung open the car door. But there was no getting away from it. All her life she'd accepted things at face value. Now she couldn't shake off the feeling that it was time to start scratching below the surface. And no matter how impossible the challenge might seem, she just had to accept it.

Joe would have relished the chance to pit his wits against the police, would probably have asked God for strength and guidance and even thanked Him for the opportunity. But the nagging conviction that *He* would not respond to *her* still persisted.

The early evening sun had lost none of its heat but a gentle breeze blew off Derwentwater as she set off on the track which would take her along the shoreline and back to the car via Catbells. She needed to clear her head and work out what she should do next.

She looked at her watch. This had been one of Ruth and Ben's favourite walks when they were little. Then the circular had taken well over two hours. But without the children to slow her down while they'd collected wild flowers and coloured stones, she calculated it would probably take around one and a half hours. The shadows were already lengthening but she pressed on, not worried that daylight would be fading by the time she arrived back at the car.

But the long dry spell which had plagued the countryside had made the ground hard and ungiving and she stumbled over tree roots growing through the path. Jagged slate and stone caught at the soles of her feet through her lightweight casuals and the hope that the walk might miraculously refresh and inspire her faded fast. How stupid to think that it would be cooler up here, she thought, pausing to dab her face with a tissue. The uphill slog had drained her and her head was throbbing. It was then that she remembered she'd had nothing to eat or drink since lunch-time.

Dark shadows began to overtake the hillside and five-foot-high ferns, which only minutes before had seemed to line her way, now threatened to submerge her. She glanced around. Anyone could be lurking in the deep cover. Even the sheep were fully camouflaged, only showing themselves as they bounded away, startled by her approach. Liberty shuddered and glanced behind her. Of course there was no-one hiding there. Why on earth should there be? The whole idea was ridiculous.

It exasperated her that she could be spooked so easily. How on earth could she ever hope to clear her name if she was such a pathetic wimp? She tried to concentrate her attention on the lake below which wallowed in a pink glow. Yet the fear persisted, sending tiny shivers up the small of her back.

At last she began her descent, coming out of the undergrowth onto the deserted road. The sun had sunk out of sight and the birds were deathly silent. She heard it then - a faint tap, tap - like footsteps. But when she swivelled round she could see no-one in the deepening gloom. She quickened her step. Rounding the last bend her car came into sight and she broke into a run, convinced by now that her imagination was not playing tricks. Someone really was following her.

On the dash along the winding roads back to Lowthwaite House, Liberty scanned her rear-view mirror and tried to catch her breath. But as far as she could make out among the twilight shadows, no car was pursuing her.

By the time she turned into the driveway the moon, which had lit her way like a beacon at sea, had disappeared behind a thick bank of cloud, throwing the house and garden into an inky darkness. She stopped the car outside the stable block and sat for a moment gripping the steering wheel, listening to her laboured breathing.

She glanced at the clock on the dashboard. Ten minutes past nine. The time Joe was murdered. Her tongue clung to her parched lips and she knew that if she didn't make a move now she'd be paralysed by fear.

She pushed the car door open and almost threw herself out, running blindly across the cobbled courtyard, towards the path round the front of the house. But as she reached the front door the gravel crunched behind her. The sound made her freeze and she held her breath like a rabbit caught in a car's headlights. A panting sound, heavy and uneven, mingled with the terrifying din of footsteps. Someone was running towards her.

Her shaking fingers pulled at the bunch of keys, trying desperately to find the right one. But it was too late. The footsteps were right behind her. She spun round to face her attacker.

The voice was high and unmistakable. 'Libby, darling, did I startle you? Oh you poor thing. I'm so sorry.' Liberty clasped a hand to her chest. Tears of relief swelled in her eyes and for a moment she thought she would burst into tears.

'Sondra. You nearly gave me a heart attack. Why didn't you let me know you were back?' Liberty tried to control the shaking in her voice and wondered at her friend's sense of timing.

'Oh, darling. It's so awful,' she purred, spreading her arms wide under her wrap as if she were attempting to fly. 'I just had to come as soon as I heard. Timothy broke the news when he picked us up at the airport.'

As Sondra leapt forward, Liberty braced herself. But the warmth of her friend's embrace was a welcome antidote to the stresses of the day and, as she leaned against the soft wool, a heavy perfume filling the night air, Liberty felt the tension in her muscles ease.

But five minutes later, as they sat on the sofa, Sondra holding a Campari and soda, and Liberty washing down two paracetamol with a large gin and tonic, she felt herself tense again.

'You *are* joking, aren't you? Tell me it's a wind-up. I mean you can't possibly think you can do the job of the police. It's just so ridiculous,' Sondra gave an imperious wave of her free hand. 'Just think of the danger you might be in. Oh Lib, don't be so silly. I mean, you're such a mouse. You wouldn't know where to start.' Sondra tilted her face, a worried smile playing on her brightly-painted lips. 'Besides, you need a devious mind to think like a criminal, or a policeman for that matter. And you haven't got a devious bone in your body.'

She tossed her head back, shaking the mane of lustrous red hair which was normally held in place by an exotic assortment of tortoise-shell combs and chiffon scarves.

Liberty took a sip from her glass, pausing to enjoy the numbing sensation on her lips. She wasn't surprised by Sondra's reaction. The whole idea of her turning detective must seem totally ridiculous and melodramatic, unreal almost.

She shrugged and said: 'I've got to try, Sondra. For my own sake as well as Joe's. If it had been me who'd been murdered, he wouldn't have dithered and worried about whether he was up to the job. He'd have got on with it and probably shown the police a thing or two in the process. What does it say about me if I don't do anything?'

'But you don't have to prove yourself, Lib. Not to anybody.' Sondra gave her a look of pity and took a long drink.

'I know I don't, but I need to try for my own peace of mind. The police are looking for a burglar and any evidence which might disprove their theory is just ignored. But it's not just that . . .' She hesitated, wondering how much to say. But she and Sondra had trusted each other with their secrets since their first meeting at ante-natal classes. Liberty swirled the ice round her glass and continued, 'They think I might have something to do with Joe's death.'

'What?' Sondra half-choked, lurching forward and nearly spilling the orange liquid down her cream silk trouser suit. 'They think you killed Joe?' She made a noise somewhere between a laugh and a snort before descending into a fit of coughing.

'I know, it *is* ridiculous, isn't it? But it's true.' Liberty suddenly saw the funny side and burst into hysterical laughter as her friend shook uncontrollably, dangling the glass in front of her until the coughing had ceased.

A moment later Liberty sighed and wiped the tears from her eyes. 'I'll tell you all about it another time but for now I'm whacked and my head's banging. Would you mind terribly if I had an early night?'

'No, of course I don't. I should have realised. But I really do think you should reconsider . . .'

Liberty raised a hand and stopped her in her tracks. 'Do stop worrying,' she said, noting with surprise and pleasure the reassuring, decisive tone in her voice. 'If I don't do something now I may never know the truth about Joe's death. I need to know, Sondra. In fact, I need to know the truth about a lot of things. But don't worry, I'm not about to go looking for trouble. Just make a few discreet enquiries, that's all. Then I'll take any important information to the police.'

'I still think you've taken leave of your senses,' said Sondra running her carefully manicured fingernails up and down her bronzed neck. 'Derek will be horrified when I tell him.'

The thought of Derek's usual disinterested grunt in response to anything Sondra told him made Liberty almost burst out laughing again. Instead she checked herself and put on her 'difficult' face, as Ruth called it.

'It doesn't matter. I've made up my mind. I know it won't be all smooth-sailing but I couldn't live with myself if Joe's murderer got away just because I was too much of a coward to do something about it. And what if it happened again? What if someone else was killed . . .?' She shook her head and stood up. 'No, I must do something,' she insisted, almost adding that the murderer might even turn out to be someone they both knew - a local perhaps, someone from the golf club or even, God forbid, a parishioner of Holy Cross. But she thought better of it and said nothing.

CHAPTER 5

Next morning Liberty awoke late feeling surprisingly refreshed. The hint of a breeze was channelling its way between the bedroom curtains although the temperature, even at 9 o'clock in the morning, must already have been in the high 70's.

She'd worked out the night before, during the two hours she'd lain awake, what her first task must be. And, although uneasy about her ability to 'interview' people, she was still resolved to try. She picked up the bedside phone before she had the chance to change her mind and rang the incident room. She needed to know the identity of the woman who claimed to have seen someone running into the garden of Lowthwaite House only minutes before Joe was murdered. But, in a tone she recognised immediately as deeply suspicious, DCI Leatheringham was less than helpful.

Shaking off the feeling that she'd scored another own goal, she decided to start her investigations closer to home. She found Jacob dead-heading the roses in the bed alongside the patio. His wiry body bent and stretched with a mechanical yet weary rhythm. Then he paused and straightened up, his hands pressed firmly into the small of his back and she caught a glimpse of the deep lines etched into his weathered face. As she reached him, she thought she caught a look of wariness, almost fear.

'I was just about to come up to the house,' he said apologetically.

'It's OK Jacob, I thought I'd save you the trouble,' she said. But the sight of Jacob's red-rimmed eyes made her wonder whether her sense of timing may be lacking. 'How's Ellen today?' she asked.

'Not too good today, Mrs Westerman. She had a bit of a bad night, like. But I'll tell her you was asking about her.'

'Yes, do that, Jacob. Tell her I'm thinking of her,' she said, wondering how she could most delicately begin her questioning. But she needed to be sure of certain details and Jacob was in possession of vital information. She reminded herself that the police wouldn't let a personal tragedy stand in the way of an investigation. And, if she was serious about finding Joe's killer, *she* couldn't afford to either. She shuddered, remembering Chief Inspector Leatheringham's intense, unsympathetic approach.

Jacob had placed his secateurs on the pile of petals and dead rose heads in the wheelbarrow and was gazing at her expectantly. She made up her mind not to waste the opportunity.

'I hope you won't mind, Jacob,' she said softly, 'but I'd like to ask you a few questions about the night Joe was murdered.'

His eyes narrowed and she saw his lip twitch, but he didn't speak.

'I just want to ask you about the car you and Dr Firth saw parked opposite the path.'

He nodded uncertainly, wiping his soiled hands down the side of his pants. 'Like I told the police, I didn't get a good look at it. The light was fading, like. But I could see it sticking out. I said to Dr Firth as it was a funny place to park.'

'What colour was it? Do you remember?'

'Some sort of blue or grey as I remember. But, like I said, I didn't see it that well.' He shrugged and snapped the withered pink head off a tall rosebush.

'And the make? Have you any idea what the make was?'

He shook his head. 'No. No, I don't know one from another,' he said, not meeting her gaze. 'Now if it'd been a rose you wanted me to tell you about . . . only I'm not very good with cars, like. Not having one myself.'

He seemed very uneasy with her questions. For a brief moment her eyes rested on the silvery water lapping the shoreline beyond the parched lawn. Should she leave him in peace? She was aware that yesterday she would have done.

'Jacob, I'm sorry to ask all these questions,' she said.

"Ain't no trouble at all, Mrs Westerman.' But his dark eyes seemed to be saying something else.

'Just a couple more, then I'm finished. What time was it when you saw the car?'

He seemed relieved. 'Oh, that would be about half past eight. That's what I told the police. I'd cycled down to Dr Firth's house after

Mass to see if he could take a look at Ellen. I was worried about her and he said he'd come right away. He stuck my bike on the back of that car of his and we set off there and then. Must 'ave been about half past eight, give or take a couple of minutes, by the time we passed here.'

'Now I'd like you to consider this last question very carefully, Jacob. Did you see anyone in the car?'

'I wasn't taking much notice to be honest. I was too worried about Ellen. She'd taken a turn for the worse, you see. There was somebody in the car but who they was and what they looked like I couldn't say.'

'Not even whether it was a man or woman?'

He looked blank, shrugging his shoulders and making a gesture with his hands which told her he had nothing further to offer.

She thanked him and walked back to the house. None of the information she'd gleaned had been a great revelation but the exercise hadn't been entirely fruitless. It had set her off on the road to unravelling some of the mystery surrounding Joe's death and, in the process, had given her the confidence to believe that she might, just might, succeed in uncovering some crucial evidence overlooked by the police.

She allowed herself a faint smile of satisfaction before ringing Dr Firth for an appointment to see him after his morning surgery.

The red brick Victorian detached was set back from the Keswick to Cockermouth road, perched precariously on the hillside under Whinlatter Forest. The sprawling house, with its assortment of windows and high, red-tiled roof, had always seemed cold and functional though, she conceded, when it was first built it would probably have been considered the height of sophistication and grandeur. Its only redeeming feature, as far as she was concerned, was its position, overlooking Bassenthwaite Lake and directly opposite the sheer slopes of Skiddaw. But she would never have dreamed of swapping Lowthwaite House for it and wondered why the doctor hadn't moved to a smaller place years ago after his wife left him. It wasn't as though he had any children or grandchildren to fill its empty rooms.

The surgery was round the back, reached by a narrow, crumbling path which wound its way in a zig-zag along the side of the house. Liberty checked her watch and noted that she had five minutes to spare before her 10.30 appointment.

As she settled herself in the empty waiting room the consulting room door opened and she looked up from a magazine to see a familiar face. She recognised Alan Walters immediately although she could hardly believe how much he'd changed in the two weeks since she'd last seen him at Westerman & Brock's. It seemed to her that Joe's traffic manager was a very sick man indeed. Rivers of sweat ran down his grey face and his eyes, blood-shot and watery, stared blankly at a point somewhere in the distance.

She watched him amble towards her, wondering what kind of illness could transform the athletic, well-proportioned body of a man in his mid-thirties into that of a shuffling, sagging old man. The thick, black hair, usually so glossy and healthy now looked limp and lustreless. His clothes too showed a marked deterioration. For someone who had prided himself on being the local stud, his crumpled, light-coloured trousers and faded black t-shirt did nothing for his image.

She tried to catch his eye but decided against calling out as he passed within feet of her, a prescription crushed in his hand. Something told her that at this moment he would prefer not to be disturbed.

When she entered the consulting room a few moments later Dr Firth was extracting a print-out from the printer on his desk. The movement revealed a large, damp patch on the under arm of his short-sleeved shirt. Beads of sweat had also formed on his bald head. The heat was obviously getting to him too, she thought.

'Take a seat please, Mrs Westerman,' he said and smiled, displaying the row of gold teeth which had gradually replaced his own.

She perched on the end of the upright chair reflecting how he'd always addressed her formally even though he'd called Joe by his Christian name. But that had been because he and Joe had grown up in the same close-knit community.

Not that they'd been particularly close either then or later. The doctor had been about five years older than Joe who'd been packed off to boarding school when he was seven.

'Now, what can I do for you?'

She wondered how many times he must say that in the course of a day. He squinted at her over half moon glasses and curled the edge of his excessively long handle-bar moustache.

Liberty gripped her fingers together between her knees and took a deep breath. 'I need to ask you about the night Joe died,' she said.

The doctor raised an eyebrow. 'What would you like to know?'

Suddenly wishing she'd contacted him out of surgery hours, she said, 'I'm sorry to bother you. I know you must be busy. But it *is* important. I won't keep you long.'

He was nodding, almost impatiently she thought.

She got to the point. 'It's about the car you and Jacob saw outside Lowthwaite House on the night Joe was murdered. I know you've already given the police a statement but I doubt if Chief Inspector Leatheringham will let me see it. So if you don't mind . . .'

He smiled, flashing the gold teeth. 'Of course, but I'm afraid I can't tell you much.'

In fact his answers varied only in minor detail to Jacob's. The car was a pale blue as far as he could make out, the make unknown but might have been a Vauxhall. The person sitting in the driver's seat had on a black or dark t-shirt. Whether the car was still there later the doctor couldn't confirm since he'd had another call after he'd attended to Ellen Newington and had taken the Carlisle to Keswick road home.

Liberty could barely disguise her disappointment and stood up to leave. The trail seemed to have gone cold already.

But, as if sensing her mood and wanting to help, he added, 'Have you spoken to Veronica Nadle?'

'Sorry?'

'Veronica Nadle. The lady who saw someone entering your property that evening.'

'No. I'd like to. But Chief Inspector Leatheringham preferred not to tell me her name.' She could barely contain her contempt.

'I see,' he said, frowning. 'But it's hardly classified information.'

Liberty shook her head, baffled. 'But how do *you* know her name?' she asked.

He tapped the side of his nose with a forefinger. 'There's not a lot I don't get to know about. In a little place like Lowthwaite there's always somebody with a tale to tell.'

And what they don't know they guess, she wanted to add, but she resisted.

'Do you know where I can find her?' she asked, feeling her optimism growing.

'She works at the Somerby Hotel in Keswick, I believe. A waitress. You'll probably find her there.'

Liberty felt like hugging him. Instead, she thanked him profusely and left. It was only when she reached the car that she realised she'd not explained - and he'd not asked - the reason behind her questions.

Veronica Nadle was a small, pinched looking woman with narrow lips, greasy hair and a disconcerting habit of alternately gazing at her nails and chewing them. Liberty thought she must be approaching forty, but the way she slouched in a shabby armchair in the hotel foyer seemed more appropriate to a teenager.

When Liberty explained who she was, adding vaguely that she was curious to discover more about the car and its owner, Veronica Nadle eyed her suspiciously. But then she shrugged and turned her attention once more to her chewed-down nails.

'Sure. I saw the car all right,' she drawled with an accent Liberty took to be American in origin but which had been influenced by years of living in the north of England. 'And that guy too. Ran straight across in front of me. I had to slam my brakes on. 'Damn fool,' I yelled but he'd gone. Didn't think no more about it 'til I heard on the radio the cops were asking for people who'd seen anything suspicious.'

'And you're sure he ran down the drive to Lowthwaite House?'

'Yeah. Didn't know its name then. But the cop with the crooked nose said that was it. Right opposite that big hall place. Can't see it for trees.'

Liberty nodded. 'Yes, that's Lowthwaite. Now, can you be sure it was a man you saw and not a woman?'

'Not right positive. But I reckon it'd gotta be a man. Looked like a man, anyhow. But I guess a woman might dress like that too,' she added with a shrug.

'How was he dressed? Can you describe him?'

'Not real well. Like I told the cop, I nearly didn't see him. The light'd gone and it all happened in a second. I could see he was medium-build though, dark hair. All dressed in black. Slacks, t-shirt, the lot. But I didn't see his face.'

Another wasted journey, thought Liberty watching the waitress uncross her black-stockinged legs and cross them again.

'And what time was this?' The questions were drying up.

'Oh, about ten minutes after nine, it'd be. I was on my way to Cockermouth. Had the night off, see. But I told the cops all this before.' She glanced at her watch.

'Yes, I'm sorry to bother you. I wouldn't take up your time unless it was important.' But Veronica Nadle had already pushed her chair back and was standing up.

'I gotta get back now,' she said and walked off towards the dining room.

On the way back to Lowthwaite, Liberty found it impossible to dispel the feeling of failure. She'd learned very little so far and had no new leads to follow up. Approaching the roundabout at the far end of the town, she decided to take the Keswick to Carlisle road home. It was a slower route, but less busy than the Keswick to Cockermouth road which skirted the other side of Bassenthwaite Lake. She needed time to think.

Winding the window down she savoured the warm wind on her face and tried to work out why Chief Inspector Leatheringham had wanted to keep Veronica Nadle's identity from her. Was it police procedure in order to protect witnesses? Or did he think she might try to influence the waitress's version of events which, as they stood, made the police theory about Joe being murdered by a burglar more plausible?

The timing was perfect too. According to the waitress the man had run across the road only minutes before Joe was killed. Just long enough to find Joe's toolbox on the shelf at the back of the stables and sort out the ideal weapon for prising open a window. Then, just as he was about to leave the stable, crow-bar in hand, Joe had arrived. It all fit in beautifully. But was it what had really happened?

She pulled over into a lay-by and sat looking at the glittering lake. The wooded fells on the opposite side rose up into a clear sky but the air was still unpleasantly warm. It would all end in a massive storm, that was for sure.

She tried to make sense of the clues in her possession, irritated that she couldn't even rely on the police for information. As far as she knew there was no forensic evidence to trap the murderer. No fingerprints, footprints, hairs or pieces of fabric, nothing. The only lead was the sighting of this person who couldn't even be positively identified as a man. But the thought that a woman might be capable of smashing a man's skull seemed too remote a possibility.

She gazed miserably towards the Scottish mountains across the Solway Firth. It all seemed hopeless and pathetic. She'd been a fool to even imagine that she could solve a crime which had baffled the police for nearly two weeks. She leaned back and closed her eyes, feeling the sharp stab of tears behind the lids. What was the point of pretending any more? She was a hopeless failure.

The figure of Sister Monica flashed into her consciousness. The nun's rosy face encased in a black veil was as clear in her mind today as in her schooldays. Each morning at assembly Liberty had lapped up, with a childish reverence, her headmistress's every word. And those pearls of wisdom - practical as much as spiritual - had sustained her long after the uncertain days of her youth. But what words of encouragement would she have offered now?

The phrase came to her without effort. 'The greatest failure is the failure to try,' that's what she would have said. She could almost hear the shrill, sure voice.

Liberty switched on the engine. Should she persevere, at least a little longer? But if she did, what course would her investigations take? She glanced in the rear-view mirror and was surprised to find that a red car had parked behind her. She hadn't heard it. But no matter. A quick glance at her watch told her she was running late.

She pulled out into the road remembering how Bob had rung her in desperation the previous evening, soon after Sondra had left. He'd managed to keep all the plates in the air, he'd said, but there were delivery notes, invoices and cheques all over the place. And if he could get his hands on that good-for-nothing Alison Grant he swore he wouldn't be responsible for his actions. He'd gone on and on, until Liberty's bedtime mug of tea was cold, about the secretary who'd left without explanation two days before Joe's death.

In a last-ditch effort to get Bob off the phone rather than from any great desire to return to Westerman and Brock's, Liberty had agreed to be there by one.

Since it was now twenty minutes past twelve she decided to skip lunch and drive straight there. She could grab a coffee later, when she'd had time to settle in. But the thought of returning to Westerman and Brock's was already causing her stomach to churn.

The high, wild flowers which edged the Kildale road had become shrivelled and brown since the last time she'd made this journey. She changed into top gear, realising with a sinking feeling that there would be other far more upsetting changes to face before the day was out.

But her thoughts were suddenly interrupted when she glanced in the wing mirror. Wasn't that the same car she'd noticed in the lay-by? It was a long way back but it certainly looked like it. She slowed, trying to make out the driver's face. The car slowed too.

It was with a sense of relief that, a few moments later, she turned into the yard of Westerman and Brock's. She switched off the engine and twisted herself round in her seat, but she wasn't quite quick enough. The car had sped past.

She sighed, as much in frustration as in relief. Was her imagination playing tricks on her now?

The loading bays were deserted except for a lone trailer painted in the familiar livery of Westerman and Brock (Hauliers). The ten-foot high gold letters stood out more starkly than usual against the deep royal blue background.

Wiping her clammy hands on a tissue, she made her way towards the portacabin which Joe had maintained would be quieter for her than the main building. The silence was eerie and she glanced round her nervously. But there was no-one about.

Quickly she unlocked the door ready to duck inside but, as she did so, a wall of heat surged out. She gasped and stood back, momentarily fighting the urge to shut the door again and go back home. But Bob had said he was desperate and she didn't want to let him down. She wafted the flimsy door back and forth. But she knew she was wasting her time. The sour heat, along with the pungent smell of melting plastic, refused to give way. She gave up and made for her desk in the far corner. A half-empty mug of fungus-covered coffee sat next to her phone and she remembered that she'd left it there the day before Joe's death.

There'd been a flap on about some lost cheques and Joe had called her into his office to try to find them. It wasn't usually part of her job to work directly with him but, with the sudden departure of the secretary he and Bob shared, for once he'd needed Liberty's help. She'd spent all afternoon searching for the cheques but not found them. In the end she'd left at about five o'clock, returning to the portacabin only to lock the door.

It occurred to her at that moment that she never did find out the reason for Alison Grant's sudden departure. Perhaps that was one line of enquiry she should follow - and soon.

She picked up the mug and emptied the lumpy contents down the sink in the adjoining wash room. Nobody had disturbed anything else on her desk as far as she could see. The delivery notes she'd been filing still lay in a neat pile, next to the mail still waiting to be franked.

She flopped back into her swivel chair and gazed up at the water-stains on the plastic ceiling. Whatever else the future might hold, she knew then that it didn't include this synthetic cage and mundane job. Perhaps a working partnership with Bob might be the answer after all. But she wasn't able to cope with that kind of decision yet and, picking up a notebook and pen, she went through to Bob's office.

'What am I going to do about all this, Liberty?' He wafted a hand over the mess on his desk. 'And the e-mails haven't even been looked at. I don't have a clue about that bloody computer. Most of it's addressed to Joe but if you can print it out, I'll have a go at answering it.' He ran a hand through his thick hair and tilted his head on one side. 'But I'm not very good at that side of things. And with all these new regulations to sort out . . . I'm hopeless without a secretary. If I wasn't desperate I wouldn't have asked you to come in so soon after . . .' He paused and for a moment she had the feeling he was searching for the right words. But all he said was, 'I've had folk on my back all week wanting this and that. I appreciate you coming in.'

'It's all right, Bob,' she said, eager to get away now. 'I don't mind. I was going to come back on Monday anyway.'

'Yes, but . . .' he gazed at her with a look she couldn't interpret but it made her feel uncomfortable.

'Really, Bob. It's OK.' The sharpness in her voice must have been apparent as he didn't say another word.

He just nodded with that hang-dog expression he sometimes had when he'd failed to clinch a deal.

He'd been right about the mountain of paperwork. Envelopes and packages had been dumped, mostly unopened, in the middle of Alison's desk. With a feeling that she'd rather be anywhere else, Liberty glanced round the empty open-plan office.

Bretherton and the new accounts clerk must still be at lunch, she concluded, suddenly aware that this might be an ideal opportunity to discover more about Joe's business acquaintances without arousing suspicion. If Joe did know the person who killed him, the clue to his identity might be right here in this office. But where?

A letter from Whitchurch and Jones (Solicitors) revealed nothing new. It was common knowledge that Westerman and Brock were planning to expand by opening another depot in the Midlands. Economically it was a sound move, Joe had explained on one of the rare occasions they'd discussed the business. Apart from being more central for sorting and distributing goods to southern regions, it would also cut down on the number of return journeys up north with an empty trailer. Deliveries would be less costly, since the distances between them would be shorter and overnight stays for drivers avoided. The solicitors' letter, signed by Amos Whitchurch himself, was merely a clarification that the vendors of the premises, yet to be converted, were hoping to sign contracts in three weeks' time.

It reminded her of the countless times she'd typed similar letters when she'd worked for a firm of solicitors in Cockermouth just after she'd married Joe. But it also reminded her that without Joe to mastermind the new venture, Westerman and Brock's would be unlikely to proceed.

She shrugged, unwilling to take any more problems on board and put the letter in the pile for Bob's attention. As far as she could see, there was no indication here of a motive for murder.

A statement from financial advisers Trevor Needham and Associates meant little to her. But figures had never been her strong point. Even though she'd managed to gain five 'O' Levels at St Hilda's, maths hadn't been one of them, much to the disappointment of her mother who had high hopes of her working in a bank like her brother Eric.

But Eric hadn't found working with numbers to his liking either and had packed it in to travel the world. She wondered where he was now and whether he knew, or cared, about Joe's murder. That was if he himself was still alive. The last she'd heard of him had been a postcard from Thailand nearly twenty years ago.

The Fletcher family seemed to have made a profession of rejection, she reflected, not for the first time and not without a twinge of resentment towards the father who'd abandoned her at the impressionable age of four, together with her pregnant mother.

She squinted at the maze of columns and numbers in front of her. But not knowing what she was looking for, it seemed pointless to keep on analysing everything. Half an hour later she'd had enough of opening the post and switched on the word-processor to sort out the e-mails. When it had been installed two years ago, she'd wondered how she would ever get used to this enemy on her desk. Now, although she was still illiterate when it came to performing more complex tasks, she embraced its efficiency in running off stock letters and contracts.

But twenty minutes later a gnawing ache over her eyes soon told her that a headache was coming on and she went into the little kitchen adjoining Joe's office to make a cup of coffee. Returning to the general office a few minutes later she noticed Bretherton standing by the photocopier, his dark blue security uniform hanging off his sagging frame. For a moment his brows furrowed and he tucked a sheet of paper into his top pocket. His normally doleful voice seemed strangulated.

'Good afternoon, Mrs Westerman. I didn't expect to see you here.'

'No, I didn't expect to be here. But Bob asked me to sort out this backlog.' She pointed to the still-unopened envelopes. 'I thought he might have mentioned I was coming,' she added, wondering why no-one in this company ever seemed to know what anyone else was doing.

He shook his head vaguely, a shock of pepper-grey hair swaying above his bloodshot eyes. Then, with a look of puzzled annoyance, he walked back to his desk in the far corner next to the warehouse door.

It was then that she noticed the new accounts clerk who had been hidden behind a pile of cardboard boxes outside Bob's office. She'd already decided during their first meeting, after Joe's funeral, that there was something about Ken Dewhurst's plastic good looks that she didn't like. She had the same vague unease now but it was too soon to make a more precise judgement. He nodded and flashed a wide smile in her direction.

Liberty smiled uncertainly and picked up an invoice from Norman Cullinson who, with the help of his son had built every one of Joe's twenty trailers. There had been few occasions when this partnership had been less than successful, in spite of Norman's irritatingly relaxed habit of leaving the final touches until the day he handed over each vehicle. Joe had always spoken highly of his work and there was nothing here to suggest there had been any friction between them.

Realising that her search for significant information in this mess was like trying to find a pebble in a field, she decided to look elsewhere. But where? Her head was throbbing now as she took a pile of correspondence to Bob. If she could grin and bear it a little longer, at least get all the urgent correspondence sorted, then she'd have time to inspect Joe's office.

But when she returned to Bob's office half an hour later for his replies she could see he was clearly floundering. With a look of exasperation and a shrug he passed the pile back to her, having scribbled no more than a couple of muddled comments on a scrap of paper. Clearly, being Sales Director of a nationwide transport company for over twenty years hadn't improved his basic communication skills. But Joe had been the administrator, the intelligent, educated one who'd given Westerman & Brock its professionalism and the edge over its rivals.

Liberty settled herself in front of her PC and wondered how long the company could survive without him.

It was just after four when she looked up from the screen, the pain in her head making her eyes water. When would she ever learn that she couldn't get away with missed meals any more? she wondered, wishing she'd not used the last two paracetamol in her handbag after Sondra had left the night before. If it got any worse she'd have to ask Bob for some, but she'd rather not give him the opportunity of passing more work onto her this late in the day.

It was just after five when she saw Bob's car pass the window. Armed with a pile of letters ready for signing, she tip-toed into Joe's office and placed them on the oval rosewood desk. If anyone came in now, her presence wouldn't set any alarm bells ringing. But then she saw the empty armchair. For a moment she could see Joe leaning back in it, his hands behind his head in that way he had of looking relaxed and in-charge.

Quickly, she turned away, gazing instead at the gallery of photographs on the rough stone wall. Gold and blue trailers dominated picturesque locations and one photo showed Norman Cullinson handing over a new trailer to Joe. Her husband's self-satisfied grin, half hidden under his moustache said it all. Lorries had been his life and he was never happier than when he was among them.

She gazed at the trim figure, barely able to comprehend that his infectious energy would no longer fill this room. Suddenly she recognised the black and gold cufflinks she'd given him the previous Christmas and felt the familiar lurch of her stomach and the lump in her throat. She gulped and looked away. This wasn't the time or place for sentimentality or for letting her emotions get the better of her.

Fighting the urge to give up her plans and go home, she walked over to the filing cabinet and pulled out the three drawers one by one, glancing quickly at the names in the bulging cardboard files. It would be impossible to study this lot, she decided, and for what reason? Did she really believe Joe's death had anything to do with a disgruntled customer, or a rejected supplier? There had to be more to it than that.

She went back to the desk and pulled at the top drawer but it didn't move. She rattled it impatiently, feeling her head pounding with every move, but the drawer wouldn't budge. Then she remembered the bunch of keys she'd found in Joe's briefcase. She hurried to the portacabin and took them out of her bag. Clasping them tightly she returned to the office, first making sure that Bretherton and Ken Dewhurst were nowhere to be seen. Bob was still out, presumably visiting a customer.

It only took a few moments to find the right key. The drawer slid out easily and she knew straight away that she'd found what she'd been looking for. The black leather address book lay on top of a tray containing pens and pencils. She could hardly believe her luck.

But as she reached into the drawer to take it out the office door swung open and Bob stood there, his face a curious mixture of pleading and pain. She closed the drawer.

'What is it, Bob?' she asked, at once alert and concerned.

He said nothing but closed the door silently and took a couple of strides into the room. Alarmed now that something must be seriously wrong, she waited for him to explain. But he said nothing. Like someone in a trance, he walked towards the desk, then paused, towering over her. His eyes, narrow and brooding, gazed into hers.

She'd never seen him so serious, so intense and her stomach tightened.

'What's wrong? Tell me what's wrong, Bob,' she pleaded.

He smiled uncertainly, his lips unusually pink and full against his shadowy chin, and shook his head.

'Nothing's wrong,' he said, almost whispering. 'Liberty, I've got to talk to you.' He moved effortlessly round the side of the desk and she could feel his breath on her face, smell the stale cigar.

'If it's about that partnership you mentioned . . .'

He looked hurt. 'No, no it's not about that. But I do need to talk to you about . . . about . . . Oh, Liberty, you must know.' He held out his hands in a pathetic gesture and his eyes seemed glazed.

It was then that she realised what he was finding so hard to put into words. Instinctively she stepped back and stared.

He wasn't unattractive. She'd known that from the day Joe had first introduced them in this very office over twenty years before. Now approaching 50, Bob's body showed no signs of ageing under the expensive white shirt. And someone half his age would be proud of his thick slicked-back hair, in spite of a few silver strands mingling with the dark brown.

But how could he imagine she would take kindly to his amorous advances? And Joe barely cold in his grave. The idea was repulsive. Quite apart from the fact that he was a married man.

He smiled, a weak, pathetic smile and reached out to touch her. She stiffened, feeling the hot finger tips brush against her arm, and startled at the strength of her revulsion. Yet she was painfully aware that a wrong word or action could very easily put an end to a valued friendship. Together with any future partnership.

In desperation she turned and grabbed the pile of letters, thrusting them into his outstretched hands.

'Oh Bob, I can't talk now. I've got the most awful headache but I didn't want to leave before you got back. I've sorted all this lot out. Have a look through, will you? And sign them. I'll finish the filing tomorrow. Only I must get home now before a full-blown migraine develops.'

His head jerked back and his eyes took on the look of a surprised animal.

'Oh, right. Yes, of course. I'm sorry. I hope you feel better soon. I . . .I'll see you tomorrow then? If you feel better.' His voice had almost trailed off.

She watched his long fingers curl tightly round the papers.

'Yes. I'm sure I'll be fine after a good night's sleep,' she said breathlessly. 'I'll try to get in by nine.' His little-boy-lost look reminded her of Ben years ago when she'd chastised him for stealing apples from the orchard at Bagley Hall. He opened his mouth as if to speak but no words came out. She sensed he wasn't going to be fobbed off so easily and tried to control the panic in her voice as she added hastily, 'By the way, tell Susan I'm sorry I didn't get the chance to catch up with her news at the funeral.' She held her breath and watched the square jaw clamp shut in an unwitting display of frustration and anger.

'I'll do that,' he said coldly and turned towards the door.

Liberty leaned back against the wall, feeling the cold rough stone through her blouse. She waited until he'd closed it behind him before opening the desk drawer and pulling out Joe's address book.

Making a snap decision not to open it until she got home, she tucked it under her arm and made straight for the portacabin where she grabbed her bag, locked up and left.

Unable to quell her confused emotions during the five minute drive, she pulled up outside Lowthwaite House in a highly excited state. Switching off the engine she clasped her hands together to try to suppress the shaking. But unsure whether her unwelcome reaction was anger that Bob had ruined a good friendship or excitement at the prospect of examining Joe's address book, she couldn't say. But a soothing glass of wine would help calm her nerves, she decided, at the precise moment a car engine revved noisily behind her before fading into the distance.

'Damn,' she cursed between gritted teeth. In all her confusion she'd forgotten to check whether the red car had been following her.

CHAPTER 6

Liberty settled herself on the settee in the cool, north-facing sitting room. Pinching the bridge of her nose to try to stem the pain now exploding in her head, she downed two extra-strong paracetamol and a glass of Joe's finest Burgundy. But her fingers still trembled as she pulled the address book out of her bag and flicked through the well-thumbed pages, her eyes widening in disbelief at the sight of so many names.

As she thumbed more slowly through the entries, experiencing a surge of regret at the sight of Joe's familiar neat script, she realised that a good proportion of them were different telephone numbers and addresses for the same person. Presumably Joe's acquaintances moved around a lot. But not, she saw with a faint smile of satisfaction, very far from Cumbria.

She scrutinised the names more closely. It wasn't as bad as she'd thought, but there must still be more than thirty names in the book. And none of them was familiar to her. Who were these people? And why had Joe kept their contact numbers hidden away? But more importantly, was it possible that one of these acquaintances had murdered him?

It wasn't difficult to decide what to do. She knew she must contact all the entries. But how? That was the hard bit. She could easily find the addresses of those with only a telephone number by looking in the directory. But then what? Should she phone, send a letter or question them in person? And what would she say? If any of them had anything to hide they would hardly volunteer the information readily. And without a policeman's expertise in interrogation how would she know when someone was feeding her a pack of lies? But there was no way she was handing the book over to Detective Chief Inspector Leatheringham, of that she was sure.

Her head had stopped throbbing now and she went outside, hoping that a gentle trot on Merry along the lakeside path might help her to think more clearly.

The sky had clouded over and a pinkish glow had descended on the slopes of Skiddaw. At least the sun wasn't setting on a completely wasted day, she thought, making for the stable block. But she must make sure that tomorrow was even more productive.

She awoke with the dawn chorus and arrived at Westerman and Brock's a few minutes before eight. At least with an early start she had a chance of being finished by lunch-time. And in the afternoon she'd have time to contact some of the names in Joe's address book. The trouble was she still couldn't make up her mind how she would do it, although a quick phone call seemed by far the easiest way.

As she hurried towards the portacabin, sunlight bathed the loading bay. Bretherton, his uniform already sweat-stained, leaned over the edge shouting instructions to two drivers loading a trailer. Suddenly she stopped. It was like a light being switched on.

Of course. Who better to advise her? She looked at the stooping body with renewed interest. Long worry lines seemed etched more deeply into his face than she remembered and his expression as he examined a triangular-shaped parcel betrayed a troubled soul. But whatever his problems at home he'd always been willing to put himself out for others.

For a moment she stood undecided at the door of the portacabin. What if his wife had had one of her 'turns' as he called them? Doris had been having turns since their five-year-old daughter was killed in a road accident more than twenty years ago. He'd never spoken about it directly and no-one really knew the details, except that it had traumatised his wife. A frail woman to start with, she'd gone steadily downhill, spending more time in the psychiatric wing of Carlisle City Hospital than out of it, according to Ben who'd let it slip that he'd nursed her on numerous occasions before his move to Sheffield.

But even on her good days Doris rarely ventured out of the house. Liberty had met her only once, at the Co-op in Penrith about two years ago. Bretherton had been pushing the trolley and Doris, looking older than her sixty or so years, had been leaning against him, as if she needed propping up. Her pale, sickly complexion, sunken eyes and dark grey wiry hair dragged into a bun had reminded Liberty of the mad woman in a film of Jane Eyre she'd seen on TV. But then it had occurred to her that once she'd probably been a striking, raven-haired beauty. Bretherton had seemed agitated and after the briefest of introductions had led Doris towards the check-outs.

Liberty wondered now whether it was wise to involve someone in her investigations with such a volatile private life. At that moment Bretherton turned away and was making for the sorting area. She made a snap decision.

'Bretherton,' she called, her voice sounding surprisingly loud above the clatter of boxes being thrown into the back of trailers. He stopped and glanced back, not seeming to see her. She waved and hurried across the cobbled yard. 'Can I have a word with you? When it's convenient.'

He looked surprised but his voice was flat when he answered, 'Of course, Mrs Westerman. I'll come now.'

He followed Liberty like a lap-dog into the portacabin. The airless, plastic room smelled just as foul as the day before. She put her hand over her mouth and glanced at Bretherton. But he seemed not to have noticed, engrossed as he was in meticulously wiping his feet on the coconut mat behind the door. Liberty sighed and wondered how long he might take to complete the ritual if his shoes were really dirty.

She gestured towards the swivel chair she kept for visitors. In effect it was rarely used as most of the drivers who came to her with their time sheets and wage queries preferred to stand. Bretherton lowered himself warily onto the edge of the chair, his heavy eyes following her.

Wishing she had someone more dynamic to help her, she made up her mind to tell him only as much as he needed to know. At least for the moment.

'Bretherton, I need your help but just say if you have too much on your plate already.'

He nodded uncertainly but his dour expression seemed to lift and his eyes brightened.

'I'll do whatever I can, Mrs Westerman.'

She reached in her bag and took out Joe's address book.

'I need to contact all these people.' She flicked through the pages to give him an idea of the number involved. 'I have reason to believe that one or more of them might know something about Joe's murder, but I don't want the police involved. Not yet anyway.'

His expression was blank except for a slight wrinkling of his forehead. Liberty wondered whether she'd made a mistake in asking for his help. It had been eight or nine years since he'd left the police force. Perhaps he was past it? Or did he just find her suppression of possible evidence difficult to stomach?

A low humming came from between his tight lips and she waited expectantly, straining her head forward and willing him to say something. But if she felt frustrated now, how would she be able to tolerate his plodding preciseness throughout a long and protracted search for evidence to nail Joe's killer?

He looked up and began wringing his over-large hands. 'There are numerous ways of going about a task such as this,' he began. 'But I would suggest that each person be visited in turn. A preliminary phone call might give them too much time to consider their position - especially if they have something to hide. But I should also point out that the interviewing of suspects should be carried out only by a police officer.'

She'd expected as much. Half a lifetime of police training hadn't been wasted on Bretherton. 'Yes, but they're not exactly suspects. More acquaintances who may be able to help the investigation.'

'Hmmm,' he murmured, but she knew he wasn't convinced.

'I wondered if you might consider helping me with the interviews.' There, she'd said it. But she regretted it almost immediately.

He rubbed his chin and shook his head.

'Oh, I don't know whether that would be a good idea, Mrs Westerman. It could be dangerous. Not that I'm worried about myself, mind. But it wouldn't be right to . . .'

'Look, Bretherton,' she snapped. 'Whether you agree to help or not, I'm going to try to contact as many of these people as possible. I just thought that, being an ex-policeman, you might relish the challenge.'

He glared as if she had hit him below the belt and spluttered. 'Well, yes. Of course, if you put it like that, but . . .' He paused to compose himself, his face screwed into a worried mask. Then, in a strangled tone: 'What would you like me to do?'

'Visit the first three names in the address book. I'll take the next few.' She surprised herself with the speed of her decision.

He nodded compliantly and she guessed he'd been less attracted by the challenge than incensed by her declaration to go ahead without him.

'You'd better tell me what information you require,' he said.

She gave him the details, mystified throughout the briefing as to how this pitiful shadow of a man had ever managed to reach the rank of sergeant with the Northumbrian police force.

At just after twelve she sat back and glanced from the pile of envelopes franked ready for posting to the almost empty in-tray. The petty cash tin and the drivers' wages too had been sorted out. Feeling pleased with her morning's work she decided it was time to take advantage of her part-time status and slipped out of the portacabin. But when she saw Bob's dark green Jaguar parked in the shade of the main office block next to her Sierra she stopped.

She'd understood from Bretherton that Bob would be out all day visiting customers in the North East. She wondered now if he'd returned early in the hope of cornering her again before she left. Her inclination was to believe that he'd got the message and wouldn't try again, but she wasn't taking any chances. She hurried across the yard without even a sideways glance at Bob's office window.

Five minutes later she turned into the drive of Lowthwaite House with the sudden realisation that she had no recollection of the journey. She switched off the engine but a car back-firing behind her made her jump and she glanced in the wing mirror just in time to glimpse a pale blue car as it sped off from the gateway. Had it been following her? She couldn't say for sure. All she knew was that it was the same colour as the one which Jacob and Dr Firth had seen parked opposite on the night of Joe's murder.

In spite of the heat in the car she shivered. What if the killer were stalking her, waiting for his opportunity to finish her off too? Suddenly she realised that those other times she'd thought someone was following her might not be the fanciful imaginings of a neurotic mind.

For a moment she sat inspecting the high wooden doors of the stable block. One day soon she would find the courage to clear it out – and in the process, uncover the spot where Joe died. But not today. Her temerity irritated her and she found her mood changing to one of anger.

What was the point of kidding herself that she could help catch a ruthless killer if she was too timid to confront her fears and too distracted to notice she was being followed?

One of those quotations repeated time and again by Sister Monica sprang into her mind so suddenly that it took her by surprise: 'The only thing we have to fear is fear itself.'

She jumped out of the car and dragged both doors open. As daylight spread across the cobbled floor she reached for one of the brushes in the corner and began to sweep.

By two thirty she was on her way to Cockermouth. The old road past the golf club was the quickest and most scenic route. On such a bright day the drive would relax her. But the prospect of arriving unannounced at a stranger's door with the intention of questioning him about his dealings with a murder victim had given her more than a few second thoughts. A dose of Dutch courage with lunch hadn't helped either.

But now the mid-afternoon sun, high above the lush pasture, gave her a feeling of optimism even though she had no idea what she would say to Winston Dodd, the first name on her list. She switched on the tape in the dashboard. As Vivaldi's Four Seasons filled the warm car, Liberty loosened her vice-like grip on the steering wheel and vowed to stop letting her fears rule her life.

Her A-Z of Cockermouth had already shown her that Engleton Gardens was on one of those newly-created estates of near identical houses which had grown up on the fringes of the town. As she drove through the labyrinth of tree-lined avenues, she wondered, briefly and without concern, what Wordsworth would have made of these modern developments encircling his birthplace. What did concern her was the kind of residents these places housed. Hard-working, law-abiding families probably, she decided, hoping that Winston Dodd would fit into this category.

Engleton Gardens was a particularly charmless cul-de-sac of semi-detached box-like houses. The curtains across the downstairs window of number three were closed and she could make out no signs of life as she parked on the pavement in front of the overgrown lawn.

Suddenly the foolishness of her quest hit her. What on earth could she hope to achieve by coming here? Winston Dodd was probably no more than a business acquaintance too insignificant for Joe ever to have mentioned.

But something inside drove her on. She'd come this far, what harm would it do to speak to Dodd? And if nothing came of it, then at least she'd tried.

She stepped out of the car and smoothed down the creases in her beige linen skirt. The open-plan garden, a postage-stamp lawn surrounded by a bare border of soil, gave the impression that the house had only recently been built. She wondered how long Dodd had lived here. But there had been no previous address for him in Joe's address book, she remembered, concluding that Dodd must have been a recent acquaintance. The quickness of her observation both surprised and pleased her, giving her the confidence to stride up the tarmac path towards the garish green front door.

No bell was apparent so she rapped on the flimsy letter-box. The wait seemed endless. What if Dodd was a shift worker trying to get some sleep? He wouldn't be too pleased at being disturbed. She shifted nervously from one foot to the other, fighting the urge to retreat. After a few moments and two unanswered knocks, she decided to give it one more try. But as she took hold of the metal flap the door swung open, almost catapulting her into the thick-set figure of a tall, muscular man wearing only boxer shorts and an off-white vest.

The expression in the heavy, muddy-brown eyes was not only suspicious but openly hostile. She gasped and took a step backwards. This wasn't the kind of resident she'd expected in Engleton Gardens. For a moment she was speechless.

'Yeah?' he demanded, his breath thick with the smell of beer.

Suddenly she felt vulnerable. If only she could think up some excuse and get away. But why *did* she should feel so threatened, on a sunny summer afternoon in the middle of a sleepy housing estate?

'Winston Dodd?' she asked, feeling the words croak from the back of her throat.

'Who's askin'?' he grunted, flexing his broad shoulders and jutting his chin forward.

'My name's Liberty Westerman. I believe you knew my husband, Joe.' She paused, wary of his reaction and poised to make a dash for the car. But then she saw with disbelief his tight mouth spreading into a wide smile revealing a row of discoloured though perfectly aligned teeth. It wasn't what she'd expected and she didn't know how to interpret it. The mocking, contemptuous face unnerved her, but in the absence of any reply she gabbled breathlessly, 'As you probably know, he was murdered almost two weeks ago and I'm contacting all those who knew him in the hope that . . .'

He didn't let her finish. 'How'd you find me?' he demanded, his grin fading.

Gripping her shoulder bag tightly she looked him in the eye. 'Your name was in my husband's address book.'

'You're kidding,' he muttered clenching and unclenching his fists. Then he shook his head. 'That guy sure was trouble.'

'Sorry? How do you mean?' she asked.

'Hey, lady, if you don't know I ain't gonna tell you.' He stepped back to close the door and she saw the tattered suitcase behind him. Something told her he wouldn't be around long.

'Please. Just one more minute. How did you know my husband?'

He looked at her, his dull eyes seeming to light up with mischief. 'He didn't tell you, did he? I knew he was a cagey one, that one. Let's just say he hired me to watch his back. Never knew why, not really. Watch his back on his little trips to Ireland, that's what he said. Didn't say nothin' about when he was home.' He gave a sly grin as if he were enjoying a private joke.

'What trips? When did Joe go to Ireland?' she interrupted, conscious of the irony of asking a total stranger about her husband's movements.

Dodd drew himself up so that he seemed more menacing and even taller than the six foot she had guessed at earlier. 'I gotta go,' he growled, eyeing her suspiciously and slammed the door shut.

Liberty stood transfixed for a few moments, trying to take in what he'd told her. She had no reason to suppose he was lying but it all sounded so unreal. She shook her head in bewilderment and turned towards her car.

Was it just a coincidence that this was the second time in 24 hours that the subject of Ireland had reared its head? Or had she stumbled on the mystery behind Joe's murder?

As she drove back along the by-pass she felt drained and light-headed, realising just how much of a battering her nerves had taken. But, mixed with her exhaustion was a vague feeling of elation at having managed to extract at least some information from Dodd. This first unnerving interview over, she felt sure that the rest must get easier.

The telephone was ringing as she opened the front door and she ran to answer it.

'Lib? It's me, Sondra. I've been tyring to get hold of you for ages. Bob said you'd finished at lunch-time. Where've you been?'

Liberty smiled. It was her friend's favourite greeting when she'd had to ring more than once, although why Liberty always felt obliged to apologise for not waiting around to answer the telephone she couldn't say.

'Sorry, I had someone to see.'

As usual, Sondra wanted to know the details and Liberty found herself giving Sondra a carefully edited version, along with a toned-down description of Dodd's appearance and aggressive manner. Ireland wasn't mentioned. Only that Dodd had worked for Joe.

'He sounds just like the landlord at the Dog and Duck in Ambleforth - and you know what Joe said about him.'

Liberty grunted vaguely.

'Don't you remember? It was your birthday . We'd all been to Cockermouth for a Chinese and Derek fancied a pint on the way home. But Joe took one look at the landlord and said there was no way he was going to patronise someone like that. Derek was really miffed, I can tell you. Surely you remember, Lib. We ended up at your place and played dominoes instead.'

'Yes, I remember,' she said, not wishing to pursue the conversation.

Joe had been in a particularly difficult mood that night, she remembered. They'd had a row before going out because Liberty had arranged to meet up with Sondra and Derek. Their preoccupation with the golf club and amateur operatic society irritated him and he always avoided them if he could. Yes, thought Liberty, he was extremely fussy about who he mixed with, either socially or at work. 'Seems funny, doesn't it?' Sondra persisted, 'that Joe would hire someone like that? A lorry driver, was he?' Liberty heard a sudden gasp. 'You don't think he could have had anything to do with . . .with . . .you know . . . Joe's . . .?'

'Murder?' suggested Liberty, determined not to wrap up the facts in euphemisms.

'Well, yes. He sounds just the type. Don't you think you should inform the police?'

'No,' replied Liberty rather more firmly than she intended. 'There's no need for that.'

'Well I just hope you know what you're doing, Lib. Those sort of people can be very dangerous.'

'Don't worry, Sondra. I'm no heroine. I won't take any chances.'

CHAPTER 7

Just after seven o'clock that evening Liberty tipped the remains of her chicken stir-fry in the waste bin and made a decision to postpone the whiskey and soda she'd promised herself. Instead she would call on Bretherton.

Buoyed up by a strangely unsettling curiosity, she'd been unable to get Winston Dodd's words out of her head. She switched on the dishwasher and decided she needed to find out more. Bretherton might have some information for her and she had an uncontrollable urge now to find out precisely what. She could telephone him of course, but a drive seemed more appealing. The heat from the hob had made the kitchen unbearably hot and she judged that a drive to Wigton would cool her down. If he wasn't in she would just have to try to get hold of him over the weekend.

It had been some years since her last visit to Bretherton's home - a red brick, end-of-terrace with the gable-end shored up - but she remembered, before she reached it, that the front door was never used. A notice on the inside of the glass panel requested that visitors use the back entrance. Liberty made her way along the path at the side of the house where, until ten years ago, another house had stood before it was demolished in a road-widening scheme.

Reaching the back door, its blue paint cracked and faded, she stopped to check her watch - 7.25. Bretherton should be home by now. She knocked on the door but, at that precise moment, an explosion of sound, like breaking glass, filled the night air.

Instinctively she jumped back, wrenching her ankle on the rough cobbles, her heart racing. Off balance and in pain, she tried to locate the crash but almost immediately it was followed by an ear-piercing shriek. This time she knew at once that the sound had come from inside the house. She gasped and grabbed the door handle. Someone was in trouble.

Without a thought for her own safety she pushed her shoulder against the door, rattling the handle. But it wouldn't budge. What should she do? She glanced about her, rubbing at the burning sensation in her ankle. A small window over a disused coal bunker had been left open. She hobbled over to it, wincing at the pain as she clambered up and cursing her clumsiness. But as she pressed her face to the window and peered cautiously past the white pot sink she caught sight of Bretherton's bear-like figure framed in the doorway to the lounge.

He had his back to her and was holding the side of his head. At his feet lay the remnants of a china vase. As she watched in horror, a drop of blood trickled through his fingers and ran down the back of his broad hand.

She froze, watching the vapour from her breath spread over the glass. What should she do? Did Bretherton need help? But the weary-looking body which now sank against the door-jamb gave her the impression that, whatever might have happened, he was not in need of rescuing at this moment. She half turned away, but out of the corner of her eye she spotted another figure, smaller and frail, push past Bretherton.

Liberty bent her head closer and recognised Doris immediately. Her tangled hair, a mass of grey curls, half-covered her sickly face but Liberty could still make out the wild, flashing eyes which gazed unfocused towards the ceiling. Her skin, dry and wizened, hung loosely over her cheek bones.

Suddenly she spun round. 'You . . . you make me sick. Always running round like some pathetic lapdog.' She wagged a painfully thin finger at her husband.

It was unforgivable, eavesdropping like this. Liberty knew she should leave at once, but she couldn't help herself.

'Doris, please.' Bretherton's voice was low and weary.

'Don't you 'please' me. You don't give a damn about me . . . how I feel. Do you? Go on, admit it.'

'Doris, that's not true.'

'Don't deny it,' Doris continued. 'You can't wait to get me out of the way. Then you can go on running errands for that...' The querulous voice rose in a crescendo.

Liberty couldn't believe she was doing this. She felt like a voyeur, one of those ghouls who frequent the scenes of accidents in the hope of catching a glimpse of some poor victim and their injuries. She tried to convince herself that she wasn't like that. She wasn't like the rest of them, the vultures who'd made her life a misery since Joe's death. This was different. She was only doing this in order to discover the truth. But did that really make her any less guilty of intruding on other people's personal tragedies?

She bent her head, averting her gaze, but a gut feeling told her that she couldn't afford to be scrupulous. She pushed her face up to the glass, suddenly regretting her decision to enlist the help of someone about whom she knew so little.

Bretherton had turned to face his wife now, his arms wide and pleading. Liberty could see clearly the long narrow cut above his temple which still oozed blood. A red band had formed on his white collar and the memory of Joe's fatal injury flashed into her mind.

'Doris. Please. Calm down. It won't do you any good to get yourself all upset.' Bretherton's tone was pleading, although Liberty thought she detected a note of desperation.

' 'Calm down, calm down' is that all you can say?' Doris waved her arms frenziedly, her baggy cardigan flapping like impotent wings. 'How can I calm down when you insist on doing everything to spite me? And what about poor Jane? If you'd loved her you'd never have gone working for that . . . that . . . devil.'

Bretherton's body seemed to crumple under the onslaught and he leaned against the rickety kitchenette.

'That's not true. You know it's not. Why do you always say such cruel things?' He sounded desperate. 'You know as well as I do that I had to take that job. We couldn't have managed on my police pension. And there was nothing else. I didn't like the idea any more than you.'

'Like? Like? I loathed the idea.' She spat out the words, her face twisted with hatred. 'I begged you not to go. But you wouldn't listen. You had to do it. Now look at me. Look what you've done to me.' She flew at him, her fists pounding into his chest until he caught hold of her wrists and gently restrained her.

Liberty could hear herself panting and had to fight against an impulse to run. She tried to make some sense of what was going on but she couldn't. Suddenly Bretherton let go of his wife and turned away. Liberty ducked down so that he wouldn't spot her, but not before she'd caught a glimpse of the tears welling in his eyes.

'For God's sake, Doris.'

'Look at me. Just look at me.'

For a moment neither of them spoke. 'You've not been well since Jane died,' he said finally.

'Died? Died?' Her voice was getting louder, as if she were coming over to the window. Liberty crouched down beside the coal bunker. 'Jane didn't die. She was killed.'

'Please, Doris.'

'Go on, admit it. Killed by that murdering swine. And if you cared a toss for her you'd get down on your knees and thank God he's dead too.'

Liberty shook her head. Surely they couldn't be talking about Joe. Joe hadn't killed their little girl. The woman was obviously off her head.

'Please, Doris. Don't talk like that. He didn't kill Jane. You know that.' But Doris wouldn't be convinced.

'I hope he rots in hell. And his ever-loving wife with him.' Liberty couldn't believe how someone she'd hardly met could hate her so much.

'Doris, please. Don't do this.'

'You... you pathetic... why don't you tell her? Tell her how her precious husband killed our daughter . . . our lovely. . . beautiful . . .' Her voice trailed off and Liberty thought she heard a sob.

'It won't do any good.'

'No. You won't tell her, will you? Ah, you're a pathetic wimp of a man.' Liberty shivered and sank to her knees on the rough shale. The woman was clearly deranged - and possibly dangerous.

'*I'll* tell her then.' Doris's voice sounded triumphant. 'I'll tell her he admitted it when you told him who you were.'

'I never told him.' Bretherton sounded breathless now and defeated. 'He never knew Jane was my daughter. He wouldn't have taken me on if he'd known.'

'But . . . he must have known.'

'Why should he? It was nearly eighteen years before. Just another road traffic accident as far as he was concerned.'

Neither spoke for a moment, then Liberty heard Doris's voice, low and whining.

'But you said . . . you said you told him. You said he begged forgiveness, admitted he was to blame. You said.....'

'I lied.' Bretherton interrupted, barely audibly.

The sobbing, loud and abandoned, followed almost immediately.

Liberty could listen no longer and crept silently away, wincing at the pain in her ankle and convinced that it had been a terrible mistake to have stayed.

In spite of what she'd heard, she couldn't believe that either Bretherton or his wife had anything to do with Joe's murder. And yet. Could she really trust Bretherton to have her best interests at heart? And what was the true story behind Jane's death?

She would make it her business to find out.

But for the moment she felt drained and sullied, with an unshakeable conviction that a long soak in the bath wouldn't even restore her body, let alone her spirits or peace of mind.

CHAPTER 8

Liberty awoke earlier than ever next morning. Even though it was a Saturday she threw back the sheet, eager to get on with what she hoped would prove a fruitful day. The violent dreams and images of the night were best forgotten lest they cloud her mind and colour her judgement.

She dressed quickly in a sleeveless top and cotton skirt. The low, strappy sandals, she hoped, would be cool and comfortable for her bandaged ankle on what she supposed would be a long and arduous visit to Manchester. She'd made the decision the previous evening some time between her bath and crawling into bed. She'd decided too that she either carried on alone checking the names in Joe's address book or gave it to DCI Leatheringham. What was not an option was to put more pressure on Bretherton.

The Fox and Ferret, a public house in the heart of the city, was the next entry in the book, but no contact name was included. Liberty planned to arrive just after opening time. If she left it much later, she reasoned, it would probably be full of city shoppers.

It wasn't yet eight o'clock when she threw open the patio doors. But the stagnant wall of heat which greeted her promised an even more unpleasant day than yesterday. Even in perfect weather she invariably found Manchester tiring and oppressive. And the temptation to postpone the visit was growing stronger.

In the hope that a short stroll might restore her resolve, she set off across the lawn, spending a few minutes in the paddock fussing over Merry before hobbling along the path by the lake.

It was cooler under the trees but the thought of the long, hot drive down the M6 and the uncertainty of what she might discover at the Fox and Ferret made her even more convinced that the hunt for Joe's killer was beyond her. She gazed out blankly over Skiddaw and saw that the sun was starting to break through the thick haze.

The weather forecast last night had given little hope of a let-up in the heat but the sight of clear blue patches spreading across the skyline gave her a feeling of optimism.

But as she entered the kitchen a loud rapping on the front door startled her. She glanced at her watch, irritated that the simple pleasure of being able to start the weekend at her own pace was to be denied her. She pulled back the bar and turned the key in the oak-panelled front door. Giles Tranter's burly figure almost filled the doorway.

Until now she'd only heard about his aggressive, intimidating manner, but one glance at his curled-up lips and the narrowed eyes staring from behind puffed-out cheeks and she was in no doubt that she was about to witness it for herself.

Before she had the chance to invite him in he pushed past her, waving a rolled document tied with a red ribbon.

'I can't wait any longer,' he began. His voice was thick and forceful. 'Time's running out and I need to speak to you urgently. I've left it as long as was decent after. . .'

Liberty nodded, recognising the familiar awkwardness of even the most confident person when the subject of Joe's death came up.

'I have to go out in ten minutes,' she said, deciding on the spur of the moment to catch the train rather than drive to Manchester. She'd ring the station later to find out the times but it was important now not to be delayed. She decided to keep him in the hall.

Tranter gripped the roll between thick fingers, tapping it loudly on the palm of his other hand. 'I'll not beat about the bush. I need your signature on the land-deal I had with your husband. I've brought the documents with me. It'll only take a minute. He was ready to sign two weeks ago but then . . .'

Liberty felt as though she was being bull-dozed into something but she wasn't sure what. 'I'm sorry, Mr Tranter, but I have no idea which land you mean. Joe told me nothing about any agreement.'

His mouth twisted in irritation and she could feel her face flushing. She hated being involved in business deals, mainly because she understood little of the jargon, or the psychological warfare employed, usually by men, when pushing through 'a good deal'.

For what seemed like the millionth time she wished that Joe was still alive. He wouldn't have let Tranter brow-beat him like this. And why the rush? She couldn't imagine what Giles Tranter wanted more land for. Bagley Hall was surrounded by hundreds of acres of woodland, pasture and farm-land. So why did he want some of Lowthwaite's twenty-five acres? It didn't make sense.

She hoped he wasn't going to create a fuss, but one look at his puffed-out, scarlet cheeks and she knew he wasn't going to be put off too easily. Well two could play that game. She met his glare but as she did so a totally unexpected thought struck her. He looked just like an overweight goldfish. It was all she could do to hold back a nervous giggle.

His eyes flashed. 'Now look here, Mrs Westerman, I had a deal with your husband and I expect you to honour that. It was a gentleman's agreement and I've got a witness to it.'

Liberty shuffled uneasily. Dealing with legal matters wasn't something she'd ever had to do before and she had no idea how a court of law would rule on the matter.

'What land are we talking about, Mr Tranter?'

'Why, the strip from the bridge, between the road and the lake. Up as far as the house. About twenty acres in all.'

'But that would only leave me with the garden.'

'More or less. But you'd be getting a good price for it. You'd not get a better offer anywhere else.'

'That may be. But I don't want to sell the land. And I can't believe Joe would have agreed to part with it. It was left to him by his aunt along with the house.' She shook her head vigorously. 'No, he would never have agreed to sell it. Especially not without telling me. I'm afraid there must be some mistake.' She tried to sound convincing but a seed of doubt had planted itself at the back of her mind. There were a lot of things Joe hadn't told her.

'There's no mistake.' Tranter unrolled the document and waved it in her face. 'And if you think you can wriggle out of this, you're mistaken. I'll take you to every court in the land - the European court too - before I'll give up.'

There were a host of questions she would need answers to but now wasn't the time. She took hold of the door handle. 'I have no intention of wriggling out of my obligations. You have no need to worry on that score. But I'm sure you understand that I need to know the details of the agreement before I sign anything. And, as you can see, you've caught me at an awkward moment. I have a train to catch so I'll have to discuss this with you another time. If you'd care to come back . . .'

'Oh, I'll be back all right. I'm not giving up, you can count on that.' His face a dark purplish mass of fury he jabbed the papers like a dagger into her stomach and left.

Liberty closed the door quickly and leaned her back against it. Was she being over sensitive or did his parting words sound very like a threat? The man might be a moron, a chauvinist pig with the manners of a lager-lout, but she couldn't afford to ignore him.

The encounter had unsettled her and she wondered whether she had the stamina for her planned visit to Manchester. The grandfather clock chimed the half hour. If she was going to make it to the Fox and Ferret for soon after opening time she needed to be on her way.

It only took a few minutes to put a notebook in her bag and check that she had enough money for the journey. Tomorrow she would concentrate on Tranter and his claims. But for now she preferred to forget him.

There were no hold-ups on the half hour drive to Carlisle and she arrived on the platform with minutes to spare before the through train to Manchester was due to arrive. A current of cool air blew through the station and she allowed herself a brief moment of renewed optimism. But it was short-lived.

As she settled back in her seat, watching sunlight and shadows alternately flitting across the carriage, she realised someone was watching her from across the aisle. It was only a fleeting glimpse and almost as soon as she'd noticed, he lowered his eyes. But she was convinced this wasn't just the idle curiosity of a bored passenger. She'd noticed him first on the platform. The hooded eyes under thick brows, the bushy black hair and over-large head were quite distinctive and she'd concluded that he must be an immigrant, from Romania or the Balkans probably. But just because his appearance was a little unusual didn't mean she should be suspicious of him.

She unfolded the Daily Mail which she'd bought at the station kiosk and wondered if all this cloak and dagger stuff was making her paranoid. But as she turned the page her attention was drawn to a short piece outlining police fears of a possible terrorist attack in the North of England within the next few days.

Her mind wandered back to the cutting she'd found in Joe's study and wondered vaguely whether there could be any connection. But why should there be? She shut the newspaper, her mind made up to resist seeing intrigue and danger round every corner.

When the train pulled into Manchester Piccadilly an hour and a half later she was already standing by the door. The foreign-looking man, who'd shown no further interest in her and had slept for the remainder of the journey, was only just rousing himself. She walked quickly up the platform without a backward glance.

But as she hurried past the ticket office she realised she'd forgotten to check the timetable for the return journey. She stopped, wondering whether to bother. But it would probably be useful to know. She let out an irritated sigh and swung round.

It was then she saw him. There was no mistaking his intention this time. He was following her, peering out from behind a display of newspapers like a cat stalking its prey. Her heart leapt with the realisation that she was his intended victim. But what should she do? She glanced about her, swivelling her head round, trying not to look at him. Surely she'd read somewhere that all stations are now patrolled by the police. And with the threat of a terrorist attack there must be at least one. But there was none to be seen.

A loud buzzing in her ears almost drowned out the click of heels on the concourse and the low drone of voices. Clutching her handbag tightly to her chest she pushed her way through the surge of people rushing towards the exit. But as she emerged into the daylight she saw with a sinking heart that a queue had built up at the taxi rank. She stopped in her tracks, buffeted by a sea of bodies and bags, unable to decide on her next move. Suddenly, not daring to look behind her, she turned into the stream of people heading towards Piccadilly and the shopping centre.

Half limping, half running she pressed on, petrol-filled fumes seeping into her every breath. At the first cross-roads she paused, gasping, and stole a quick glance behind her. Please God, don't let him be there, she prayed. But the thick-set figure was clearly visible, rising head and shoulders above the crowd. People were dispersing now, up side roads or into one of the small shops along the route.

Only a young couple and a woman pushing a buggy were in front of her and she began to feel increasingly vulnerable. The traffic, which seemed light for a Saturday, rushed past unconcerned. She scanned the road ahead, desperate for the sight of a vacant taxi but none came. The tap-tap of her sandals on the pavement sounded unnaturally loud now as she increased her pace, trying to ignore the painful dryness at the back of her throat and the throbbing pain in her ankle.

She could see the red and blue buses parked in the distance but the oppressive heat was sapping her strength. She couldn't keep this pace up for long. Then one of the buses started to move off. It was coming this way. Trying to ignore the pain that was now spreading up her calf, she sprinted towards it. But the spiky-haired youth at the bus stop leaped quickly on board and it looked as though she'd missed her chance. With a last desperate effort she lunged forward and flung herself onto the platform just as the doors closed.

She had no idea where the bus was heading so she paid for a ticket to the terminus and collapsed onto a seat hoping she hadn't done any permanent damage to her ankle. But at least she'd shaken off her pursuer.

Staring blankly out of the window, she struggled to make sense of it all. Who was this man and why was he following her? The obvious conclusion was that he was Joe's murderer and the thought sent shivers up her spine. If that was the case her own life was in danger too. But she had her doubts.

If his motive was murder he'd had his opportunity on the station at Carlisle - and on the train too. And if he knew who she was and where she lived, why was he following her to Manchester? It just didn't add up.

Too hot and exhausted to think clearly, she sat rigid, aware only of the ache in her leg and the lurching of the bus. But after a few minutes she turned to watch the shops and hotels go by. If she wasn't careful she'd end up miles from her destination. She waited a few more stops then got up and hobbled off to look for a phone to call a taxi.

Half an hour later the cab driver turned off the road and stopped under a viaduct.

'OK if I leave you here, love?' he asked leaning over the back of his seat and revealing a mouth full of decayed and nicotine-stained teeth. 'Only the last time I went down to the Fox and Ferret I ended up with two punctures. There's glass all over the place. Landlord doesn't even bother to clear it up now.' He shrugged and pointed under the arch way. 'It's just down there. You can't miss it. Just follow the canal. That'll be eight pounds sixty.'

Liberty took out her purse and glanced down the narrow cobbled street. A train rattled noisily overhead and she felt her heart beating faster with the vibration. Was it madness to continue her search in what she increasingly felt was a hostile environment?

The temptation to hurry back to the familiarity, if not safety, of Cumbria was difficult to overcome. She longed to ride Merry along the shores of Bassenthwaite Lake, the wind in her face. But then what? Give up? Nobody else would do this for her if she did.

It was at that moment that she felt the full weight of the loneliness she'd been struggling to fight off since Joe's death. Now, like a pillow over her face, it seemed to suffocate her.

'You goin' or not?' the driver sounded impatient. Was she or wasn't she? 'Yes, yes,' she replied fumbling for the money. 'Eight pounds sixty, you said?'

She gave him a ten pound note and climbed out, surprised and not displeased that she'd refused to take the easy option. Tossing her head back, she tucked her bag under her arm and walked under the archway, carefully side-stepping the cardboard debris left by a vagrant who, by the look of it, had resided there the previous night.

The buildings to her left had been boarded up and the street was deserted. All she could hear was the dull crunching of her heels on the pavement as she followed the low stone wall beside the canal. The vile smell of stagnant water and diesel, which she had noticed only vaguely at first, now assaulted her nostrils.

The crystal clear water of the river Cocker, which flowed under the bridge at the edge of Lowthwaite's land seemed a lifetime away. She picked up speed, spurred on by the thought that the quicker she concluded her business here, the sooner she'd be back home. It was still only half past eleven. With a bit of luck she could be back by tea-time.

A few moments later a garish, red building came into sight, wedged between a derelict mill and a fenced-off piece of spare land. The sign above the door confirmed that this was indeed The Fox and Ferret.

She crossed over the cobblestones, treading carefully for fear she would twist her ankle again or that the glass grinding under her sandals would cut her feet. She hoped that the public house might not seem as bad close up. But the peeling frontage, rotting window sills, the pitted and battered door, all confirmed her worst fears. Her heart was thumping as she stopped outside, apprehensive about the sort of people she might have to deal with. But it was no use giving up now. She took a long, deep breath and stepped into the dimly-lit passage.

The stench of beer and cigarette-smoke made her stomach lurch, but before she could cover her nose a heavily-built man pushed past her knocking her off balance. She gasped, flattening herself against the wall and watched the figure stagger out into the light. Blowing the foul-tasting air from her mouth, she turned towards the dingy saloon which even at this early hour was thick with a cloud of smoke.

If Joe had had any dealings with this place, and she could scarcely believe he had, there was no doubt in her mind that he'd never set foot in the place. He could never have tolerated the filth and the stench.

She pushed her way through the scattered stools towards the bar, not daring to look in the dingy alcoves, but it felt like a hundred eyes were trained on her, watching her every move. It was unnerving. Surely she should be the one eyeing them up and down, not the other way round.

She reached the bar, its surface littered with dirty glasses and full ashtrays which she was sure couldn't possibly have accumulated just this morning. Had the place been open all night? she wondered, leaning against the bar and searching for someone in charge. But only the leering face of a drunk gazed up at her from where he lay slumped on a stool at the other end of the bar. It was then that she realised, with surprise and some satisfaction, that she hadn't thought about alcohol for more than twelve hours.

The seconds seemed like hours before a small, wiry man with receding hair and a face resembling the ferret on the sign outside emerged from a door at the far end of the bar. A filthy tea towel was slung over one shoulder. He didn't ask what she wanted.

'I'm looking for the landlord,' she said.

'So?' he asked, barely moving his tight lips.

'I need to speak to him. Privately. Can you tell me where I can find him?' The smoke burned at the back of her throat and made her cough.

'You've found him,' came the unenthusiastic reply through congested lungs. Liberty thought she detected an Irish accent but couldn't be sure. She gave an involuntary smile but his expression was far from friendly.

'It's about my husband. He died two weeks ago and I'm trying to trace some of his friends and acquaintances. His name was Joe Westerman . . .'

Even to herself her words sounded formal and, in this setting, mildly ridiculous. His eyes narrowed and his nose twitched almost imperceptibly but he said nothing. She was sure the name had meant something to him.

'He had the name of the Fox and Ferret in an address book. I just wondered if he might have done business with you in the past.' Something flickered behind the motionless dark eyes.

'You wondered wrong. Now d'you want a drink or what?' His rasping, breathless voice was now tinged with hostility.

To her, drinking was a comforting, relaxing experience. It could never be that in this environment. She shook her head. It had been a fruitless journey, only serving to increase her conviction that not only was she totally out of her depth but that the truth about Joe's life and death might never be uncovered. And in the absence of the truth, she wondered how far DCI Leatheringham might be prepared to manipulate half-truths in order to get a result.

CHAPTER 9

The hall clock was chiming five and the telephone was ringing as Liberty unlocked the front door of Lowthwaite House.

'Mum, where *have* you been?' The voice was unmistakably Ruth's and the emphasis on the 'have' made Liberty feel as though she were sixteen again and being scolded by her mother for staying out late. But she'd already decided that, unless it became absolutely unavoidable, she would disclose nothing about her investigations to Ruth and Ben. They would only try to talk her out of it, pointing out that mothers, especially mothers fast approaching fifty, don't do that sort of thing.

The Autumn term had already started at Holy Cross Primary School and Liberty hoped now that Ruth would be too busy looking after her new charges to keep tabs on her. Ben was less of a problem since his phone calls were usually short and to-the-point and, since he'd moved to Sheffield, not very frequent.

'Have you been trying to get hold of me?' Liberty asked, forcing herself to sound cheerful after a journey from Manchester marked by frustrating delays, stifling heat and a debilitating throb in her swollen ankle.

'Of course I have, silly. What d'you think I'm trying to do now?' Ruth paused. Her tone was teasing and affectionate, not tinged with annoyance as Liberty had expected. 'I've been worried about you, mum. There was no answer when I rang last night and then today . . . I thought . . . well, it doesn't matter. As long as you're OK.'

Liberty smiled. The need to explain had passed. 'I'm fine,' she reassured her daughter.

It was usual in their regular phone conversations for Ruth to do most of the talking and Liberty settled herself in the chair by the hall phone, thankful that, for the most part, she need only listen. Her daughter's colourful anecdotes about life at the village school, punctuated by cries of indignation at the increasing amount of paperwork, were a welcome distraction from the stresses of a wasted day and Liberty found herself inviting Ruth and Crispin to an old-fashioned Sunday tea the following day.

Half an hour later, after she had put the phone down, made herself a cup of tea and taken two painkillers, Liberty decided that her flagging energy levels were restored enough to take the short walk to Bagley Hall.

The early evening sun cast deep shadows across the parking area at the front of the 16th Century baronial hall. The ivy, which almost covered the mullion windows of the east wing, glowed pinkly in the evening light. She glanced up at the ornate facade only vaguely remembered from her only other visit, a couple of years before, when she'd been collecting for a charity whose name now escaped her. The stone seemed cleaner, the stained-glass windows more brightly-coloured and the Virginia creeper, which now stretched its red-tinged fingers across the arch of the doorway, seemed more vibrant and alive.

Suddenly she had the feeling that, possibly for the first time in her life, she was seeing things as they really were.

She banged on the lion's-head door-knocker. A moment later, Giles Tranter pulled back the door. He didn't seem surprised to see her and didn't wait for her to speak.

'Come in,' he said gruffly, leading her through the flagged entrance hall, past the wide, open staircase and into a huge oak-panelled room which, she supposed, could once have witnessed the comings and goings of the landed gentry, royalty even.

She gazed in awe at the trophies of tigers, bison and buffaloes which adorned the walls and wondered how someone so unlike a lord of the manor had come to own this magnificent building with all its trappings. But Giles Tranter had always been a man of mystery.

Before him, the hall had been owned by four generations of the Crook family who'd made their fortune from quarrying. But rumour in the village had it that Charles Crook, the last in line and a renowned gambler, had lost the estate to Tranter about ten years ago in a series of poker games. Whether this was true or not no-one had been able to confirm, and since Crook, who had been in his 70's, had died shortly afterwards, leaving no immediate relatives to challenge the loss of their inheritance, Tranter had been free to assume control.

Little was known of his past, except that his real name was George Tranter and he had worked as a game-keeper for Lord Melchet on his estate near the Scottish border. His financial situation was also something of a mystery. It had been assumed that revenue from the farms, which took up most of the land belonging to Bagley Hall, had been sufficient to support him, his common-law wife and grown-up son.

But according to Millie, who cleaned here two half days a week, he was contemplating turning the hall into a hotel. Could this be the reason for wanting more land?

Tranter leaned his plump arm against the veined, pink and black marble fireplace and smirked.

'Like it?' he asked, indicating the room with a slight movement of his head. 'Impressive, eh?'

Liberty nodded. 'Very,' she said. But she was in no mood for gushing. She tried to assume a business-like control.

'You know why I'm here, Mr Tranter. I need to know more about this . . . this arrangement which you said you had with my husband. As I told you earlier I don't intend to wriggle out of my obligations but I will need to know more.'

He smiled and glanced at the portrait of a naked woman reclining sensually above his head. It was only a fleeting glimpse but it was enough to make her feel uncomfortable. It had been quite deliberate, of that she was sure, but if he'd hoped to intimidate her, he'd failed.

'You'd better take a seat then,' he said. Liberty chose a leather chair next to a table containing an ivory chess set. Tranter remained standing, his back to the fireplace.

'There's nothing more to tell. We shook hands on the deal. It was all sorted. Joe agreed to sell me the strip of land along the edge of the lake - about 20 acres in all. We agreed forty pounds an acre.'

'Forty pounds an acre? For the most desirable shoreline on Bassenthwaite?' She could hear the contempt in her voice but she didn't care. The man was taking her for a fool. 'That's ridiculous. Joe wasn't stupid. He had a keen eye for a good deal. And that certainly isn't one. Even I can see that. Besides, he wasn't hard up for a few hundred pounds.' She shook her head. 'No, I'm sorry. It just doesn't add up.'

'Are you calling me a liar?' A pulse in Tranter's bulging neck throbbed but his facial muscles were taut.

'No, I'm not calling you a liar. I suggest that there was some mix-up in communication. It's easily done. I'm sure there's a simple explanation.'

'There's no mix-up. It's only scrub-land, worth next-to-nothing without planning permission. And it's mine by rights. If you don't believe me, ask my son, Richard. He was there when we shook hands on it. He'll tell you I'm not lying.'

For a moment Liberty was stuck for words, desperately trying to work out how valid his son's testimony would be. Surely the word of a near relative would be suspect? But she didn't know. Only someone knowledgeable about British law would be able to give her the answer. She thought of Sondra's husband, Derek. He'd been Joe's solicitor before he retired.

'It's such a small piece of land compared with all the acres you have here,' she said. 'Why is it so important to you? Of course I realise you don't have private access to the lake at present, but surely it can't matter that much. Joe never put any restrictions on people fishing or sailing. And the public footpath goes right through the land. So I can't see what you hope to gain by buying it.'

He didn't speak but walked over to a large, framed sketch which was leaning against a Chinese urn. He picked it up and held it at arms length. Liberty noticed at once the look of undisguised approval. But it was only when he flipped it round to face her that she understood. It was a plan for a hotel complex on the site of Bagley Hall and she could see clearly that the strip of land which he so coveted had been earmarked for a sailing club.

'It's a winner,' he gushed. 'No doubt about it. There'll be horse-riding, swimming, shooting, sailing, tennis, you name it. I aim to make it the biggest man-made attraction in the Lakes. I've done my homework. It's what people want. Especially the ones with money. Five star accommodation, fantastic scenery and plenty of action. The lake's the thing that'll sell it. We'll have yachting, canoeing, some rowing boats and, in summer, organised competitions and games for guests and their children. They'll love it. But it won't work without a club-house on the shore - to change in, keep boats and equipment in - and get refreshments. That sort of thing. Surely you can see that.'

Liberty was horrified. Lowthwaite's peace would be shattered.

'I'm sorry, Mr Tranter, but the land's not for sale.'

He scowled at her and dropped the sketch onto a chaise-longue.

She wondered if she was about to witness his legendary fiery temper. He'd once, according to Millie, grabbed one of his tenants by the scruff of the neck and frog-marched him to the door. Liberty had no intention of suffering the same indignity.

She stood up and faced him. 'I'm sorry but there's nothing else to discuss.'

'Oh, but there is.' Tranter moved towards her and she stiffened. Would he really use force to get what he wanted? He stood now only inches away, in an obvious attempt to intimidate her. His face was almost purple as he fixed her with desperate eyes. 'Don't think I'm going to let this drop. You'll be hearing from my solicitor. And soon. That land belongs to Bagley Hall and I'll not rest 'til I have it.'

She decided against further argument. 'I'll see myself out,' she said and turned to go, all the while sensing his penetrating glare on her back and half expecting him to grab her from behind.

As she walked down the rhododendron-lined path towards the road she was filled with a mixture of quiet satisfaction that she had refused to let Tranter bully her and a dread that she might in the end have no choice but to succumb to his demands. But uppermost in her mind was the realisation that Tranter was quite capable of murder. And if he'd murdered once, there was every chance he would murder again.

CHAPTER 10

It was with a heart as heavy and troubled as the weather that she turned away from Joe's grave and entered the porch of Holy Cross Church next morning, two minutes before the 10.30 Mass was due to begin. Her eyes wandered to the inscription over the arched doorway: 'Live that you neither fear nor regret.' She'd read the italic lettering many times before but today the words seemed strangely appropriate.

She slipped quickly into the bench nearest the door, conscious of being torn between a need for spiritual sustenance and doubts that her prayers would ever be heard, let alone answered.

When she emerged three quarters of an hour later she could remember little of the service or who'd been present. And she was only vaguely aware of the bustle and chatter which hovered round her but which curiously caused her no concern. She didn't care if they were talking about her. Even when one parishioner after another stopped to enquire how she was she felt no return of the feelings of antagonism towards a curious and often intrusive public that had weighed her down since Joe's death. She responded with uncharacteristic optimism and a reassuring smile.

By the time she reached Lowthwaite House she was raring to go. She'd already worked out her plan of action on the short walk home from Holy Cross and went straight to the phone. Her first task was to enlist Derek's help, but she'd need to get hold of him before he and Sondra left for the golf course. Derek would know exactly how she should react to Tranter's demands.

'Leave it with me,' he said. 'I'll do a bit of digging. If he contacts you again, tell him the matter's in the hands of your solicitor. I'll get back to you as soon as I can.'

'Thanks. Derek. I owe you one.'

There was a pause. Liberty knew what was coming. 'What's this Sondra tells me about your brush with DCI Leatheringham?' he asked. 'Do you want me to have a word with the Chief Constable?'

'No. No, I don't,' she replied sharply. 'Look, I've got to go,' she added, replacing the receiver with a sigh of relief. At least she could leave one problem on the back-burner for a while.

She went through to the kitchen and made herself a mug of instant coffee. The percolator, she decided, would take up too many valuable minutes. Today was going to be action-packed.

While she sipped the surprisingly refreshing drink she took Joe's address book out of the dresser and opened it at the page after the Fox and Ferret. George Grundy, Ewood Grange, Carlisle was the next address. She could find the house number from the telephone directory and be there in less than half an hour. Gone was the dread of failure and repetition of the fear and frustration she'd felt during her visit to the Fox and Ferret. In its place was a mood of quiet determination and acceptance of her limitations. She could only do her best. And if that wasn't good enough, then so be it. She wasn't superhuman.

But George Grundy revealed nothing of significance. In answer to her questions the squat, almost-bald man with reading glasses hanging round his bare, scraggy neck, grudgingly told her he was the Managing Director of a company making fertilisers just outside the city. No, he could not recall ever having met Joe or of having done business with Westerman and Brock.

He'd been very convincing. Only once, when she'd thought he was about to shut the door on her and she'd blurted out: 'Do you or your company have any connection with Ireland?' had his surly face shown any expression other than irritation. It was only a fleeting movement. His neat, curved eyebrows had jerked upwards and she'd thought he looked surprised. But it could have been a natural reaction to the abrupt question. His reply, that some of the company's products were sold in Ireland through a distributor, was delivered in the same monotone as his other answers.

Ivan Kelly, the next name in Joe's address book, revealed nothing she couldn't have found out at the depot. After an hour and a half's drive down the M6 all she'd discovered was that he was the owner of the paper-making business, Fairfax and Kelly situated near Preston. She recognised the name from invoices she'd dealt with. Westerman and Brock had carried consignments of raw materials from the docks to the factory as well as transporting the finished products, mostly toilet rolls and tissues, to the warehouses of supermarket chains. But Ivan Kelly could shed no light on why Joe should keep his home number in a private address book. Neither had he any connection with Ireland other than that his grandfather had been born there.

It was almost five o'clock when she arrived back at Lowthwaite House, hot and hungry but determined to contact at least one more of Joe's acquaintances after a quick sandwich and shower. But when she saw the purple VW Beetle on the drive she realised instantly that she was already in hot water.

According to Ruth, who was stony-faced and obviously put-out, she and Crispin had been sitting on the patio waiting for her since half past three. It just wasn't on that her mother, whose habits had always been fairly predictable, had suddenly taken to disappearing for hours on end. And even though no time had been arranged for them to come to tea, surely they had been expected before this time. Crispin on the other hand had been pleased with the opportunity to relax and sketch the yachts on the lake.

Liberty, not unhappily, resigned herself to an evening of domesticity. Her search would have to wait until tomorrow.

'Come on,' she said, putting a guiding arm round her daughter's shoulder. 'You can help me with the veg. It's too late for a roast but I'm sure we'll find something that won't take too long.'

Her optimism surprised her. Not that long ago she would have been in a flap, cursing herself for forgetting and frantically rushing round trying to cover her mistake. Something had definitely changed. And for the better.

CHAPTER 11

Monday turned out to be a fairly uneventful and disappointing day although Liberty refused to be despondent. She'd spent the whole morning virtually alone in the portacabin at Westerman and Brock's, sending out overdue invoices and chasing unpaid accounts. Bob had been visiting a customer in Edinburgh, which had meant that she could put off, for at least another day, an embarrassing meeting and a difficult decision.

But his absence had also given her the opportunity to leave before midday to visit two more addresses from Joe's address book. Unfortunately both had proved fruitless.

At the first, a shabby two-up, two-down in Lancaster no-one had answered her persistent knocking. At the second, on the outskirts of Liverpool, a well-made-up, pinched-looking woman had informed her that her boyfriend, Mark Newton, an insurance salesman, was 'away on business.' But there was an evasiveness in the woman's answers which had given Liberty the impression that she was being fobbed off.

In spite of the long, tiring drive she didn't regret her decision to visit rather than telephone. She was beginning to learn a great deal about body language from her limited contact with these people. And if any of them were telling lies she reckoned that she had a better chance of detecting their deceit face to face than over the phone. But the journey had served one more purpose: to convince her that she really was being followed.

There was no point contacting the police. It might be them following her. And if not, DCI Leatheringham would only think she was making up yet another story to divert attention away from her guilt. And yet she must do something. But what? She wondered why she wasn't terrified at the prospect of someone, possibly Joe's murderer, stalking her. But as she relaxed in front of the television that evening she could feel no more than a mild anxiety and curiosity about the driver of the red car she'd spotted at various intervals during the afternoon. If he - and she was almost certain it was a man - if he had wanted to harm her there had been numerous opportunities during the last few hours - at traffic lights, road junctions, in motorway services, driving on the motorway even. And, if the aim was to kill her, why tail her day after day? Surely the obvious place was here while she was alone?

Gradually her thoughts cleared. The police obviously suspected she'd murdered Joe but had no proof. By following her they might discover . . . what? What might they discover? That she had a secret lover perhaps? She smiled at the thought of the Chief Inspector trying to make some sense of all her comings and goings.

But the prospect of being investigated by the police wasn't to be taken lightly. If she wasn't careful she could end up facing a murder charge. After all she had the opportunity, the motive might not be too difficult to come up with and evidence could always be planted by an unscrupulous police officer who was convinced of her guilt. Realising with a shudder that her search for Joe's killer must be stepped up, she switched off the television and went up to his study. She was sure now that the mystery of his death was inextricably tangled in the complexity of his life.

The crude cardboard badge she'd discovered on the evening of Joe's funeral lay where she had left it on his desk. She picked it up and ran her fingers over its rough surface. What was it about this childish piece of junk that was so important to Joe? He wasn't a hoarder. In fact, quite the opposite. His study had been kept systematically neat and impersonal. Perhaps the badge had a sentimental value? she wondered. But Joe had never been one for logos or badges of any kind, even the discrete kind on designer jumpers and shirts. In fact, he'd refused outright to wear them, declaring: 'There's no way I'm going to pay for the privilege of advertising somebody else's goods.'

She turned the badge over and examined the rusty safety pin on the back with the uneasy realisation that Joe would never have kept something so worn-out and potentially hazardous as this unless it was of immense importance. She had to find out more.

It didn't take her long to find Anthony Simon's number in the address book next to the hall phone. If anyone could shed light on the badge's significance, he could. He and Joe had shared a room for five years during their time at St Ambrose School for boys near Kendal. And although they'd lost touch over the past few years, except for the exchange of Christmas cards, Anthony had probably been closer to Joe than anyone else, apart from herself.

CHAPTER 12

Anthony Simon ran an insurance company from home and had appointments arranged for most of the next day. But he could 'fit her in,' he said, at 11.30. How would that do?

Liberty had readily agreed and rang Bob to tell him she wouldn't be in until Wednesday, probably not 'til after noon. The business was half hers now, so why shouldn't she take the day off when she needed to? And Bob's surprised, almost disapproving tone wasn't going to make her feel guilty.

The day had started promisingly enough, with a whisper of a breeze and a clear sky marred only by the odd trail of white cloud. A ride out to the coastal resort of Littleport would provide a pleasant change from driving up and down the motorway. But the brightness soon gave way to a grey haze which almost blotted out the Scottish Lowlands behind the pink-tinged sands of the Solway Firth. Liberty gripped the steering wheel, determined to fight off the spectre of impending gloom that was descending like a familiar cloak and wrapping itself tightly round her almost to the point of suffocation.

Although Littleport was no more than twenty miles from Lowthwaite, Liberty had been there only twice before. Once when she and Joe were engaged and they'd walked hand in hand along the picturesque quayside where fishermen threw boxes brimming with slithering fish from brightly painted boats. And once, when Ben and Ruth had been recovering from whooping cough, she'd brought them in the hope that the sea air would help their convalescence. But it hadn't. She remembered the chilly breeze blowing off the Irish Sea and Ben's fit of coughing so severe she'd had to usher him back to the car choking and distressed. When she'd told Joe later that evening he'd made some comment about any fool knowing that an eight-year-old with whooping cough needed to be kept warm. She hadn't been back since.

It soon became clear that things had changed. The once-bustling quayside was deserted except for an elderly woman walking a toy poodle. Only one fishing boat, its paint-work faded and peeling bobbed silently in the harbour. She parked the car in the empty car park and set off towards the three-storey, pink-fronted building further along the quay where Anthony Simon had directed her. A pile of nets, tangled and broken, lay discarded on the cobbled walkway in front of her but before she reached them the repugnant, nauseating stench of dog-fouling reached her. Instinctively she flung her hand across her nose and mouth and hurried past, saddened at the decline of an ancient and once proud way of life.

The sound of raised voices behind her made her spin round. Two men, dressed almost identically in jeans and grubby white T-shirts, were locked in a heated argument outside a public house, each one shouldering and pushing the other. Vaguely noticing the sign, The Ship and Shamrock, over their heads she concluded that they were probably the worse for drink and was about to turn away when she caught sight of a familiar figure through the open door. What on earth was Fr. O'Malley doing in this seedy pub so far from his parish?

But, for the moment, she had more pressing matters to deal with. Andrew Simon had informed her that he lived on the top floor of the terraced Victorian building. She found his name on the intercom straight away and pressed the bell. 'Yes?' barked a man's voice, gruff and unfamiliar.

'It's Liberty Westerman. I . . .' But before she could finish a loud buzz announced that the lock had been released. She pushed the door and was confronted by a young girl in a skimpy red top and shorts who almost ran into her. Liberty stepped aside and surveyed the white-washed entrance hall in which a half-moon wicker table and chair were the only pieces of furniture. But before she reached the polished wooden staircase a head popped over the banister.

'Hi. Come on up. It's good to see you after so long.'

She recognised now the happy-go-lucky tones which she remembered from their last meeting fourteen or more years ago. She climbed the two flights of stairs aware that he was watching from the top of the stairwell. At once she became conscious of her appearance, suddenly and inexplicably realising she'd not had her hair highlighted for several weeks. From that angle the greying roots must be quite visible through the blonde streaks. The shoulder-length bob too was probably in need of attention. She plucked at wayward strands of hair which she now felt sticking to her warm face and made a mental note to make an appointment at her usual salon in Keswick. But when she saw Anthony's receding hairline and remembered how proud he had once been of his thick black hair she couldn't help wondering at her own vanity. What made her think that *she* could be any more successful at holding back the passage of time?

'I'll not keep you long,' she said as he steered her into the surprisingly light and airy apartment. A glance around the scantily-furnished room confirmed that he was still living alone.

Files, computer print-outs and manuals littered the floor and table at the far end of the room. Caricatures of famous people, mostly footballers, covered the wall to her right while the other three remained almost bare. The room had an unlived-in, uncoordinated look. Liberty couldn't imagine any woman placing a cream and white striped settee in the middle of a grey carpet without at least trying to tone it with complementary cushions or a rug. And it looked as if no-one ever sat on it.

The lack of colour co-ordination also extended to Anthony's clothes, a lime green shirt and red polyester tie. But his lived-in, baggy black trousers were, to her, the most telling indication of his bachelor-hood.

'Look, I'm sorry about Joe. I would've come to the funeral but I was in London. Sales conference. Nothing much but I had to go.' He held his arms out in a gesture of helplessness and shrugged. Liberty nodded and he continued, 'It was a terrible shock when I read it in The Times. I was going to write but . . . you know how it is. I'm not very good at that sort of thing. Would you like a drink?' He twisted his neck awkwardly and ran a finger along the inside of his collar.

Liberty smiled. He may like to give the impression of being a hard-nosed businessman, but buried underneath was the same insecure adolescent she remembered.

'No thanks,' she said, sure that at this early hour it would be non-alcoholic and aware of the unwelcome pang of disappointment. 'I just need to ask you a few questions about your schooldays - yours and Joe's.'

The furrows on his brow tightened and he pointed to the settee.

'Take a pew and fire away.'

Liberty perched uncomfortably on the edge wondering whether she should start by catching up on his news. It had been at Joe's 40th birthday party when they'd last met. But even now she could recall vividly the look of horror on her husband's face as he'd entered the dining room to a chorus of Happy Birthday. He'd tried to cover up later but it had been clear to everyone that the surprise party she and Sondra had arranged had been a big mistake. She decided to get straight to the point.

'Tell me about Joe,' she said, realising as she spoke that it wasn't the question she'd planned to ask.

'Don't say you need *me* to tell you about your husband. For God's sake you were married to him for nearly 30 years.' He gave a hollow, dismissive laugh and turned, embarrassed, she thought, to shuffle the papers on his desk.

Liberty cringed at her clumsy approach but the plea had been from the heart, the result of her growing, disproportionate conviction that she had never fully understood what made Joe tick.

'What was Joe like as a boy?' she asked in a deliberately measured tone.

Anthony paused and she thought for a moment that he was about to question her reason for asking. But instead he pulled the straight-backed chair from behind the desk and straddled it thoughtfully.

'I'm not sure I can tell you an awful lot. You probably know most of it already.' He spoke softly now, as if sensing her desperate need to fill in the gaps. 'As you already know, we were room-mates for five years, but Joe was always a loner. Never liked talking about himself and kept his feelings firmly in-check mostly. I presume he didn't change much when he got married?'

He inclined his head and she nodded, seeing in his steady gaze that he understood.

'I was mad on cricket and rugby,' he continued. 'But Joe wasn't interested in team sports. Oh, he'd play them. It was impossible to get out of them when Fr. Maguire was P.E. master, but if he got half a chance he'd be off fishing in the stream that ran through the school grounds. I used to joke with him that he only put his heart and soul into something when he could win all the glory for himself.' He hesitated and rubbed his chin. 'Don't get me wrong. I got on well with Joe. He was a good mate. But he was never one of the lads.'

'That was very perceptive of you.' But then Anthony had always struck her as more sensitive than other men. Maybe that had something to do with the friendship floundering.

'Not really.' He shrugged. 'I remember just before we left - at the end of fifth form - we decided to have a midnight feast. You could say it was tradition. Like a stag night before a wedding. I think the priests turned a blind eye to it, to be honest. Sister Agnes, the nun in charge of the kitchen, certainly did and it was her larder everybody raided. Just for a few packets of biscuits and some lemonade, that's all.' He smiled, as if remembering happier days. 'We knew what we could get away with. But Joe said he didn't want anything to do with it. Some of the others called him 'holier than thou', but he just said it was childish and pathetic and that he had better things to do. I can remember it quite clearly. While the whole dorm gathered round scoffing anything they could lay their hands on and telling jokes, Joe sat in bed trying to outwit himself at chess.'

Liberty nodded. She'd always known Joe liked to be different from the crowd. Anthony wasn't telling her anything new but it felt good to share these memories of Joe with someone who had been close to him.

'Go on,' she said.

'I think Joe found it difficult to lighten up. He was a real deep thinker. Not like me. I was more interested in pop charts and the girls from St Chad's who came for debates and discos. But I think his upbringing had a lot to do with the way he was.'

He stood up and walked to the large picture-window as if deliberating over his next words. The lightweight curtains fluttered gently when he pushed open the top pane.

Liberty took a deep breath of the welcome air, her eyes now resting on the harbour scene below. The fishing boat, so weather-worn at close hand, seemed at a distance restored as it bobbed in the clear blue water. The pink-paved quayside glowed in the midday sun.

Anthony coughed sharply before continuing. 'I don't suppose him being brought up by a maiden-aunt helped. I mean, it must have been a bit embarrassing at open days. All the other chaps had parents who had a bob or two. They'd turn up in Jags, Bentleys, Mercs, you name it. And they'd be dressed to the nines. There was a lot of one-upmanship - who could get an invitation for coffee with the headmaster, that sort of thing. So, you can imagine his aunt . . .' He stopped and looked embarrassed.

'What about her?' Liberty tried to give him an encouraging smile.

'Well, no disrespect, but she stuck out like a sore thumb. A real plain, no-nonsense type of woman, she was. Always wore a tweed suit and heavy brogues even in warm weather. And she'd insist on walking from the station about three miles away. My parents offered her a lift on a few occasions but she always said the same: 'Thank you, but the walk will do me good'. Anthony mimicked the broad, north-country accent and Liberty smiled, affectionately remembering Joe's Aunt Cecilia. 'She was a lovely person, don't get me wrong,' he continued. 'The sort that'd do anything for anybody. But there were no frills or flannel with her. What you saw was what you got. But you knew her too, didn't you?'

'Not long enough, sadly. She died just before Joe and I got married.'

'That's right, I remember now. But I didn't get the impression she and Joe were close.'

'Oh, I don't know about that,' Liberty protested.

'Well, I do,' he retorted with a grin. 'Joe would go to any lengths to stop her coming. I remember once he got a sixth-former to ring her and pretend to be one of the teachers. He told her Joe was in quarantine with measles or something and couldn't receive visitors. The old girl fell for it hook, line and sinker.'

Anthony laughed, then paused, eyeing her quizzically. She stiffened, sensing that he was about to reveal some aspect of Joe's past that she might not like.

'What else?' she urged.

He paused, pulling his chair closer in a conspiratorial way. 'If I were guessing,' he began thoughtfully, 'I'd say the father was Joe's biggest problem. I only saw him the once. When we were in third form. It was a bit of a surprise to be honest, because nobody really believed Joe when he told them his father was a Major. Then this day he turns up as large as life in full uniform. Well, I can tell you it caused quite a stir. We were in the middle of a French exam and he just waltzed into the classroom and asked to speak to Joe. Of course I could see by Joe's face that he hadn't expected his old man. His mouth just fell open. He couldn't believe his luck when Brother Bernard said he could finish the exam later. You never met his father, did you?'

Liberty shook her head, impatient for him to continue. Major Thomas Westerman had died soon after Joe left school and until now her opinion of him had been founded almost totally on what Cecilia had told her. But Liberty had long suspected that, being a loyal and loving sister, she'd been hopelessly biased.

Joe himself had imparted little information willingly. And when Liberty had pressed him, mostly in the early days of their courtship, he'd become irritated, snapping that he'd had very little opportunity to get to know his father since he'd been stationed in Germany for most of Joe's childhood. Sensing a raw wound and mindful not to rub salt in it, Liberty had ceased her questioning.

'What do you mean by his father being his biggest problem?' she asked, anxious now to shed light on an aspect of Joe's life that had always intrigued her.

'As I said, I only saw them together on that one occasion. And then for no more than a minute or two. When Brother Bernard said Joe could go with his father, it was as if a light had suddenly gone on inside him. I'd never seen him look so happy. He was just beaming at everybody and then at his dad. But the Major never smiled. I remember that. A real surly bloke he was, kept curling the end of his moustache up, just like those Sergeant Major types do in war films. He and Joe shook hands – very formally - and then they went out into the corridor. I never found out what was said but when Joe came back half an hour later his face was red and blotchy. I could tell he'd been crying. But I never said anything. And he didn't.' Anthony's eyes seemed to have misted over and he gazed at the carpet as if remembering some detail of a painful past. 'Funny though,' he added. 'Joe never mentioned his father's name again.'

'I think I can shed some light on that mystery. It must have been about the time when his father remarried - a German woman – Eva, I think her name was. Cecilia told me that Joe was very unhappy about the wedding, particularly as Eva already had a son about the same age as Joe. According to Cecilia, it seemed that the boy had achieved what Joe had craved all his life, to be able to live with his father. But I don't know whether Joe himself ever spoke to anyone about it. The wedding was a quiet affair on the Rhine somewhere. None of the family were invited. But Eva and her son didn't stay long. They left a few months later. It was only a couple of years after that the Major died of a stroke.'

Anthony stood up and walked over to the table where he flicked absent-mindedly through a note-book. 'You know, I've never told anyone this before,' he said. 'But I always thought my own father hated the sight of me. He didn't of course. He just wanted to toughen me up, but he had a funny way of going about it. I only realised after I joined the Navy that he was as proud as punch of me. But Joe's dad . . . he was different. He never let Joe visit him in Germany. He was always too busy. As far as I recall he was involved in establishing a peace-time headquarters for the British Forces on the Rhine. And his work was far too important to take time out for family visits. But, you know, I honestly felt - even before that day - that he would rather Joe hadn't existed. In fact I'd go as far as to say that the guy hated Joe's guts. And I think after that meeting the feeling was mutual.'

Liberty's immediate reaction was to protest at the ridiculousness of the suggestion. But then again . . . if it were true it would explain such a lot, not least his inability to communicate with his own children. She'd soon realised that Joe and his father hadn't seen eye to eye. But hate? With all its connotations of wishing the hated one dead, surely a father could never feel hatred for a son? Or a son for a father?

'What makes you say such an awful thing?' she asked, seeing for the first time that Anthony had genuinely cared about Joe, that he was not the shallow, fair-weather type of friend she'd previously assumed.

'Look, I'm sorry. You must think me terribly rude talking about Joe's family like this. But since I read about his death he's been on my mind rather a lot. I've been going over old times. You know, the way people do when it's too late to do anything about it. I can't help feeling guilty that we didn't keep in touch these last few years. But what with the job . . . and having to travel all over the place . . . you know what it's like.'

She nodded sympathetically and he held her gaze with a sad, almost child-like expression. 'I need a drink,' he said. 'Let me buy you one. There's a little place on the quayside.'

She wanted to refuse but something stopped her. Vulnerability, she reflected, always did bring out her maternal instincts. And she too was in need of a drink.

A display of hanging baskets gave a splash of colour to the grey-fronted Boatyard Inn where a dozen or so tables were scattered haphazardly across the pavement. Anthony chose a discreetly-placed table behind a row of conifers planted in beer kegs. Liberty took the chair he held for her, struggling to remember the last time she'd sat outside a pub.

There'd been times when she and Joe had taken the children for a bar-lunch or they'd gone for a drink with Bob and Susan. But it had been in the early years of their marriage when they'd sat outside the

Swan at Colby Bridge and gazed at the river with two ciders and a packet of crisps between them. In later years, Joe was never keen on going to pubs, especially in the daytime. Instead, he would leave it till late in the evening before indulging in his own 'little vice', as he called it, of a tot of whisky or glass of wine in the comfort of his armchair.

'What will you have?' Anthony asked, nodding to the waiter.

'A vodka and bitter lemon please,' she said, noticing his eager smile and wondering if it had been wise to accept his invitation. The last thing she needed right now was for Anthony to jump to the wrong conclusion about her intentions. But surely he could never presume she'd be interested in another man so soon after Joe's death.

'Now where were we?' he asked, sitting down next to her, his thin upper lip lined with perspiration.

'Joe's relationship with his father,' she said.

'Oh, yes. I suppose their problems stemmed from the fact that his mother died when he was born. It can't have been easy for Joe knowing he caused his mother's death. No matter how innocent he was he must have felt *some* guilt. But his old man definitely held it against him, I'm sure of that. Of course Joe never said as much but he didn't have to.'

The waiter brought the drinks and Anthony almost drained his pint glass in one swallow. He wiped the froth off his top lip with the back of his hand before continuing:

'I can see his face now, waiting eagerly for Matron to bring round the morning post. Joe never got so much as a birthday card from his dad. But I suppose in the circumstances that was a day probably best forgotten. The aunt would write about once a week but you could tell that wasn't what he was hoping for. And when parents took their sons out to Sunday lunch all Joe had was the old biddy to bring him a box of biscuits. He became a bit of a social outcast to be honest. Then when his dad left Lowthwaite House to the aunt . . .' He shrugged, rolling his eyes in bewilderment. 'I can't imagine how he felt. Anyway I'm sure you know most of this stuff anyway.'

Liberty wrapped her hands round the chilled glass and nodded. The house had been jointly owned by Joe's father and Cecilia, with the estate going to Cecilia on the death of her brother. Joe had had to wait for what he had considered his inheritance until after Cecilia's death. It was not a subject Joe cared to discuss. She twisted the plain gold wedding ring round her finger and noticed the look of pity on Anthony's face.

A sudden rush of blood to her already warm face and neck added to her misery and she thrust a hand in her bag for a tissue. A sharp pricking sensation made her jump and she realised at once it was Joe's badge. She pulled it out and placed it on the table.

'Do you recognise this at all?' she asked, feeling the enthusiasm with which she had set out that morning waning fast. But Anthony's unexpected cry of surprise gave her fresh hope.

'Well I never expected to see that old thing again. It must be forty years since I saw it.'

She could scarcely contain her excitement. Was she finally nearing a breakthrough? She pushed the badge nearer to him.

'But you still remember it clearly? Can you tell me about it? I found it in Joe's study but I can't think why he would keep it all this time.'

'I suppose it's not all that surprising. It was probably his most prized possession, the symbol of his acceptance among his peers. It was the badge of the only society to which he could feel he truly belonged.'

Liberty shuffled in the rickety chair, uncomfortably aware that she was about to uncover another side of Joe that for too long had been hidden in the shadows of secrecy.

'As I said,' he went on, 'Joe was a bit of a social leper, so when he heard about the Irish Rebellion Force it would have struck a chord with him. It was a hush-hush type of organisation with no obvious function, but its members all had to have Irish ancestors. If I remember rightly both sets of Joe's grandparents were Irish, weren't they?'

Liberty shook her head and took a long sip of her drink. 'Not all of them. According to Cecilia, Joe's paternal grandmother was born in County Sligo. She came over here in the early 1890s and married Joe's grandfather, John Westerman. He was a Cumbrian, the one who built Lowthwaite House. Joe's mother's parents were Irish. They lived in Belfast all their lives. They died a couple of years before Joe was born – their house burned down while they were asleep. Local feeling - according to Cecilia - had it that it was a Unionist reprisal for a spate of Republican terrorist activities. Joe told me he visited the area soon after his father's death but he couldn't find anyone who remembered the couple. Now tell me about The Irish Rebellion Force.'

'OK,' he said and drained his glass. 'It was outlawed by the Head because of its sympathies with the IRA. So it went underground. Operating under the noses of the priests probably added to its attraction too. Secret societies were always a turn-on in those days. Well, they still are, I suppose. But Joe took it all so seriously. From what I gather he became fanatical. It didn't seem to matter that if he was found out he'd be expelled. But perhaps living dangerously turned him on. Make no mistake, the priests would have had him out on his ear if they'd caught wind of any funny business.'

'But what kind of activities did this society get involved in?'

'To be honest, I never knew a lot about it. Its members were sworn to secrecy so I only picked up the odd bit of information, mostly gossip, from some of the other lads. Joe never let anything slip. And I never let on to him that I knew about the group. But rumour had it that they'd collected quite substantial funds for the IRA over the years.'

'But how? I mean, they couldn't fundraise or anything.'

'Hardly. One theory was that they conned parents and family, probably on the pretext that they needed more pocket money. For most parents money wasn't a problem but I suspect Joe didn't have much success from his aunt. She was much too thrifty, although I don't think she was short of a bob or two. And the father . . . well . . .'

Liberty was intrigued. 'How did you know Joe was a member if he didn't tell you?'

'I found the badge. I was looking for some change for the telephone and I thought Joe might keep some in his bedside cabinet. That was when I saw it. It was in a plastic wallet with his name on it, so I knew it was his. I suppose I was impressed. The Irish Rebellion Force had quite a reputation, especially among the younger boys. But as I got older I began to wonder just how much of it was a load of hot air and how much was actually achieved. I suspect there was never any connection with the IRA although they would have liked there to be one.'

She couldn't help noticing the concerned look, as though he was worried he'd upset her. She smiled reassuringly. But the thought that the IRA could be involved in her husband's murder filled her with horror. She tried to control the nervousness in her voice.

'Do you know the names of any other members?'

'As a matter of fact I do. The leader was a bit of a tough nut. Came from Belfast. As far as I know he still lives there. His name's Michael O'Connor.'

She remembered seeing the name in Joe's address book. The two had obviously been lifelong friends – unless something had happened to sour the friendship and Michael O'Connor had killed Joe. Or had a rival organisation, a terrorist group, perhaps, been to blame?

She clung to the empty glass in her hand and tried to remember if Joe had ever expressed any leanings towards the IRA or any other group. Nothing came to mind even though he was a keen follower of current affairs. Perhaps his training in the Irish Rebellion Force had been so thorough that it had become second nature to disguise his allegiance. But to her?

It seemed totally out of character that Joe would condone terrorism. And yet somehow the pieces of the jigsaw were fitting neatly into place. Would Michael O'Connor prove to be the missing link?

She stood up quickly, almost pushing her chair backwards onto the pavement. 'Thank you, Anthony, you've been a big help. I think I know where to find Michael O'Connor.'

He looked stunned and jumped to his feet. For a moment she thought he was about to come with her. 'But surely you don't think . . . Look, let me buy you some lunch and you can tell me . . .'

She didn't give him the chance to finish. 'I'll explain another time,' she said firmly and popped the badge back in her bag.

But as she turned to leave, a sudden movement startled her. She swung round just in time to catch a glimpse of a tall, bushy-haired figure dressed in black emerging from behind a row of potted conifers and disappearing round the side of the Boatyard Inn. It had only been a fleeting glance but she was in no doubt that he was the man who had followed her on the train to Manchester.

Surprisingly, this latest sighting of her pursuer filled her not with the fear she had experienced previously but with a determination to find out once and for all who he was and why he was following her. She was almost certain he would turn out to be one of DCI Leatheringham's men but she had to know for sure.

CHAPTER 13

Later that evening she had the distinct impression that everyone was conspiring to stop her being alone with her thoughts. She'd arrived back from Littleport at about 3 o'clock, after a quick visit to the supermarket in Cockermouth to stock up her empty fridge. But since then her phone had rung almost non-stop.

First Sondra had kept her talking for half an hour about the golf club committee's preparations for their annual dinner and dance. Since Derek was Captain of the club this year, Sondra was revelling in her elevated role. Liberty found the mostly one-way conversation rather tedious but, since the event was the highlight of her friend's social calendar, she had listened patiently until the topic had been exhausted.

Five minutes later, Ben had called after his seven till three shift had finished. He'd sounded tired and dispirited, and although he'd tried hard to convince her that this was as a result of having to deal with a particularly difficult patient suffering from schizophrenia, Liberty knew him well enough to realise that he was keeping something back. It was then that the guilt returned. Was it *her* fault that her men found it so difficult to confide in her?

Ruth had been the next caller, anxious to be reassured that her mother was coping well. In between warming a pizza and preparing some salad, Liberty had received four further calls from parishioners enquiring about her welfare. She wondered idly whether Fr. O'Malley had put out a church bulletin asking people to give her a ring. But the irritation, even hostility, she'd felt initially towards callers - except for family and close friends - was not there now. It had been superseded by a calculated acceptance that although some were just plain nosy and others were intent on discovering some tasty morsel to feed to the gossiping vultures who hovered in local bars, the majority probably had a genuine concern for her welfare.

It was 8 o'clock and there had been no calls for over half an hour. She curled up on the settee with a large glass of St. Emilion, her conversation with Anthony Simon now dominating her thoughts. But the more she dwelt on the subject of Joe's involvement in Irish affairs the more confused she became.

She switched on the television but as the images of several species of wildlife flitted across her screen the questions in her mind demanded answers. Did Joe really help the IRA? And how far was this schoolboy society, of which Joe was so fond, implicated in terrorist acts of violence? She remembered the newspaper cutting she'd found in his study. Could Joe have known about that bomb - even condoned it and its terrible repercussions for the poor boys left orphaned? Never. It would have to be proved to her beyond a shadow of a doubt before she'd believe anything like that.

But if he had nothing to do with terrorism, why the need to employ the thuggish Winston Dodd as his minder on trips to Ireland? She had the unnerving feeling that the hunt for Joe's killer was leading her into dangerous, uncharted territory. In danger of being overwhelmed, she gulped down the wine and switched channels furiously on the TV's remote control.

At that moment the telephone rang again. This time she was thankful for the interruption and almost ran to the phone. She recognised Derek's voice immediately but it was more insistent, more intense than usual.

'You haven't signed anything for that Tranter fellow, have you?'

'No I haven't, although he was pretty obnoxious when I refused.'

'Good. That's all right then. Not good that he was obnoxious. Good that you refused, of course.' He made a low, deep noise somewhere between a grunt and a laugh. 'As long as you've not agreed in writing to sell the land, he hasn't a leg to stand on.'

Liberty breathed a sigh of relief. 'You're sure?'

'I've checked with the Land Registry and there's no record of any change of ownership taking place. The land is still registered in Joe's name. So, even if there was a written agreement, which I very much doubt, there's been no change of title as far as the Land Registry is concerned and that's all that matters.'

'Well that's good news,' she said, thankful that at least one problem seemed to be sorted out.

'I wouldn't mind betting the scoundrel badgered Joe to sell him the land, but Joe told him to get lost. Then, when Joe was killed, he spied his opportunity to get your signature under false pretences. The man's a con artist. He should be locked up, trying to take advantage like that. But he's the sort who covers his tracks. There'll be no evidence left lying about.'

'He probably thought I'd be a soft touch and all he needed to do was spin me a yarn about it being my moral duty to go along with Joe's last wishes. Well, it would probably have worked not that long ago. But I'm beginning to get wise to the subtle treacheries of men. Sorry, I don't include you in that, Derek.'

'I'm glad to hear it. But Liberty . . .' he sounded alarmed.

'What is it?' she was suddenly apprehensive.

'I don't suppose he could have . . .' He paused.

'Could have what?' She heard the impatience in her tone.

'Well, you know . . . could have killed Joe.'

She couldn't deny that the thought had occurred to her. She'd suspected almost every man who had had any connection with Joe. But she wasn't going to admit it to Derek and have him think she was becoming neurotic.

'Surely a piece of land isn't motive enough for murder, even these days,' she said coolly.

'Oh, don't be too sure about that. Old ladies get mugged every day for the change in their purse. A few acres of land that are crucial to a lucrative hotel complex are more than enough reason for greedy, ruthless people. And I dare say Tranter fits into that category. But it would be a bit of a gamble. There was no certainty he could persuade you to sign over the land. And then he'd have to get planning permission. No, on second thoughts, I can't see anyone committing murder in those circumstances. He probably just thought it was worth a try. But all the same . . . you do need to be careful. I really think you should have some police protection, if it's only . . .'

'No, Derek. No police protection.' She almost shouted down the receiver. 'I can't live my life under the gaze of Detective Chief Inspector Leatheringham. In fact, you've given me an idea.'

'Something I can help you with?'

'Perhaps. But not now. I need to work something out first.'

'Well, if you're sure.'

'I'm sure,' she said decisively. 'Thanks for the information about Tranter. Is Sondra there? I'd like a quick word.'

CHAPTER 14

Next morning, Liberty calculated that Sondra would arrive somewhere nearer eleven o'clock than ten. She'd agreed the night before to meet at the earlier time but Sondra was very rarely punctual and certainly never early. She drove Derek to distraction over her time-keeping and even golf club dinners had been known to start without the Captain's wife.

The air felt less oppressive as Liberty stepped out onto the patio, although a thick haze still obscured the fells. She'd decided to make good use of her waiting time and set about sweeping the dead leaves, rose petals and bits of honeysuckle which had gathered round the door. Jacob was mowing the lawn but he seemed oblivious to her. She leaned on her brush watching him mechanically pushing the petrol-driven mower backwards and forwards, its whirring drowning out the delicate bird-song.

The gaunt face and sunken eyes were clearly visible even at this distance and she thought he looked ill. If he didn't look after himself, she decided, he and his wife would end up together in Holy Cross cemetery.

She took in the familiar, fresh smell of newly-cut grass and was surprised to discover that it gave her a welcome reassurance of the continuity of life, that death and destruction were not the end, merely an essential part of an inexorable cycle.

As she'd expected, at 10.45 Sondra came rushing along the path from the courtyard where she'd parked the Mercedes sports car that Derek had bought her last year for her 50th birthday.

'Sorry I'm late, old thing. Thelma - you know Thelma Duckinfield, don't you? President of the Netherwood Women's Guild. Well, she rang to discuss our charity lunch next Wednesday. We're having a guest speaker, you know. Gregory Darcy-Smith. He's the food-buff from the Daily Post and he's coming to talk about entertaining on a grand scale. Sounds exciting, doesn't it? Perhaps you'd like to come along?'

Liberty pushed the last mound of rubbish onto a shovel.

'I think my days of entertaining on a grand scale are well and truly over, don't you?' she replied.

Sondra's thin, carefully-painted lips parted and her clear green eyes stared in horror.

'Oh, Lib. I *am* sorry. I'm such a clot at times. Derek tells me my big mouth will get me into trouble one day. He says I don't put my brain into gear before I jump straight in. Something like that. Anyway, pretend I just arrived. What was it you wanted to talk to me about?'

Liberty wiped her forehead with the back of her hand and emptied the shovel into a black bin-liner.

'Let's go in the house. It's cooler in there,' she said, leading the way into the kitchen. Sondra flung herself onto the battered two-seater settee in the far corner while Liberty switched on the coffee percolator. 'I think somebody's following me. In fact I know somebody's following me but I don't know who.'

'What?' Sondra sat bolt upright so fast that her chestnut hair swung like a curtain in front of her eyes. Carefully replacing it behind her ears she continued. 'I told you it was dangerous to get mixed up in things you don't understand. Oh, Lib, you must go to the police straight away. This is all getting out of hand.'

'Why does everyone want me to go to the police? I'm afraid Chief Inspector Leatheringham isn't the great detective everybody thinks he is. In fact, as far as I'm concerned, he's clueless. Pardon the pun.'

'Yes, but . . .'

'Look, Sondra, he's got it in for me one way or another. I really believe if he can pin it on me he will. Either that or he thinks I'm a neurotic woman who's making it all up.'

'The man's an idiot then. But you don't need to go to him. He must have a superior. Lib, you really must report this. My God, it could be a murderer who's stalking you. In fact . . .' She paused and clasped her hand to her mouth. Her eyes widened. 'He might be out there right now.'

For a moment, Liberty was gripped by a spasm of fear and her fingers tightened round the handle of the percolator. Could Sondra be right? Was Joe's killer at this very moment parked outside? No, the idea was preposterous. She poured the steaming coffee into two earthenware mugs.

'Strong, black, no sugar, just as you like it,' she said, handing one to Sondra and noticing her friend's shaking hands. It wasn't like Sondra to panic. Sondra was the one who looked on life as a game, to be played and enjoyed to the full. She rarely took anything too seriously. 'Come on, Sondra. You're always telling *me* to lighten up and let my hair down. You're the one who says life's too short to worry.'

Sondra sipped her coffee and flashed a wary glance at Liberty.

'I hardly think it's worrying unnecessarily to suggest you inform the police about a potential psychopath following you.'

'But that's the point. I don't think he is dangerous. In fact I'm convinced he's one of Chief Inspector Leatheringham's men. And I want you to help me follow him, to catch him out.'

Sondra screwed up her finely boned nose.

'You must be kidding,' she exploded. 'Tell me you're just joking. Please. I don't believe you can possibly be serious.' She paused and Liberty could see she would need some convincing, but instead of the denial which Sondra obviously hoped for, Liberty flashed her a reassuring smile.

'Of course I'm serious. But I've not taken leave of my senses, if that's what you think.' She settled herself into the sagging cushions next to Sondra, determined that she was going to win the battle of wills. It was, to a certain extent, an alien feeling since for most of her life she'd been on the receiving end of other people's persuasion and manipulation. It had started with her mother who had kept her firmly in place and receptive to every demand by barely disguised blackmail. Any failure to comply with her wishes, Liberty was conditioned to believe, might easily result in a return of the depression which had dogged her mother since her father's departure.

But Joe had been an expert at it, achieving what he wanted either by switching on his not-inconsiderable charm or by convincing her that it was in her own interests to acquiesce to his wishes. Either way she'd usually gone along with him. It would only have caused one quarrel after another if she hadn't and probably not changed his mind. And, after a while, it had become second nature to bow to his superior judgement and, in the process, she'd learned not to harbour resentment.

In fact their marriage, especially in the last few years, had been virtually without argument and she had gradually come to accept that in most instances he had probably been right anyway. In a strange way, giving in to his way of thinking had lifted much of the burden of decision-making from her shoulders. She'd understood that only too well over the past few days. She'd missed Joe's decisiveness. But did that make it right to employ the same kind of tactics?

With the reluctant admission that a certain amount of ruthlessness might be necessary from time to time, she soon dismissed any qualms about pressing her friend against her will. Placing a hand firmly on Sondra's shoulder and leaning forward she said:

'Look, Sondra. I've thought it through very carefully. Just hear me out, will you? I'm almost certain that Chief Inspector Leatheringham has put a tail on me - that's the expression isn't it? To discover if I might have a secret lover or accomplice, presumably. But if he's had me followed everywhere, and I rather think he has, he must be wondering what the hell I'm up to by now.'

Sondra fingered the rim of her mug and gazed sympathetically at her. But she didn't look convinced.

'Surely he wouldn't do that. Not with somebody who'd just lost her husband. You might have been terrified out of your wits. In fact, I don't know why you're so calm. I'd be on to this Chief Inspector what's-his-name's superior like a shot if I thought he was having *me* followed.'

'But if he thinks I'm implicated . . . Don't you see, he could argue that he was justified. And he'd have evidence by now that I was behaving very suspiciously . . . visiting seedy pubs in Manchester, having a cosy drink with an unknown male acquaintance.'

She stopped as Sondra's mouth dropped open. 'What male acquaintance?'

'Ah!' Liberty bit her lip. 'Never mind that now. But you can see my point, can't you? Then there's always the chance that if I go over his head, it's his word against mine. Without proof or witnesses, he might choose to deny the whole thing. And if it did turn out that it isn't the police following me . . . they really would have a field day. They'd be convinced I'm making the whole thing up to deflect attention from the fact that I really did kill Joe. Surely you can see that, can't you?'

Sondra shook her head. 'But what if it is a psychopath? Oh, Lib, you could be in terrible danger.'

'I don't think so,' she said, but seeing Sondra was about to protest, she continued: 'OK. So there's a slight possibility that it might not be the police. Very slight. But I really do believe it is. Oh, I know I don't always get things right but I reckon this time I have. Whoever he is, he must have been following me now for at least a week. It really freaked me out at first, I can tell you. But don't you see? If he'd intended to do me any harm he's had loads of opportunities - at work, at home, when I've been out in the car. Most of the time I've been on my own.'

Sondra was fluttering her long, mascaraed eyelashes, her face a solemn mask of doubt.

'But you've got to do something.'

'My point exactly. That's why I need your help.'

'What do you want me to do?' She held her hand up. 'Just as a matter of interest, mind. I can't see me being much use.'

Liberty smiled, sensing that her friend was weakening. Her gaze fell on the elegantly manicured fingernails which tapped nervously on the mug.

'I don't want you to do anything risky. That wouldn't be fair. Look, I'll explain what I have in mind. If you don't want to get involved, I'll understand.'

CHAPTER 15

At just after 12.30 that afternoon Liberty arrived at Westerman and Brock's. She was acutely aware that Bob would be wondering where she was. But she'd been deliberately vague about what time she'd be in, suspecting, rightly for once, that she might have other matters to attend to.

Hoping that she would be able to get away soon, she released the portacabin door, standing back for a moment until the foul air had been replaced by, if not cooler, then more oxygen-filled air. She wafted the door back and forth, her eyes falling on bits of cardboard and polystyrene foam scattered about the yard. It was less than three weeks since Joe's last day here but already she sensed a relaxing of attitudes. A certain energy was lacking too - the vitality and enthusiasm which had generated orders, kept the trucks on the road and made the bank manager happy. She doubted whether it could ever be replaced.

She turned away and strode into her portable office. Someone had placed two piles of mail next to the bulging in-tray and she decided to start by opening that. But before she'd taken her paper knife from the desk, the phone rang. It was Bretherton and he spoke quietly, as if he were afraid of being overheard. Could he speak to her as soon as possible, in his office?

Five minutes later she stood outside his glass-fronted office at the far end of the warehouse. Bretherton leapt up immediately and rushed to open the door. With a furtive glance to his left and right he beckoned her to sit down. Then, without speaking, he walked round his desk and lowered himself into a battered swivel chair. His dark-rimmed eyes looked heavy and tired and she thought he looked ill. A thin cut was visible just below the hairline.

'I think I've stumbled across something important,' he said breathlessly. 'I've had my suspicions for a while but until now I . . . the thing is, I think there's been some falsification of tachograph records.'

Liberty looked at him blankly. What possible connection had this to her investigations? He seemed edgy and strained and his bottom lip trembled. She wondered if he might be having a nervous breakdown.

'I don't understand,' she said, trying to suppress her irritation. The last thing she needed now was to get side-tracked by operational matters.

'You know that tachographs record the length of time a driver spends behind the wheel and the vehicle's speed?'

'Yes, I know what tachographs are for,' she interrupted sharply. Did he think she'd worked for a transport company for ten years without knowing what a tachograph was? It was insulting to her intelligence.

'Right. Of course. Well . . .' he hesitated and shot her a nervous glance. 'I've managed to get hold of some tachograph charts and, in my opinion, they've been tampered with.'

'But why are you telling me this? Surely Bob's the best person to handle that sort of thing.' Her patience was wearing thin now. 'I was hoping you might have a report for me on those names in Joe's address book.'

'Yes, yes. I have. But don't you see? This could be the breakthrough you're looking for.'

How on earth could this be of any use to her? She watched him wringing his big hands as if he were desperately trying to squeeze life into them. She knew then that it had been a mistake to involve him and screwed up her face.

'I'm sorry. I don't understand what tachographs have to do with Joe's death.'

'Let me explain.' He seemed to relax a little and sat back in his chair as if preparing for a long explanation. 'I'm not talking about the odd driver who has falsified a chart so that he can get back home and avoid an overnight stay. I'm talking about regulations being broken on a massive scale. Where employers, drivers and the traffic desk conspire together. I'm talking about hundreds of charts. Wholesale abuse of the regulations. A total disregard for the public's safety. And what for? For money, that's what. For profit.'

'Just hang on a minute, Bretherton. Just who are you accusing here?' Suddenly her irritation turned to outrage and indignation.

'I'll need more time before I can be sure. But the whole aim of such fraud is usually to boost profits, to allocate work to drivers knowing it's impossible to complete within the legally permitted number of hours. And with each driver doing more deliveries per day, competitors working within the law are at a distinct disadvantage. That can only be beneficial to those who own the company. Not to the drivers who would have to go along with it or else lose their jobs. But the traffic manager would have to be involved too.'

'So you're saying that Joe and Bob - and Alan Walters - were all in this together?' She fleetingly recalled Walters' gaunt appearance coming out of Dr Firth's surgery.

'Not necessarily. Alan Walters must have been in on it. As Traffic Manager he allocates the deliveries. He's very experienced and would know precisely how many drops and pick-ups each driver could do legally in one shift. As for Mr Brock and Mr Westerman - it may have been that only one of them was involved. But it was Mr Westerman's job to oversee the traffic office.'

'You can't think Joe would be party to anything like that. Surely not. He could have been in serious trouble with the law. Gone to prison, even. What would have happened to the business then? No, I don't believe Joe would ever have put the business at risk like that.'

Bretherton shook his head and fixed her with a sceptical and, she thought, desperate look. 'It's not just the business that would be at risk. What about people's lives? A tired driver behind the wheel of a heavy goods vehicle is lethal. He can maim and kill, destroy whole families.'

He stopped suddenly and dropped his head onto his chest, his breath coming now in short gasps. Liberty shuddered as if an icy hand had touched her back. At that moment she knew exactly how his daughter had been killed.

'I'm sorry,' she began, wondering how much she was apologising for. 'I'm sorry but I don't see what all this has to do with Joe's murder. Do you think there's some connection?'

It was a few moments before he could speak. Liberty watched the bloodless lips part, then clamp firmly shut as if he'd suddenly realised he'd said too much already. She waited, the weight of her own loss adding to the pity she felt for him, and wondering at the mammoth self-discipline which had kept his grief in check over the years. Suddenly his whole body became rigid, the muscles in his face stiffening and twisting so much that his eyes seemed to bulge.

'I . . .' his voice was barely audible. He paused. 'I think it's possible that there may be some connection. But . . .' His energy and brief enthusiasm were spent and he slumped back, deflated and apathetic. 'I suggest you speak to Alan Walters,' he concluded.

When she found him five minutes later, Alan Walters was leaning heavily against a concrete pillar watching a fork-lift truck manoeuvre a stack of pallets into a 40 foot trailer. He pushed himself away rather too quickly when he saw her approaching. Liberty thought he looked more than just a little guilty. But she'd always thought of him as the shifty type. How Joe had managed to work with him for nearly fifteen years she couldn't imagine. Fortunately, her job involved little contact with the traffic manager.

'Can I have a word with you? In private.' Her words sounded ominous even to herself.

He looked as if he might say something but seemed to think better of it. Instead he shrugged and shuffled towards the next loading bay. Liberty followed, unable to avoid the smell of stale cigarette smoke mixed with a particularly offensive body odour. The sweat which had soaked through the back of his shirt was now seeping into the fawn trousers making a damp patch above his belt. His limp, unwashed hair clung to his collar. Liberty was amazed that someone so renowned for his womanising could have gone downhill so suddenly and so completely.

He stopped by a pile of boxes labelled 'Fragile - Handle with Care' and turned to face her.

'This'll be more private than the office,' he said, resting his elbow on the boxes. She noticed now that his eyes looked inflamed and he had a sore in the corner of his mouth.

Was everyone round here cracking up? she wondered.

'I'll not beat about the bush,' she said, the urge to get far away from him suddenly taking over from her resolve to approach him warily. 'I'd like to know if you had any problems with the way Joe ran the business.'

The question struck her as stupid even before she'd finished it. If he were up to his neck in some tachograph scam, pulling the wool over her eyes would be a doddle. Why hadn't she planned her questions more carefully? But it was too late now. She bit her lip and gazed at Walters' perspiring, impassive face wondering if he too were incredulous of her naivety.

But to her amazement he laughed, a low and bitter laugh of self-deprecation.

'It's a bit late now, isn't it?' he said, his mouth twisted scornfully. 'What does it matter what my problems with your husband were?'

Liberty struggled for an answer. What could she say without accusing him outright? She had no proof of his guilt, only the suspicions of an emotionally disturbed employee.

She fidgeted with her wedding ring and walked over to the sheer edge of the loading bay. The yard below was alive with activity and the vehicle Walters had been watching was now revving, sending clouds of dust and fumes into the air. A smaller boxed-trailer and a van were negotiating the limited space to allow it to pass. She felt a surge of regret that Joe would never watch the comings and goings of his fleet again.

'Did you know that when Joe bought this depot it was just a warren of derelict farm buildings?' The question had been prompted more by her need at this moment to look back rather than to change the subject - and take stock of Joe's considerable achievements. But it was also possible that this could be the best tactic to gain Walters' confidence.

He nodded, puzzled.

She continued, 'It was 1978. The children were only babies and I remember bringing them with me to look at the place with Joe. He could see the potential but I told him to forget it. Fifteen thousand pounds was a lot of money in those days. But he stuck to it that he could make a go of it. And he was right. He brought Bob in as a partner and they set about restoring the buildings they needed and demolishing the ones they didn't. He was very clever.'

She stopped, aware that she was gabbling. What on earth would Walters make of all this? She had no idea but it had helped to remind her of the good times she and Joe had shared. She coughed self-consciously and looked across the yard at the sheep grazing on the hillside.

'He was clever all right.' Walters spoke as if thinking out loud. 'Too bloody clever for his own good.'

Liberty, jolted out of her reminiscences, swivelled round and saw that he was about to light up a cigarette.

'You . . . smoking's not allowed, you know that,' she protested.

'Dangerous, is it? You think we might all go up in smoke?' He gave a thin smile and drew deeply on the cigarette. 'I should be so lucky.'

She could see that he had no intention of putting it out. She was wasting her breath and decided it might be wiser to let the subject drop, although it did cross her mind that if she became a working partner she would need to be much firmer in enforcing the company's health and safety regulations.

'What do you mean, Joe was 'too clever for his own good'?'

'Just that.' He shrugged, blowing a stream of smoke down his nostrils.

She decided on a change of approach.

'Have you ever thought of giving them up?' She inclined her head towards the packet in his hand and attempted a friendly smile.

He fixed her with an icy stare.

'What the hell for? The good of my health?' He let out a convulsive laugh that shook his body and left him coughing and choking.

For some moments she watched horrified as his body was gripped in a supreme effort to regain control, but the coughing spasm had left him doubled up and gasping for breath. He stamped on the cigarette and ground it into the concrete floor.

'Wouldn't be any point giving up, would there?' he muttered.

'Sorry?' she asked, puzzled.

'No point. Giving up.' He eyed her up and down and she wondered what was the point of the whole conversation. She might as well give up, even if he wouldn't. At least for now. 'I'll be dead anyway this time next year,' he added in a matter-of-fact tone.

The statement asked for no sympathy and she could think of nothing to say that wouldn't be totally inadequate. He rubbed his unshaven chin and continued:

'Syphilis. Not cigarettes.' The smile, pained yet mocking, made her shiver.

The frank admission was intended to shock her, she knew that. And it had succeeded. He had taken control of the conversation and she had no doubt it had been his aim. But she had to concede that it was an original tactic to divert her from quizzing him about the tachograph irregularities.

Feeling a sudden flush of heat on her neck, she fanned herself with the lapels of her blouse. 'I'm sorry . . . I didn't know,' she muttered pathetically.

But he didn't seem to hear. He stood motionless for a moment staring vacantly ahead, his fist pressed hard against the pile of boxes. Then he rubbed his knuckles and scowled at her.

'You want answers? I'll give you answers. But they won't be the ones you want. And I've got nothing to lose. The police won't be able to touch me now.'

Liberty could hardly believe her ears. Was he really ready to confess some crime? And if so, what? Trying to disguise her excited, if somewhat nervous anticipation, she leaned against the cold stone wall, held her breath and waited.

'I'll tell you about your precious husband. But you won't like it. You don't want to hear that he didn't give a damn about anybody else. All he cared about was screwing every penny's worth out of people. He didn't give a monkey's for the drivers he sacked who wouldn't go along with him. Or for the lives he put at risk.'

Liberty's heart sank. She wanted to protest, to object bitterly to the accusations Walters was making, but a part of her had already accepted that Joe wasn't the man he'd led her to believe.

'You're talking about the falsification of tachographs, I presume?' she asked, trying to sound business-like. But she knew Walters had the upper hand.

He sneered and propelled himself towards her. His face was twisted with contempt.

'Yeah. False tachographs and a hundred other stunts that could make him a quick buck or two. But he never got his hands dirty. Oh no. Not that one. He left that to me. Holier-than-thou Joe. That's what he was. He doled out money to local charities and pretended to be whiter-than-white. Mostly, people fell for it. But I was the one on the front line if anybody got wise to his little scams.'

She shook her head, outraged but nevertheless unsure of her ground. 'But Joe didn't give money to charity to make himself look good. He had a naturally generous nature,' she protested. 'He never made money his God.'

His eyes narrowed and he seemed to be thinking. 'No. You're probably right.' His tone was much calmer now, more calculated. 'It wasn't the money he was after. It was the power. Money gave him power. He was the great benefactor, the successful businessman, and everybody looked up to him. He could get what he wanted from people that way.'

He turned away from her, panting, and wiped his forehead with his hand. He seemed to have exhausted himself and neither of them spoke for a moment.

Liberty felt deflated and weary, her will to search out the truth broken. But Walters hadn't finished. With a last surge of venom he spat out his hatred.

'Want to know what I think? I think he pushed some poor sod too far and got his head stoved in for it. He had it coming to him. No mistake. I'd have done it myself for tuppence. But he was worth more alive than dead to me.' He grinned, his white, perfect teeth looking incongruous in the half-dead face. Liberty shook herself from her lethargy.

'What do you mean?' Suddenly she knew. 'Blackmail? Is that what you mean?'

He nodded, pressing together cracked lips. 'Yeah. I wanted to get back at him for all the crap he'd dropped on me. I figured I had nothing to lose. He'd never dare go to the police. And if I'd succeeded I could've lived it up for the rest of my life.' He paused and gave a hollow laugh, obviously realising the irony of his words. 'But the cunning bastard sussed that Alison was in on it and called my bluff.'

'So that was why she left so suddenly.' It had never occurred to her that the sudden departure of Joe's secretary the day before his murder might have been suspicious. But why hadn't it?

'Yeah. He knew I wouldn't risk her going down. I couldn't care less about me. But she's different.'

He spoke softly now, as if he were regretting that he'd not met Alison earlier in his life. Perhaps if he had she could have saved him from the sexual liaisons which had led to the illness now chomping its way, like a hungry caterpillar, through his vital organs. The thought repulsed her and she could no longer look at his vacant, watery eyes. She turned and walked quickly away.

When she got back to her office she found an envelope propped against her telephone. The words Private and Confidential were scrawled across the top in red ink. She recognised the rounded, child-like handwriting immediately and assumed that Bretherton had been unable to face her so soon after their earlier discussion.

At that moment her heart went out to this man who had suffered so long in dignified silence, reluctant to apportion the blame for the death of his only child. In the throes of her own sorrow she could empathise with his grief but not with his reluctance to act on his suspicions and bring the person responsible for her death to justice.

She wondered now whether that failure had compounded his and Doris's loss to such an extent that they had been unable to come to terms with it. The dead child had become as much a part of their lives as any living one and probably, for Doris, just as real.

She shivered and opened the letter. It was a report, set out in the kind of formal, factual style she imagined he'd used regularly during his years as a police officer. The content was even more mundane.

He'd contacted the three names she'd given him from Joe's address book. On Saturday 21st August he, Bretherton, had visited a Victor Adams at an address in Barrow. The person in question worked at the docks in Whitehaven. His acquaintance with Joe was purely through business, he had claimed, mainly in relation to Westerman and Brock's Irish traffic. End of report.

Liberty bit her lip. Surely Bretherton could have dug deeper? But he was obviously past his best. His eye for detail and that essential quality which all good policemen possess, the ability to read between the lines, seemed to be missing. She could only imagine the fire that had once burned brightly in him but which now struggled to maintain even a flicker of a flame.

As with the first contact, the reports of Bretherton's interviews with the second and third were brief to the point of being useless. Peter Ball, an accountant living in London - whom Bretherton had telephoned owing to the distance involved - had spoken to Joe on only one occasion. As far as he could remember, it concerned a dispute over a contract to carry fertiliser. Anne-Marie Broughton, one of the few women in Joe's book, had no recollection of ever having spoken to or met him. She had also been unwilling to answer any further questions.

Liberty threw the reports on the desk. If any of these people had anything to hide, they had certainly been given plenty of warning. But Liberty had gleaned nothing. Or virtually nothing. The Irish connection had raised its head once more. She pulled Joe's address book from the top drawer and looked up the name, Michael O'Connor. A visit to Ireland was long overdue.

CHAPTER 16

The morning of Thursday, 26th August started uneventfully enough with the usual pile of mail on her desk, but Liberty was convinced that a breakthrough in her search for Joe's murderer was imminent. There was no rational explanation for her sudden optimism but it nevertheless spurred her on to complete the drivers' wages in record time. By half past eleven she had cleared her desk and was on her way across the yard to her car.

Bob had made some comment about it being all right for some but she hadn't cared. Today she had more important business to attend to. And Ireland was at the top of her list of priorities. She might even have time to take the ferry from Stranraer, she decided, turning out of the yard towards Lowthwaite.

But as she turned the bend, a startled ewe darted out from the rough grass which bordered the narrow lane and made a dash for the other side. She braked hard and swerved, the animal momentarily disappearing under her offside wing. But there was no bump.

Breathing a sigh of relief she turned to her wing mirror and watched the terrified beast scamper safely through a hole in the hawthorn. It was at that moment that she spotted the small red car hurtling round the bend behind her. She could see clearly the startled look on the driver's face just before he braked and came to a juddering halt. It was only a glimpse, but in that brief second she recognised him instantly. It was the man who had followed her on the train to Manchester the previous Saturday.

While the discovery unnerved her, she was surprised that the hairs no longer stood up on the back of her neck. Instead, she felt strangely elated, almost heady with the intoxicating awareness that she might soon be in control of the situation. As long as Sondra hadn't dragged

Derek off on a shopping trip . . . or gone to the golf club. It was at times like this when she wished she'd taken up Joe's offer to buy her a mobile phone.

For the next three miles she gripped the steering wheel tightly, hoping and praying that her pursuer would hang around long enough for her to put her plan into action. Previous sightings suggested he would tag onto her until he had something worthwhile to report.

Her hands wet with sweat she flicked down the indicator and turned into the driveway of Lowthwaite House. Glancing in her mirror she saw that the car behind had pulled onto the grass verge outside Bagley Hall - the exact spot where that other car had parked on the night of Joe's murder.

She pulled up in front of the house and jumped out expecting the familiar jelly-like feeling in her legs. But it wasn't there. She strode into the hallway, the clacking of her stilettos on the tiles resonant and unfaltering. This was her chance to fight back. And she could do it too, she decided, dropping her bag on the floor and grabbing the telephone.

'Sondra? Thank goodness you're in. Are you and Derek free for a couple of hours?' she crossed her fingers and held her breath.

The voice was hesitant : 'Y . . es. Why?'

'It's time for Operation Quick Switch. Are you on?'

'If you're sure this is going to work.'

Liberty hesitated. It was one thing to be reckless for her own ends but it wasn't fair to rail-road her friends. She had to give them one last chance to back out.

'*I* am. But if you're having second thoughts . . .'

'No, no, we want to do it. Well . . . I do. And Derek's OK about it. As long as we don't take any risks.'

'Good. You know what to do. The car's parked outside Bagley Hall. It's a small red car. But don't be tempted to look at the driver. You might scare him off.'

'OK. Don't worry. We'll be with you in fifteen minutes.'

Liberty went upstairs and took off her blouse, noting with a satisfied smile its distinctive floral design. Laying it carefully on the bed she donned a plain red t-shirt over her white skirt. Now to work on her appearance. It wouldn't be easy, she conceded, facing herself through the oval mirror in her en-suite bathroom. But her disguise needn't be too detailed. Her experiences over the past few days had confirmed that, unless they were close up, faces seen through rear-view mirrors were notoriously difficult to define.

Slapping on a heavy coat of foundation she got to work with the blue eye-shadow and eye-lash thickening mascara that Ruth had left behind. Finally, two dark circles of blusher and a generous coat of cherry-red lipstick completed the make-over.

She stood back to admire her hard work.

'Great,' she said screeching almost hysterically and observing that the gap between her front teeth exaggerated the clown-like appearance.

The brown and gold chiffon scarf had been waiting on top of the mahogany dressing table since she'd formulated the plan with Sondra the day before. Now she wrapped it round her head, carefully obscuring from view all but the tiniest wisps of honey-blonde locks. From a distance the turban-like scarf just might be mistaken for auburn hair.

The door-bell began to ring as she descended the stairs. It was a sharp, demanding ring and her heart lurched erratically.

'Please God,' she whispered and opened the door.

'God, you look awful, Lib.' Sondra broke into a raucous peel of laughter and inched past her into the hall. 'It's a bit of a laugh, this cloak and dagger stuff, isn't it? A bit scary though. Derek says we need our heads testing but what does he know? He always was a stick-in-the-mud. No sense of adventure. Now, where do I change?'

'Upstairs. My room.' It was said without thought, but the point was not lost on her that only three weeks ago the possessive pronoun would have been plural.

'Righty-ho. I'll be down in a tick.' And with an imperious wave she glided up the stairs, her ankle-length red dress flowing behind her.

Liberty paced the hall, the slow click-clack of her heels on the tiles reminding her of a clock ticking away the moments. She glanced at her watch. It wouldn't be long now. But what if she'd got it wrong yet again? She didn't think she had. But what made her so confident she could change the habit of a lifetime?

Five minutes later Sondra reappeared. 'That blouse looks better on you than me,' Liberty said with a nod of approval. 'But I hope my hair doesn't look anything like that.' She smiled. The short blonde wig, discovered at the bottom of a trunk of amateur operatic society costumes, was Sondra's own contribution. 'Now you're sure you know what to do? The keys are in the car.'

Sondra's porcelain face was animated with the kind of excitement rarely felt by most women after girlhood. 'Trust me. This is what I'm good at. You never did see me in the Pirates of Penzance, did you?'

Liberty shook her head.

'Pity. Everybody said I was the star of the show. This'll be a cinch by comparison. Right. Time for off.' With a theatrical flourish Sondra threw open the door.

'Do be careful, Sondra. It's not a show. This is the real thing. And if the bloke in that car's not one of Chief Inspector Leatheringham's men, you could be in serious danger.'

'Worry not. I can take care of myself.' She stepped out into the sunlight and pulled the door behind her.

With a sudden unnerving rush of panic Liberty grabbed the handle. 'No, wait. I can't let you . . . It's too dangerous.'

'Too late, old thing. I'm on my way,' came the reply a split second before the door banged shut.

Liberty leaned against it and listened. An engine exploded into life and she could hear it revving, then fading as it reached the end of the drive.

Quickly, she swung into action. Slamming the door behind her she ran to the cobbled area by the stable block. The maroon BMW was waiting. With barely a glance at the driver she jumped into the soft leather seat. The air-conditioning greeted her like a wall of ice.

'Thanks, Derek. I owe you one,' she said, clicking the seat belt into place. 'We'd better get going.'

Derek frowned and threw his cigar out of the window. A moment later the car purred into action.

'I can't believe I've let myself be dragged into this hair-brained scheme. It's just ludicrous,' he said, his small, grey-blue eyes meeting hers.

They'd reached the end of the path and she saw, as she'd hoped, that the red car was no longer parked opposite.

'Quick. Or we'll lose them,' she urged.

Derek turned right, as arranged, towards the Keswick to Carlisle road. No cars were in sight.

'I hope you know what you're doing.' Derek's voice sounded gruff, almost threatening and his normally relaxed manner was edgy. 'If anything happens to Sondra . . .'

Liberty scanned the road ahead. 'Don't worry. She'll be fine,' she said, more confidently than she felt. 'We don't need to be too close behind. We know where they're heading. At least I think we know.'

Derek tapped his fingers on the steering wheel and put his foot down. Trees and hedgerows began to flash past.

'It's a damn fool thing to do. No matter how much planning you've done, things can go wrong. And I should know. I've seen the best laid plans of people a lot more intelligent than you two go wrong.'

'Thanks,' she muttered, giving him what she hoped was a withering look.

'Sorry, but you might as well know, I've tried my best to talk Sondra out of it. I don't know what you've told her but she's got the idea this is some sort of game. I'm only here because I couldn't let you - either of you - go tearing around the place on your own.' He swerved sharply round a cyclist and she lurched towards him.

'Relax, Derek. I wouldn't be doing this if I thought it was dangerous. And I certainly wouldn't have involved Sondra. This guy's been following me for days. If he'd meant me any harm he's had plenty of opportunities.'

'Yes, yes. Sondra's explained all that. But you're only guessing that it's one of Chief Inspector Leatheringham's men.'

'I suppose so. But . . .' She held her breath as they rounded a tight bend. Then she saw it. About 50 yards in front of them was a red car. She knew instinctively that this was the car following Sondra. Derek too seemed instantly alert and pulled back. Neither of them spoke.

Liberty wondered whether Derek was thinking the same as her. Where was Sondra? But the winding road and high hedges conspired to blot out their view of the road in front of the car. She glanced at Derek. His steady gaze didn't waiver. Only his hands, wrapped tightly around the steering wheel, betrayed the tension he was so obviously struggling to control. The age-spotted skin, stretched tight across his white knuckles, was thin and strained.

Liberty gripped the door handle, more for reassurance than a need to steady herself. She had made this journey hundreds of times before but somehow it felt like a completely new experience. Her senses were so heightened that gardens on either side seemed to explode into colour as they passed. She tried to concentrate on the car's number plate but it was too far away. And they daren't risk getting any closer. Sondra was still nowhere in sight.

The trees to the left and right became more dense and sunlight streaked through the overhanging branches. Liberty realised with mounting unease that they were fast approaching the spot where they would discover once and for all whether or not Sondra was safe. The road curved sharply to the right, past a shaded lay-by, then opened up in front of the Traveller's Rest car park. Liberty leaned forward, straining to see over a low hedge. A figure was emerging from a white car parked directly in front of the hotel's main door.

Liberty recognised the car and the brightly coloured floral blouse almost at the same moment as Sondra whipped off the wig and shook her Titian hair with a victorious flourish.

'Look, there's Sondra,' she gasped, her relief at seeing her friend tinged with the uncertainty and fear of what might happen next. 'Pull back,' she added.

Her gaze moved to the red car which had almost reached the car park entrance. The brake lights flashed on and the driver twisted his head towards Sondra. Liberty held her breath. Surely he would realise his mistake now. Surely he would see that the figure now making her way into the hotel foyer had duped him. But then what?

This had been the difficult part of the plan. But they'd decided that, whoever he was, he wouldn't risk giving away his identity by following his prey into the hotel. She would be safe there. By that time, hopefully, it would be obvious to him that Sondra had acted as a decoy to facilitate Liberty's escape.

But would he assume that there was no point returning to Lowthwaite House? Liberty's money was on him heading straight home or to the person who had given him the surveillance job in the first place. Either way, he would give away his identity.

Sondra had pointed out that he would probably have a mobile phone and may be given new instructions. But Liberty hadn't been put off. If this was one of DCI Leatheringham's men, he would probably be told to report back to the station. One way or another, they would have their proof. But what if he was neither a policeman nor a murderer?

There were a lot of 'ifs' and 'probablys'. Liberty was suddenly overcome with doubt. She glanced at Derek's mobile phone in the space between them. At least, in an emergency . . .

At that moment the red car accelerated forward with a screech. Derek glanced at her. With his faded mousy hair hanging low across his forehead and a stubborn reluctance set in his chubby features, he reminded her of Ben when he was little. She knew immediately what he was thinking. The man they were following, whoever he was, wasn't making for the police station. That was back in the opposite direction.

'We've got to go after him, Derek. We can't give up now we're so close. But keep your distance.' She tried to sound confident but he nodded unconvincingly. 'Don't worry about Sondra, she'll be fine.'

She heard the revs increase and felt the car gently pick up speed. A surge of adrenaline made her heart beat faster and she savoured the excitement it brought.

Neither of them spoke as Derek negotiated the tight bends. Their quarry was out of sight for most of the time but now and again, on straighter pieces, it flashed briefly into view before disappearing again behind a wall of greenery.

The traffic was comparatively light for a Saturday afternoon and their journey proceeded at a fast, though not reckless, pace. One other car had come out of a side road to separate them but Liberty was not unduly worried. In fact, she judged, it would probably make their pursuit far less conspicuous to a suspicious driver. The sun streamed through the windscreen as the car rocked her back and forth lulling her into a false sense of security.

But, as they reached the rise of the hill where the road narrowed, a coach loomed into view. Derek swerved, scattering leaves and branches in the hedgerow. As he did so, a car suddenly appeared from a hidden side-road to the left, its nose jutting out into their path. Derek let out a loud hissing noise and hit the brake.

Liberty gasped, her feet searching for a non-existent brake pedal. Her body lunged forward and was caught, almost simultaneously, by the seat belt a second before the car screeched to a halt. It rocked in the slip stream of the coach as it hurtled past. Liberty let out a long sigh. They might have avoided an accident but had they any hope of catching up now?

Derek waved impatiently for the car to move. It seemed to take forever. But then he revved hard and they shot forward. Liberty felt as though she were in an aeroplane taking off, although she'd never had the real experience to compare it to.

As she'd expected, the red car was nowhere in sight. To her right she could make out the end of the lake and knew that they would soon be approaching the roundabout just before Keswick. If they hadn't caught up by then they'd only be able to guess which of the three routes to take.

Liberty chewed at the ends of her fingers, willing Derek to go even faster though she knew they were already going too fast. A few moments later the road widened and straightened just as they came up behind an old Rover sauntering along at no more than twenty miles an hour. As Derek sped past, Liberty glanced at the white-haired man, wondering if she might have him to thank for holding up the mystery driver. With Skiddaw's peak now to their left she realised they had little chance of making up the lost ground before Keswick but, against the odds, her hopes remained high.

Then, as they rounded a wide bend almost on two wheels, she saw it, a fleeting glimpse of red, as it veered off to the left a few yards before the roundabout.

'There. Left. Next left,' she yelled, unable to hide her excitement.

Derek nodded but his narrow eyes were fixed on the road ahead. She had the feeling for the first time, that he too was relishing the chase. As he negotiated the sharp turn into a single track road, he braked gently and glanced in her direction. Had he also realised that the road led only to Holme End and a few scattered dwellings? Perhaps the man they were following lived in one of them? Or was he reporting back to the person who'd set him on her tail? They'd soon find out - if they didn't lose him.

High hedges enclosed them as they sped along, recklessly now, the big car weaving clumsily round hair-pin bends. She clung to the door handle terrified that they would meet a vehicle travelling in the opposite direction. As they shot past hidden driveways and farm tracks she craned her neck to see whether their quarry had disappeared up one of them. But it was impossible to know. Their only hope was to go forward.

But as they careered round a left-hand bend a tractor blocked their path. Liberty gasped and tensed herself for the expected crash as Derek slammed on the brakes once again and they skidded to a halt inches from the front of the tractor. With an apologetic wave to the farmer he reversed into a gateway and they waited in frustrated silence for the tractor to pass.

As soon as they set off again she saw with dismay that the road split. Derek slowed and she knew they'd lost the object of their chase.

'Which way?' Derek flashed a desperate look.

Liberty shrugged and shook her head. Left was to the village and the more obvious choice. But somehow it didn't feel right.

'Up there,' she snapped, pointing to the right-hand fork.

The track took them upwards, into the foothills of Skiddaw which loomed over them, its dark summit obscured by a thin trail of white cloud. Then she spotted it. The red paint seemed to gleam from under a high screen of rhododendrons lining the curved driveway.

'Stop!' she yelled, the strength of her voice surprising her. 'That's it. I'm sure that's it. Let's take a closer look.'

Derek pulled up on the grass verge and Liberty jumped out.

'I'll be back in a minute. You wait here,' she said, shutting the car door before he could protest and walking back towards the drive.

At first sight the cottage appeared much like many others scattered around the Northern Fells. The low building of Lakeland stone, evenly proportioned, like a child's drawing, with four square windows and a centrally positioned porch, sat snugly in a copse of mature trees and shrubs. A swathe of yellow roses ran across the front of the house, blending haphazardly with a cluster of deep red, larger roses around the door arch.

The sun on her back felt warm after the chill of Derek's air conditioning and she paused for a moment. The whole scene seemed idyllic and charming but she knew she mustn't be lulled into a false sense of security. Cautiously, she glanced around but there was no sign of anyone either in the garden or at any of the windows. She made up her mind to take a calculated gamble.

Running back to the car, she pulled open the door. 'Drive down the path behind me, Derek,' she said. 'Keep the doors locked and if you think I'm in danger ring the police from your car phone. I'm going to find out what's going on.'

She saw his mouth twitch and his eyes widen in disbelief, but all she heard, before she shut out his protests for a second time, was a mumbled, 'What the . . .?'

Before she had time to change her mind, she strode down the path, pausing only until she heard the revving of Derek's car behind her. Her heart was thudding but she didn't look back.

CHAPTER 17

Sunlight danced through the delicate branches of a huge copper beach that shaded her as she approached the entrance. The sweet scent of rose blossom hovered in the air. Surely no-one capable of murder could live in such peaceful surroundings, she thought, moving warily up to the porch, its sides interwoven with branches.

But before she could reach for the iron bell pull, the door swung open. Liberty gasped, more in surprise than fear, and stared in disbelief at the figure now smiling at her.

'Do come in, Mrs Westerman.'

The greeting was warm though the face betrayed the slightest hint of smugness. An elegant hand waved her inside and Liberty noted the same heavily-ringed fingers which had handed her that note after Joe's funeral. Liberty hesitated, questions rushing into her head like a waterfall after a cloudburst. She'd wanted answers and this woman clearly held the key. But who was she? And could she trust her?

The words of the note, indelibly etched on Liberty's memory, came back to her: *Joe had many enemies. One of them killed him.* Whether she was in danger or not, she couldn't run away now.

Turning towards the car where Derek sat watching through the open window she signalled to him to stay put before following the woman into the narrow hallway.

The effect on her was similar to that she imagined Aladdin might have experienced on entering the cave full of riches. Paintings, tapestries and ornamental nick-knacks adorned the walls behind hand-painted vases and bronze ornaments. Rich reds blended with golds and emerald greens. Liberty was stunned by the sheer number of antiques vying for space but she daren't let herself be distracted. She needed to keep her wits about her. And keep her eye on the olive-skinned beauty who glided bare-foot before her, the mass of jet-black curls flowing like coiled springs down her back.

Who was she? And how did she seem to know so much about Joe? Liberty found herself not so much nervous or frightened as intrigued.

In the doorway at the end of the hallway she stopped, her powers of observation uncharacteristically heightened. Although the cottage was probably 17th Century, a notoriously austere period, the sitting room achieved a fine balance between authenticity and comfort. A crushed-velvet settee, the colour of burnt sugar, dominated the centre of the room. Half a dozen tapestry cushions scattered, not evenly and precisely but randomly, gave the impression of having been leant on recently. The ashes of a half-burned log lay in the grate of the stone fireplace although, in this heat wave, Liberty couldn't imagine that it had been lit for weeks. But the illusion of a room in constant use was assured.

The woman - or was she more like a girl? - hovered smiling, as if waiting for Liberty to take in the mesmeric aura of the room. She motioned towards an armchair by the hearth but said nothing. Liberty hesitated, catching the trace of a burning joss-stick in the air before moving over to the fireplace. Rustic implements were strewn haphazardly across the chimney breast while brightly-patterned vases, jugs and bowls adorned tiny alcoves at either side.

The whole effect was stunning, the silence total but not awkward.

Liberty lowered herself into the chair, keeping her eyes fixed on the uninhibited, almost child-like movements of the woman as she flung herself across the settee. Her gypsy-style, loose smock trailed, as if by design, onto the Indian rug.

It was then that Liberty reluctantly acknowledged the obvious. Of course it had been staring her in the face since the funeral but until this moment she had steadfastly refused to believe it. This was Joe's mistress. Her stomach lurched nauseously but she didn't acknowledge it. She wouldn't - couldn't - let this woman get the better of her. And she had no intention of giving in here to the stream of emotions fighting to be released.

With an almost superhuman effort she smiled, gazing at the high cheek bones and full mouth which now pouted with satisfaction, and at the huge dark eyes, at once innocent yet full of worldly instinct. She could well understand how any man would find her bewitchingly seductive, and at that moment Liberty knew what it was like to hate someone.

The woman was clearly a man-eater. But how had she managed to ensnare Joe? Level-headed, workaholic, unromantic Joe. Perhaps he'd been attracted initially by a faint resemblance to his own daughter? Both had the kind of clear, youthful skin which needs no make-up, the same delicately-boned features and tumbling locks, although Ruth's colouring was in stark contrast to this woman's. She found herself looking for excuses for her husband's treachery.

'My name's Maria Rosa. May I call you Liberty?' The voice was thick and low, the accent faintly foreign.

Liberty could feel the anger, tinged with not a little jealousy, rising in her throat. This temptress had seduced her husband and now here she was, wanting to be on first name terms. Liberty glared, wondering what kind of woman could be so barefaced and, in the circumstances, so heartless. Should she walk out without a word? But then she might never discover the identity of the man stalking her. Or how this woman was involved.

Suddenly her attention was diverted. A peel of laughter, high and uncontrolled, rose from the doorway behind her. Liberty recognised it immediately as that of a child and swivelled round just in time to see a girl of about four race past her and into Maria Rosa's open arms.

'Mama,' she shrieked, her voice shrill with excitement. 'Come and see the puppy.'

Maria Rosa laughed, a throaty, unrepressed burst of laughter which filled the silence, suspending conversation. The two, seemingly oblivious to her presence, hugged and laughed. Liberty stared with a cold intensity, imagining Joe's face now, just inches from the mesmeric eyes and tempting mouth. She understood now how Maria Rosa's child-like abandon would have appealed to the boy in him, would have created an environment where he could enjoy the freedoms of childhood denied to him by his mother's death.

It all seemed clear to her now. And yet, only minutes before, she would never have believed Joe could be unfaithful - not because his much-hyped high moral code would prevent him but because he had never shown the slightest interest in other women. In fact he had rarely shown much interest in her. Sex, even in the early days, had been no more than a ritual, a gap in his diary where he'd fitted her in. In the last years of their marriage, it had been non-existent.

There had been no mutual agreement. It had just ceased. In fact she couldn't remember exactly when had been the last time. But for a while she'd hoped he would once again find her attractive and had even bought a see-through black nightdress. But he'd pulled that face he made when he didn't like something and told her black didn't suit her.

A pang of jealousy more painful than her loss ripped through her now as she watched mother and child shake with laughter as they rolled around trying to tickle each other. Very rarely had she and Joe laughed, really laughed, totally wrapped in each other's company. For her, he had reserved the serious, intense side of his nature, the dutiful husband and father. With this woman he would have been different.

Her eyes fell on the child who was now tugging at her mother's arm. The mass of dark curly hair and big, bright eyes had so obviously been inherited from her mother. But what about the high forehead and long face, the pinched mouth and square chin? A look of horror must have betrayed her fear.

Maria Rosa glanced in her direction. 'No. She's not Joe's child,' she said, as innocently as if she had been explaining the pedigree of a kitten. 'Her name's Sasha.'

Liberty felt a vague sense of relief, although she couldn't quite understand why. Would the presence of a love-child be so much more terrible than the discovery of Joe's infidelity?

Maria Rosa jumped to her feet, the girl still clinging to her arm. Liberty suddenly realised she herself hadn't yet spoken.

'Why are you having me followed?' she blurted out, at once irritated that her question sounded churlish and clumsy against the melodic tones of the other woman.

'Let's go into the garden. I'm sure Sasha would like to show you her puppy. Then we can talk.'

A smile lit up the irritatingly confident face before she turned and almost skipped, hand-in-hand with the child, towards a door at the far end of the room.

Liberty was left to follow, trailing behind like an obedient lap-dog, a niggling jealousy eating into her. She couldn't help wondering whether all this would have been no more than a nightmare, an incredible, impossible nightmare if she'd been more like Maria Rosa. But Liberty had never suspected that he was dissatisfied. And it was too late now.

She trudged miserably through a story-book country kitchen filled with dried flowers and earthenware pots, wishing she could have had some insight, before his death, into Joe's complex personality. Perhaps then she would have been able to satisfy his needs, even those which had never been consciously expressed, either to her or even to himself.

But as she emerged into the bright glow of sunlight her attention was immediately diverted. She stopped to gaze in wonder at the scene below her. It was as if the world had been opened up to reveal unseen, unimaginable treasures.

Bassenthwaite, which for thirty years had been her own special lake, her daily delight and inspiration, lay as if in miniature alongside Derwentwater, both of them dwarfed at the feet of endless layers of peaks fading into the distance. The deep coral blue of the sky shone in the glistening water.

Liberty had glimpsed this panoramic vista only once before, when she had climbed more than 3000 feet to the summit of Skiddaw one autumn day soon after her marriage. But on that occasion the view had been marred by scattered, wispy cloud. This picture, she decided, its crisp outlines accentuated in the afternoon sun, was without doubt the most dazzlingly beautiful she had ever seen.

The irony of making such a discovery at this moment and in this place was not lost on her. She teetered unsteadily across the steeply sloping lawn, her heels catching in the turf. Desperate not to give a repeat performance of her clumsiness at Joe's funeral, she gazed at the ground in front of her.

After what seemed like an age but could only have been seconds, she reached Maria Rosa and her daughter where they were kneeling next to a brown and cream puppy with a pink nose and soft, floppy ears. The child was dangling a rubber bone above its head. The puppy yapped and waved its paws in the air but, as it did, the bone was yanked higher.

'He's so cute, don't you think?' asked Maria Rosa, not looking up.

Liberty didn't answer. This was no time for idle chatter or playing games. And she suspected that the puppy wasn't the only creature being toyed with.

'You said we could talk out here. Shall we get on with it?'

Maria Rosa lifted her head, the deep, knowing eyes scanning her face. 'Of course. You wanted to know why you were being followed. I'm sorry if it has upset you, but you weren't supposed to know. Gregor has been very careless. I shall speak to him about it.'

The words were spoken almost imperiously, yet in the softly reassuring tone of a mother to her child. But Liberty would not be pacified so easily.

'That's beside the point, don't you think? The fact is someone has been following me for several days, scaring me half to death and I want to know why.'

'Yes, of course you do. But there was no intention to frighten you. I hope you believe that. Gregor has insisted that you were not aware of his presence. It seems that he was mistaken. But as to his purpose . . .'

She walked over to a semi-circle of log seats in the shade of an old cedar tree. Easing herself casually onto the nearest one, she beckoned to Liberty to take one of the others.

Liberty felt an intense irritation that she was expected to follow yet again. But any show of antagonism at this moment could jeopardise the amount of information this woman was about to divulge. She sauntered over to the log farthest away and sat down.

'You were telling me about your reasons for having me followed,' Liberty said, fixing her with a sullen stare.

'I think you are aware, are you not, that Joe led something of a double life?' She paused as if waiting for a comment, but Liberty felt unable to make one. 'As I wrote in the note I gave you, Joe had a lot of enemies. Some he acquired through his business dealings. I think you might already have discovered - how shall we say? - certain irregularities in the running of his company. And then there was his pre-occupation with the affairs of Ireland. I can't see the IRA being too impressed with the meddling of some amateur Englishman, can you?' She laughed with a deep, hoarse sound which seemed to be mocking.

'But what has that got to do with stalking me?' Liberty felt her patience wearing thin.

'I think stalking is not quite the right word. Gregor merely kept tabs on you from time to time to establish just how much you have uncovered of Joe's alter-ego.'

'Whatever I've uncovered is no business of yours,' Liberty snapped. She could feel the colour rising in her cheeks but she checked an impulse to say more.

'Yes, you may have a point. But it's all so very intriguing, don't you think? Joe was a fascinating specimen, so very complex. Being with him was an education. But his death . . . now that's an even greater mystery. And who can blame me for being curious about the possible suspects? After all, I alerted you in the first place to the fact that Joe knew his killer. If I hadn't, you would still be expecting the police to arrest some non-existent burglar. And . . .' She paused for effect. 'You would never have realised that your husband had another dimension to him.'

Liberty chose to ignore the implied criticism.

'But how could you possibly be sure that Joe knew his killer?'

'Ah!' she said tantalisingly, waving a finger in the air. 'You haven't guessed that? I thought you might. Gregor, of course. Gregor was following Joe on the evening he was murdered.'

'What? You were having Joe followed too?'

'Why not? As I've just said, he was a fascinating study. I was intrigued to discover the whole persona.'

'You make him sound like the subject of a psychology thesis.'

'I have no doubt he would have proved an excellent source of material for some undergraduate, but my interest was purely as an observer of human nature. I find it never ceases to amaze me.'

So she did get her fun from playing games with people. Even Joe had been little more to her than a life-study. 'And I suppose you've had plenty of mileage out of my comings and goings over the last few weeks,' she said.

Maria Rosa nodded and glanced towards her daughter who was chasing the puppy around the vast lawn and screeching wildly.

'So . . .' Liberty tried to concentrate her thoughts. 'This Gregor was the man in the blue car which was parked opposite the house on the night Joe was killed?'

Maria Rosa nodded again.

'But if he saw something - or someone - why didn't he go to the police?'

'Let's just say that Gregor has a less-than-fortunate relationship with the police. They would not have been inclined to believe him. Apart from which, he saw and heard very little that night.' It all sounded depressingly familiar.

'I think it's time you told me the full story, don't you?'

'If you like.' Maria Rosa shook the thin bracelets on her wrist and looked unconcerned. 'As you are no doubt aware, Joe was, for the most part, a creature of habit. I had already informed Gregor of the most likely times and places to catch up with him.' She laughed and wafted an invisible insect.

Liberty shuddered in spite of the warmth of the afternoon. That this stranger should be privy to the details of Joe's and her private life while she in turn hadn't even known of the other's existence, felt like a slap in the face. But she knew she couldn't afford to let her resentment get in the way. She took a deep breath and turned her gaze on the view of Bassenthwaite.

'I'd told Gregor to arrive about eight o'clock and to expect Joe between half eight and nine. But by ten past nine he was beginning to think he'd missed him and, since the light was fading, decided it would be safe to take a closer look,' Maria Rosa continued. 'Unfortunately, as Gregor reached the stable block he saw a car's headlights on the driveway and darted round the back. He could hear the doors opening and the car being driven inside. Then...' She paused and leaned forward conspiratorially until Liberty turned and met her gaze. 'What do you think?'

'I've no idea,' Liberty replied icily. 'But I'm sure you'll tell me.'

Ignoring the jibe, Maria Rosa gave her a triumphant smile and continued: 'He heard Joe shout, 'What the hell are *you* doing here?' Or words to that effect. The emphasis, according to Gregor, was clearly on the word 'you', as if he knew the person. Then the two men spoke, but Gregor couldn't pick up any of their words.' She gazed into the distance as if bored now. 'Sasha, darling, do stop rushing round,' she called. 'You'll be exhausted.'

Liberty's fingers curled round a clump of buttercups, ripping them out of the ground. 'And?' she prompted.

'Oh. That's it, really,' Maria Rosa said. 'After a few minutes he heard someone running away. When he looked inside the stable he saw Joe's body and fled just as you emerged from the house. The rest you know.'

Liberty struggled to take in the torrent of detail which, like missing pieces in a jigsaw puzzle, filled the gaps in her knowledge of events both immediately before and after Joe's death. She scattered the buttercups next to her on the log-seat.

'You should have gone to the police,' she said, hoping the note of censure in her voice was clear.

'The police are imbeciles,' Maria Rosa replied, tossing her head back contemptuously. 'They would have locked Gregor up on some trumped-up charge if he'd admitted he was at the scene of the crime. He has some past form, you see. Only minor offences, you understand. But we thought it wiser to keep out of their way. I hoped you would be intrigued enough to make your own enquiries. And I have not been disappointed.'

Liberty felt as though she should take a bow. The woman made the whole thing sound as though it was nothing more than a game, to be enjoyed and then pushed aside. Liberty was incensed. She may have been an unwitting pawn so far but not any more.

'And who is this Gregor? A private detective?' she demanded.

'Gregor? A detective?' She gave a mocking, incredulous laugh and waved to the child who now sat stroking the puppy a few feet away. 'I think he is not so gifted in that way, don't you? No, Gregor is my half-brother. We shared a father and now we share this house together.' Liberty raised a quizzical eyebrow and Maria Rosa went on: 'You are thinking that we are not so alike for brother and sister. But our lives have been so different. Gregor was the product of a brief relationship between my father and a German peasant girl soon after he arrived on the Rhine with the British Forces.'

'Joe's father was with the British Forces in Germany,' Liberty chimed. Then she remembered. This woman knew more about Joe than *she* did. 'But you don't need me to tell you that, do you?' she added with a thin smile.

But Maria Rosa was gazing indulgently at her daughter as she spoke: 'A few years later he married my mother. She was a Russian ballet dancer who sought asylum in the West, but she died when I was small.' She paused and, for the first time, Liberty sensed a weakness. But the sensation was fleeting and Maria Rosa continued, 'However, it was only when my father - a retired colonel - died three years ago that I learned of Gregor's existence.'

So that was what this woman and Joe had in common: a father with the British Forces in Germany and a mother's untimely death. Until that moment she'd been unable to see past the purely physical attraction which she'd concluded must have lured him away.

'I'd like to speak to Gregor,' Liberty said, her gaze drifting towards a low, bushy eucalyptus tree whose branches had begun to wave in spite of there being no breeze. Then a man darted from behind it and lunged forward, his outstretched arms grasping the air and a strange, menacing grimace on his face. Recognising the thick black hair and heavy features, Liberty gasped and jumped to her feet.

The next second, the child screamed and rushed towards her, her eyes wide and appealing. Grabbing Liberty's legs and almost knocking her off balance, she threw herself to the ground shrieking. Instinctively Liberty bent to shield the child. Then she heard the convulsive laughter, saw the long, uneven teeth and recognised the gaping grin of a simpleton.

She cursed herself for being so stupid. How could she have let herself be terrorised by this feeble-minded, blockhead-of-a-man? She stepped aside to allow the pair to continue their game of cat and mouse. But the man, his face taking on the sheepish expression of a naughty schoolboy caught red-handed, stopped in his tracks. The child, subdued now, positioned herself between the splayed legs of her mother.

'I hope you'll excuse Gregor. He gets a little - shall we say? - carried away.' Maria Rosa spoke as if Gregor's only misdemeanour had been his high-jinks.

What about all those times he had scared her half to death? But Liberty realised the futility of tearing into what was after all only the organ-grinder's monkey. She saw too that there was little chance of extricating any more useful details from him. But one thing puzzled her.

'Where is the car you were driving on the night my husband was murdered?'

He glanced nervously towards Maria Rosa who nodded approvingly. His thick brows lifted and, as if a curtain had been raised, his face changed. Gone was the contrite sulk, replaced by a silly, grinning smirk. The switch from one mood to another was quite unnerving, yet the ease with which the transition took place was as fascinating as it was smooth.

He blew on his knuckles and declared simply, 'I painted it red.'

So the car the police had been looking for all this time had been right under her nose. Maria Rosa eyed him with amused concern and explained,

'Gregor worked as a body-builder when he lived in Germany. He has not been lucky enough to find work here but he hasn't lost his skills. He sprayed the car as soon as we realised he'd been spotted. It might have been necessary to do more if anyone had made a note of the number plates. Now, if you've finished with your questions, I must get Sasha ready for her party. She's four years old today'.

Liberty hesitated, irritated by the abrupt dismissal and yet conscious that the child was gazing up at her with an air of expectation. It was clearly time to stop pussy-footing around this woman. Even so, Liberty hadn't the heart to spoil the girl's birthday with a verbal assault on her mother, no matter how much it might make her feel better.

Maria Rosa was already making her way up the parched grass towards the house, her hand swinging along with her daughter's.

Liberty glanced at Gregor who stood, guard-like, watching them. She dug her heels into the grass and followed, wondering if Maria Rosa was even aware of the effect of her actions on other people. Probably not, she concluded, listening to the chatter and relaxed laughter which drifted through the warm afternoon air.

Unlike herself, Maria Rosa would never be constrained by the expectations of others. She was a free-spirit, the embodiment of the wantonness that Joe had so obviously craved. His affair with her must have given him hope that one day he might jettison his past disappointments and present obligations to become part of this gloriously care-free existence. She understood him a little better now, but the irony of having been given a name more suited to his mistress than to herself was not lost on her.

Maria Rosa now stood by a wicket gate which opened onto a narrow path. Through a gap between the gate and an arch of climbing roses, Liberty could just make out Derek's stocky figure pacing up and down puffing heavily on a large cigar.

'Just one last question,' Liberty said, determined not to be shunted out just yet. 'Where did you meet Joe?'

For a brief second the shadow of uncertainty dimmed the other woman's confident features. But then it passed as quickly as it had arrived and she tossed back her hair so that each curl bobbed, as if on elastic, at either side of her face.

'We first met in the church, Joe's church, that is, and my father's - not mine. I'm not a believer.' She paused and stroked the child's hair. 'I'd gone with Sasha to tend the flowers on my father's grave. It was the week after his funeral so I didn't know where to get water. It was a Saturday evening. Joe was there and he showed me.'

'And then you made a play for him.' Liberty could no longer disguise her contempt.

'Quite the opposite. We stood talking for a while, about my father mostly. We worked out that he and Joe's father must have been stationed on the same base at Rheindahlen at about the same time. It seemed a remarkable coincidence. They must have known each other as parishioners too, before they joined the Army. Joe was fascinated.'

'I'll bet he was,' Liberty snapped.

Maria Rosa tapped Sasha on the shoulder and pointed to the house. The little girl ran off as her mother continued.

'He was desperate to know more. When I told him I had a trunk full of papers and photos my father had left, he begged me to let him see them. He hoped he might discover something about his father. He didn't, but by then we had become . . .' She paused and bent down to scoop up the yelping puppy with a wide, encircling hug. 'We had become friends,' she added with careful emphasis on the last word.

Had she decided against using the word 'lovers' to spare Liberty any more heart-ache? Liberty didn't think so. Studying the self-assured, almost contemptuous expression on the face of her rival, she realised, without doubt, that there was no room in this woman's world for sympathy or benevolence. She had no care for others except when they were useful to her.

Could it really be then that Maria Rosa had been no more than a friend, an earth-mother to Joe in his quest for parental approval? She doubted it but she took comfort from the thought.

She was ready to leave now. Not because Maria Rosa had made it clear that it was time for her to go, but because she cared little to linger, listening to the details of a relationship she had rather not know about, from a woman devoid of Christian sentiment. Thank goodness her own faith kept her from such self-seeking.

She shut the gate firmly behind her, but as she turned away, her heals crunching on the shale, she felt her recently acquired moral superiority disintegrating. Was that not part of Joe's downfall, that intolerance and bigotry which comes from believing that we are the only ones pleasing to God?

She stopped and turned to take in, one last time, the God-given spectacle below. A thundery haze was settling over the scene now but the perfection of its design still stunned her. In the foreground, Maria Rosa was sweeping across the lawn, holding the puppy aloft. Some might call the exaggerated and deliberate way she did almost everything affected. But that would be to put too simplistic an interpretation on something which was essentially as indefinable as the woman herself.

Derek was waiting in the car when Liberty reached it. She threw open the door, relishing the wall of cold air which greeted her. Anticipating his barrage of questions she held her hand up and sank into the soft upholstery.

'Not now. I'll tell you all about it later. Just give me a chance to come round. I'm whacked,' she said, taking a tissue from the bag she'd left in the foot-well and pulling the mirror on the sunshield down.

It was only then that she saw, with wide-open, thickly-painted eyes that she was still wearing the clown-like make-up she had used to disguise her features before following Gregor. And on top of her head, wound like a coiled snake, ready to perform to Indian pipe music, was the brown and gold chiffon scarf.

A hollow laugh broke out deep in her throat and she threw her head back onto the headrest, her body racked by a fit of abandoned, hysterical laughter.

CHAPTER 18

The sky was overcast next morning as Liberty boarded the twin-engined plane at Newcastle airport. She'd made an early start so that she could make the trip to Belfast and back in the day.

Making her own travel arrangements for the first time in her life had been difficult enough without the added complication of hotels and luggage. Air travel seemed such a bewildering experience but she'd managed so far, she mused, settling herself into a window seat and hoping that no-one would fill the one next to her.

Ten minutes later the plane taxied along the runway and into the low cloud. But as it left the mainland behind, the sky cleared and the Irish Sea, glistening in the sun, beckoned. Liberty was awe-struck and not a little apprehensive. But she had no intention of showing it. She refused the offer of refreshments, preferring instead to concentrate her thoughts on her plans for the day.

Until now she'd barely had time to consider what she needed to ask the legendary Michael O'Connor when she eventually caught up with him. The previous evening she'd been too busy with other matters after her encounter with Joe's mistress. For that was what Maria Rosa was, Liberty had decided, in spite of the reluctance of both women to state the obvious. Sondra had stayed late, wanting to know all the details and adding her own cryptic comments between sips of brandy and dry ginger. By midnight Liberty had collapsed into bed, her thoughts fixed solely on the husband who'd betrayed her.

The distinctive curves of the Isle of Man's coastline told her that the short flight would soon be coming to an end. But what then? She was no nearer to knowing now than when she set off. Her mission was beginning to look foolhardy and she wished she'd not come.

To think that a schoolboy group of Republican supporters might have any connection with Joe's murder was just too ridiculous. Chief

Inspector Leatheringham would think she'd finally gone over the edge if he knew. But she had to eliminate the possibility. After all, there was hard evidence that Joe had continued his early association with Ireland. The badge, the cutting she'd found in his study and Michael O'Connor's address could not be ignored.

As the Irish coast came into view a gusting wind rocked the plane and a band of heavy cloud caused it to dip and swerve. White horses on the dark sea below rolled and frothed towards a rocky coastline, reinforcing her conviction that she was in for a stormy time ahead. But as the terminal buildings at Belfast City airport loomed nearer she took long slow breaths, fiddled with the silk scarf under her coffee-coloured jacket and vowed not to be deterred.

The pelting rain had stopped by the time the taxi reached the Faulds Road. The short journey from the airport had been uneventful and Liberty had experienced a wave of disappointment that the roads, buildings and even monuments had been very much like those in any other part of the United Kingdom. Only the fortified police stations and the flags - hanging from windows, traffic signs and even cranes - gave any indication of conflict. The ordinariness and apparent peace of the rest of the city was disconcerting.

Was the picture she was seeing, of Protestants and Catholics going about their daily business, in seemingly perfect harmony, really the true face of Belfast? Or was sectarian hatred, not quelled by the peace process, bubbling beneath the surface even at this very moment? She gazed at the figures hurrying, ant-like, in and out of shops and wondered how many harboured thoughts of murder in their hearts.

But now, as the black cab bounced along uneven and steadily-narrowing streets she noticed a change in her surroundings. Gable-ends, some covered in graffiti and others exquisitely decorated with striking images, passed her by. She strained through the misting windows to read the sentiments, about peace and war, the dead and the living, scrawled on each.

Could Joe really have had strong Republican sympathies without her knowing, she wondered, clearing a section of window with her finger-tips? Then she saw it. The mural itself was fairly mundane, a mixture of abstract swirls and insignia, but the badge in the bottom left-hand corner was unmistakable. It was the exact copy of the one she now carried with her.

'Stop!' she called, rummaging to find it in her bag. 'Can you stop here?'

The taxi ground to a halt and the driver swivelled round. 'I thought you wanted Well Street?'

'Yes, yes, I do,' she replied, holding the badge in the palm of her hand so that he couldn't see it.

'I thought I recognised someone. But no, I was wrong. Sorry.'

He drove off with a shrug and Liberty glanced once more at the mural and then at the badge. She wasn't wrong. The wall-painted version was less amateurish but there was no doubting they were the same. She popped the badge back in her bag, her curiosity suddenly awakened.

Why was an organisation, thought up by a group of boys at an English public school over 40 years ago, represented in modern-day propaganda in the heart of Ulster? She was filled with a disproportionate surge of optimism that her journey might furnish her at last with some of the answers she had been seeking.

The row of pre-war terraced houses where the taxi dropped her reminded her of the one where she had been born. The street's ordinariness was at once familiar and encouraging yet disconcerting and eerily deserted.

With a growing sense of unease she viewed the outside of number three, a well-maintained house with a freshly-painted green front door and thick lace curtains on the downstairs window. Hesitating briefly to rehearse her planned spiel, she rubbed at the creases in her dress and reached for the brass letter-box. But there was no sound from inside. She tried again, aware that her fingers had made a distinctive print on the polished surface.

A clinking sound to her left made her jump and she swung round to see a plump, moon-faced woman with straggly grey hair standing at the door of the neighbouring house. Wiping her wet hands on a grubby apron, she eyed Liberty before saying:

'You won't be finding anyone at home there. They've gone away, so they have.' And with that she folded her inconsiderable arms as if waiting for Liberty to go. It was a tactic which might have put her off not too long ago, but not now. She had to think quickly.

'Oh dear, that's such a shame,' she exclaimed moving closer to the woman who, she judged with a touch of self-satisfaction, could be no more than 40 in spite of her skin and hair being in a much worse condition than her own. 'I've come all the way from England to see Michael. He's an old family friend, you see. He was at school with my husband and . . . I have some bad news for him.'

She hadn't lied exactly, but there had been a certain economy with the truth. She inclined her head and looked suitably upset, watching the woman's care-worn face for a sign that her words had been believed.

A pasty-faced toddler, its head scarcely covered by a thin layer of downy, blond hair, silently wrapped his arms round her thick-stockinged legs and stared up at Liberty. The woman's expression didn't change but the voice was less strident, although still with a wary edge.

'A family friend, you say? And what family would that be?'

Faced with the fixed, analytical gaze, Liberty tried to smile.

'My husband's name was Joe Westerman. He and Michael were together at Saint Ambrose School in the North of England. They were very close. My husband died recently and when I wasn't able to get in touch by phone I decided I must come in person.' That was a lie but she'd already made up her mind that the truth was too risky.

To her surprise the woman nodded and, lifting the child into her arms, said, 'Ah well, you wouldn't have been able to get hold of him anyways. He's been gone for . . . oh, must be three weeks or more. Ay. As a matter of fact he's staying with a friend in England.' She seemed about to carry on but instead brushed a wisp of hair away from the boy's eyes.

'England, you say? Well, I'm flying back there this afternoon. I could look him up when I get back. Do you have the address where he's staying?'

The woman's eyes narrowed and she held Liberty's gaze for what seemed an age. Then she nodded as if satisfied that she could be trusted.

'Just you wait there,' she said kindly and disappeared inside.

Liberty held her breath, scarcely daring to believe that even in this troubled province she was able to extract information so easily from a stranger. She glanced left and right along the street. An elderly man rubbing vigorously at a window was the only person in sight.

A moment later the woman returned, minus the child but clutching a piece of paper.

'Michael said I was to contact him at this address if it was important,' she said, thrusting the scrap towards her. 'I dare say he won't be minding if I pass it on to you, seeing as you're on such sad business.'

Liberty took the paper and thanked her, all the time wondering why the guilt of her small deception had to mar the triumph of her success.

Only when she turned the corner did she glance at the address.

But when she did, she had to restrain herself from shrieking out loud. Scrawled hastily in large letters was the name of The Ship and Shamrock in, of all places, Littleport.

The flight back to the mainland passed quickly, the conviction growing all the way that Michael O'Connor had something to hide. How far he was implicated in Joe's death she had no idea, but it could hardly be coincidence that O'Connor had been staying less than 20 miles away on the night of his murder.

As the plane landed at Newcastle she checked her watch. It was still early, only five minutes to four. Barring any hold-ups, she could be in Littleport by five thirty.

But after reaching the small quayside pub, the woman behind the bar was less than helpful. No, she couldn't divulge the address of Michael O'Connor. Yes, Liberty could leave a note if she wanted but she shouldn't count on receiving a reply. And yes, O'Connor came in sometimes but she couldn't say when he might be in next.

Liberty scribbled a few words to the effect that she needed to speak to him urgently and gave her address and telephone number. But why should he get in touch? Especially if he had something to hide.

On an impulse, she added: 'If I don't hear from you in the next day or so, I may have to contact the police.'

But, on her way back to the car, she wondered whether this had been a mistake. If he were a terrorist or murderer - or both - he might now be forewarned that she was on to him. But she felt drained and unbearably hot and didn't relish the thought of trying to retrieve the note or of laying herself open to the bar-woman's barely concealed animosity.

Driving towards Lowthwaite, the effect of the hours spent travelling combined with the oppressive heat of the late afternoon to convince her of the attraction of a quiet evening alone with a glass of wine. Across the slopes of Skiddaw the sun had cast a pink glow and the lake had become a mirror of blazing colour. A rare, spectacular sight, thought Liberty with a touch of humbling gratitude before the doubts and foreboding began to plague her again.

CHAPTER 19

When she threw open the curtains next morning after a fitful sleep, the scene that greeted her gave little hope of a cooler day. While the lower fells lay in dark shadow, interspersed with patches of weak sunlight, the charcoal-grey silhouette of Skiddaw now stood stark against the white sky. And at the head of the lake, a series of ill-defined cones was all she could see of the distant mountain ranges.

She thought about pulling the curtains shut again and going back to bed. After all, it was only ten past seven and, being a Saturday, no-one except Jacob would notice if she stayed in bed all morning. And it wasn't as if she had anything planned.

At that moment two grey geese, squawking loudly in playful chase, rose off the water. She watched them, envious of their freedom and mesmerised by the gentle flapping of their wings. There was no chance of her going back to sleep, she decided, dragging on an old pair of red jeans and a white cotton top.

The air in the kitchen smelled of stale vegetables but she decided against opening the window and the curtains. Instead she sat in the darkened kitchen, clasping a cup of Earl Grey and wondering how she was going to fill this bleak and empty day. Contact more of the people in Joe's address book? Perhaps. The momentum and surge of adrenalin she'd experienced since Joe's funeral had waned. What she felt now was a lethargy that threatened to bring her investigations to a stand-still. The events of the past week had taken a heavy toll, both mentally and physically.

She sipped the tea and tried to remember what Sister Monica would have said. Probably something about the greatest failure being the failure to carry on trying, she decided, smiling at the memory of the wizened headmistress who had instilled in her not only a set of Christian principles but also a down-to-earth grasp of how to cope with what fate dealt her.

Half an hour later she drew back the yellow and blue checked curtains covering the French windows to reveal a more promising picture. A light breeze from the South West was pushing the clouds along so that patches of blue opened up the sky. At once the water developed a brighter hue, feint ripples dancing in the light. A clump of trees along the left-hand side of the lake, which only seconds before had been a mass of dark green and black, seemed to light up to welcome the change. The kitchen was aglow.

Liberty's spirits lifted with the clouds and she raced upstairs eager to retrieve Joe's address book from her handbag. It had taken only a minute but by the time she returned she saw with dismay that the clouds had thickened again, banking up against the hills and forming a blanket of solid grey.

But the change couldn't dim her renewed zeal. She placed her finger in the marker for N, O and P, opening it to reveal the name of Thomas Parker at an address in Wigton. She vowed to make the short journey that morning.

But her intentions were soon thwarted. As she came out of the house just before half past nine, there on the drive was Bretherton's ageing Ford Escort. For a reason she couldn't explain, the sight of the lumbering figure, struggling out of the driver's seat and meticulously locking the door, irritated her. Surely it wasn't just because he'd turned up unannounced instead of telephoning first? Or that he had obviously taken the morning off. She knew it was more than that. It was a guilty conscience. Since her talk with Alan Walters she'd managed to avoid Bretherton, not wanting to confirm his suspicions about tachograph charts being tampered with. Now here he was seeking her out.

She waited at the door, her eyes scrutinising the security man's trundling gait. He'd probably been attractive in his younger days, although probably still gauche and awkward, but she couldn't help thinking now what a pathetic and lonely figure he cut. His short-sleeved shirt hung, crumpled and damp, half in and half out of the baggy trousers.

He caught her eye with a nervous glance.

'I'm sorry to disturb you, Mrs Westerman. But I need to talk to you.'

'Yes, of course, Bretherton. Come in. It's cooler inside,' she said, leading him through the house and into the sitting room.

She motioned for him to take one of the easy chairs but he stood stiffly, fiddling with his key ring, until she'd seated herself in the other.

Why does he have to be so damned formal? she thought, deliberately leaning forward to deter him from making himself too comfortable.

'It's a bit difficult to know where to begin,' he said, wringing his clumsy hands and gazing at her with doleful eyes and a crestfallen expression. Something was badly wrong, she could see that and she found herself softening.

'What is it?' she asked. 'Is it Doris? Is she ill?'

He nodded, his head bowed now, but she could see quite clearly the tears welling in his eyes.

'The doctor sectioned her last night. She's in Carlisle General,' he said in a voice so low she could barely hear.

Liberty remembered that the last time Doris had been ill, she hadn't been discharged for over 12 months. She wondered whether Bretherton, like herself, suspected that this time she might never come out.

'I'm sorry,' she said, aware of the inadequacy of her sentiment. 'It must be awful for you.'

There was a brief silence and she could see that he was struggling to compose himself. Once more his police training and the discipline of maintaining a stiff upper lip kicked in and submerged his natural feelings. His mouth tightened.

'It's not just that,' he said. 'I thought you ought to know. I've had time to examine the tachograph charts that Mr Westerman kept in his office. I'm afraid there's no doubt about it. A lot of them have been altered . . .falsified . . . to allow drivers to drive over their permitted hours. Various methods have been used. Fuses have been removed, clocks have been wound back and false names used. I've consulted an expert, a colleague in the force, and he's confirmed my suspicions.'

'Yes, I know,' Liberty whispered, the shame of her admission making her look away at the bowl of fading roses on the cocktail cabinet. 'Alan Walters confessed that he'd been involved. He said he'd been pressured by Joe. I'm sorry. I should have told you but I was . . .' She paused, recollecting her reasons for withholding the information. It wasn't that she'd doubted Walters. He'd incriminated himself and his girlfriend by what he'd told her. No. It wasn't that. Had she still been trying to protect Joe's good name? Even though she'd accepted that Joe had been less than honest, she hadn't been able to bring herself to denounce him publicly. It had felt too much like betrayal. But now she realised that by remaining silent about his crimes – for that was what they were – she was perpetuating his deceit. She met his stunned gaze with a heavy heart. 'I was too ashamed to admit it,' she said,

His mouth quivered and dropped and his jaws moved up and down fitfully before he finally stammered, 'So Mr Westerman was definitely in on it? I would have staked my life on it being Mr Brock. Never Mr Westerman.' He shook his head, unable to take it in. 'I never thought he could be . . .well, dishonest. I never doubted him. Not even when Doris cursed me and told me I was wrong. Why, he wouldn't even accept a bottle of Scotch from the customers at Christmas.' He looked baffled. 'And I stuck to it he'd not been to blame for Jane's death. I stuck to it.' He leaned forward staring at his trembling hands and sighed. 'Poor Doris.'

At that moment it finally sank in. With a force that felt almost like a physical blow to her body Liberty was forced to admit it. Joe's whole life had been a sham. He'd had one set of values for other people while secretly following a different set himself. But appearances had had to be maintained. `And he'd certainly done that.

She fell back into the soft cushions and closed her eyes. She'd made enough excuses for him, tried not to judge him. In spite of all the evidence to the contrary, she'd desperately clung to the memories of a good and faithful husband, father, employer, Christian who'd been tempted and fallen. But bit by bit her belief in him had been shattered. He'd deliberately and consistently deceived them all.

She opened her eyes just in time to see Bretherton brush a tear from his cheek with his sleeve. He looked dazed and for a moment she felt an overwhelming guilt, as if she had been driving the vehicle that had run his daughter down. She wanted to apologise, over and over, but she checked herself. She couldn't spend the rest of her life trying to atone for Joe's sins.

'Tell me about Jane,' she said, sitting upright and sensing a sudden and strangely-liberating desire to distance herself from her husband.

Bretherton lifted his head, a puzzled expression now on his ashen face, as if no-one had ever asked him to talk about the child before. He cleared his throat nervously.

'Jane?' he said, a far-away, glazed look in his eyes. 'She was five years old. Just started school, she had. She was the most beautiful little girl. Masses of blonde curls, just like her mother . . .' He paused, deep in thought and Liberty recalled with horror Doris's grey, tangled mop of hair. A moment later he continued, 'And her eyes . . .green they were . . .they'd light up when I came home from work and then she'd come running, her arms in the air.' His own arms made an involuntary, pathetic movement as if to demonstrate, before they flopped back onto his knees. 'We'd waited so long for her, me and Doris. Then when she came along it was as if we'd been granted everything we'd ever wanted. But then she was snatched away again.' He stopped, his face twisting in a grotesque mask of wretchedness.

'Go on,' she urged, sensing that, after all these years, and in spite of the painfulness of putting it into words, he was grateful for the opportunity to unburden himself.

He sniffed and said, 'It was nineteen years and nine months ago. I'd kissed her good-bye that morning, like I always did. But I didn't realise I'd never see her again or I'd . . . It was four weeks before Christmas . . .'

His voice quivered, then faded away. His eyes were staring but Liberty knew he wasn't seeing her. He smiled to himself then, a thin melancholy smile, as if he were imagining his poor, dead daughter. Liberty wondered whether his mental pictures were like those she'd had of Joe since his death. But she could see that Bretherton's visions held no terrors for him.

She touched his hand gently. 'I'll make some tea,' she said and went into the kitchen.

But when she came back and placed the tray on the table between them she was unprepared for the change in mood.

'*He* killed her. Just as if he'd been driving that wagon himself. He killed my Jane,' he cried, his eyes wild now. 'And now Doris is as good as dead. That man's taken everything from me. Everything.'

Liberty froze, her hand over the teapot handle. Was he going to turn violent? For a moment her heart pounded uncontrollably. She picked up the steaming teapot, quickly trying to assess the situation but fully aware that, in an emergency, she was in possession of a dangerous weapon.

'Now just a minute,' she objected, her natural instinct to defend Joe surfacing yet again. She banged the teapot down on the tray sending scalding water cascading across the polished surface. 'I think you'd better be careful what you say.'

Bretherton threw his head back defiantly and said, 'He knew what he was doing all right. And he's been doing it ever since. But he didn't care.' He clenched his fists and pressed them against his cheeks. 'I can see now what happened. That driver must have been at the wheel over sixteen hours when he fell asleep.' He glared at Liberty but she saw in the watery eyes that the brief spark of anger had once more been dampened down. His voice was calmer as he added, 'He said he had no choice but do a double shift, but I didn't believe him. Your husband was much more plausible. He said the driver was lying, that he'd taken the wagon without permission.'

He gave a long, deep sigh somewhere between a groan and a sob. His body sagged. The fight had gone out of him but she sensed he hadn't finished yet.

Liberty sank back in her chair. The tea could wait.

A moment later he roused himself. Rubbing a hand across his forehead, he said, 'It was before tachographs came in so the police couldn't prove who was telling the truth. And I was so full of bitterness towards the driver that I couldn't see past him to the real villain.' He paused and she could see how painful it was for him to remember. 'I wouldn't have taken the job if I'd known. I wouldn't.' He closed his eyes now, as if lost once more in his thoughts.

'I'm sorry,' Liberty whispered. 'So very sorry. I had no idea.' What else could she say? But even to her the words sounded empty and meaningless.

He didn't look at her. Instead he buried his head in his hands. A rush of involuntary and irregular jerks told her that the well of emotions, amassed over a lifetime of subduing his natural instincts, had finally overflowed.

She left him then, before her own grief submerged them both in an orgy of self-pity. Tears blurred her eyes as she struggled to remember why it was that she hadn't been aware of the accident at the time. But Ben and Ruth had been small, just a little younger than Jane and it had been shortly before Christmas. She wouldn't have had much time to read the newspapers or spend time chatting with other mothers at the church play-group. And Joe had never mentioned it, for obvious reasons.

The stuffiness of the kitchen took her breath away and she struggled to contain the tears. Her world was spinning wildly out of control and there was nothing she could do about it. She made for the French windows and flung them open with such force that they banged against the house wall. The glass panes rattled precariously and she waited for the tinkle of breaking glass, but to her surprise no sound interrupted the eerie silence, not even the song of a single bird.

For a moment she stood in the doorway gulping in the warm, stagnant air, her tearful gaze fixed on the thickening clouds. But the storm that was brewing would be nothing compared to the turmoil which now embroiled her.

Bretherton could be mistaken of course, or lying. But a small voice within her told her that he wasn't. Hadn't Alan Walters told her as much? But she'd only half understood the real consequences of Joe's actions, still clinging to the belief that, despite all his weaknesses, he would never have deliberately risked people's lives.

Now she saw that Joe stood condemned not only of causing the death of a child but of a cold-blooded recklessness with the lives of countless others. She shook her head, not wanting to take it in.

How could he have gone to Mass each week and received the Sacraments with the blood of a little girl on his hands? But the state of his soul, she had to remind herself, was between Joe and his maker. Suppressing a shiver she turned to go back into the kitchen.

But she had gone only a few feet when a noise from behind startled her. Realising at once that she had left the door open, she let out a gasp and swung round. There in the doorway stood Giles Tranter, his puffed-out body blocking the light, his deep red cheeks and jowls so grotesquely distended that they looked as though a pin might easily pop them. He said nothing.

'You startled me,' she said accusingly, irritated at his familiarity in coming round to the back of the house.

'Did I?' he asked, his cold, pin-prick eyes boring into her. She wasn't surprised that he didn't apologise. 'I've just had a phone call from that solicitor friend of yours. Says to lay off, that I haven't a hope in hell of getting my hands on that land. Well, I know what your little game is. You think I'll up my offer don't you? Squeeze a little bit more out of me by pretending you're not interested.' He stepped into the kitchen, jabbing a stubby forefinger into her face. 'Well it's not going to work. I know your sort. All prim and proper on the outside and slippery as a snake on the inside. But you mark my words. No woman's going to get the better of me. You wait and see. I'll get that land one way or another. Just see if I don't.'

'Now just a minute, Mr Tranter.' Liberty struggled to find the words which would put him once and for all, in no doubt about her intentions. But her earlier encounter with Bretherton, whom she presumed to be still immersed in his grief, had taken its toll. She felt drained and for a moment considered giving in to Tranter's aggressive persistence just to get rid of him. But that would be a stupid thing to do.

And the thought of him gloating about his latest victory over a woman made her hackles rise. She glared at the puffing windbag contemptuously.

'I'd like you to leave, please,' she said and side-stepped him to grab the door handle. He turned, his twisted, angry face within an inch of hers. His hot, sour-smelling breath made her stomach lurch.

'Don't you try and get rid of me,' he hissed through clenched teeth. 'I'll go when I'm ready. When I get what I want.'

She felt the thick, puffy fingers grab her arm, and when she tried to pull away the grip tightened and a hot pain shot up to her elbow. She winced and struck out with her free hand. But before she could make contact, she felt the impact of another body from behind and heard the deep groan of what sounded like a wounded animal. The pain in her arm eased and she was flung back, her head banging against the wall.

Momentarily stunned, she staggered through the open door to see Giles Tranter sprawled on the patio with Bretherton on top of him. Muffled grunts came from the pair as they rolled, like two lumbering seals, round the pink and grey flags.

For a moment she was unable to think as she gazed in amazement at the tangled bodies. There was something degrading about two grown men fighting like dogs but she felt little inclination to separate them. It would do them both good, she thought, only realising when she saw Jacob scurrying across the lawn towards them, that the sentiment was neither Christian nor acceptable.

After the earlier upheaval, Liberty had little inclination to visit Wigton to speak to Thomas Parker. But she couldn't just mope around and waste the rest of the day. Gulping down a long glass of iced water, she decided to go down to the paddock, although a ride in this heat held little attraction for her.

Storm clouds, heavy and menacing, obscured the high fells while a thick haze blurred the edges where the low fells met the lake. There could be no doubt that a storm was closing in. She welcomed it, not just for the parched lawn and shrivelled flowerbeds but for herself. A torrential downpour would bring to an end the draining heat that had dogged her search for Joe's killer. It might also prove to be a symbolical cleansing, a catharsis. She hoped so.

Merry too seemed to have sensed the approaching storm. The horse was in a highly nervous state, her ears pulled back and her nostrils flared as she pawed at the ground behind the fence as if demanding to be set free.

'Hold on, old girl,' Liberty coaxed, in the most soothing voice she could muster, and stroked the warm nose. 'I'll get your saddle.'

But even though the mare settled down as they negotiated the shaded forest paths behind Bagley Hall, Liberty couldn't shake off her own skittishness. Bretherton's words kept coming back to haunt her.

His only child. Killed by one of Joe's drivers who was too tired to keep awake. And Joe had been to blame. But that wasn't all. His deliberate and reckless disregard of safety regulations had put countless other lives in danger. And for what? Could profits - or power - really have motivated him to such an extent that he'd abandoned his principles? What about his lectures to Ben all those years ago about riding his bike round the house?

'It's *your* responsibility to watch out for others,' he'd insisted when Ben had almost run into his sister. And the little boy had taken notice of his father's words. But it had all been a sham. She saw that clearly now. She'd always looked up to Joe, and so had Ben and Ruth, but his carefully-cultivated image of concern and duty had been just that. An image. A false image to fool the world. And it had done.

But what hurt her most was the knowledge that Joe had deceived her along with the rest. Surely she of all people should have had some inkling of his true nature, the repercussions of which were only now beginning to surface? Just a few days ago she would have defied anyone who had suggested Joe had led a double life. But now she was bracing herself for worse to come.

Her head ached and she turned Merry round. The unrelenting heat and the unexpected rush of emotions had drained her physically and mentally, leaving her lethargic and morose. She wiped the sweat from her face and wondered whether she really wanted to expose herself to more revelations by continuing the search for Joe's murderer.

'Damn you, Joe,' she muttered under her breath, a sudden and intense anger gripping her.

She kicked the horse into a canter, desperate to find some release from her pent-up frustration. But as Merry slowed to negotiate a narrow gateway, Liberty slumped back in the saddle, exhausted and ashamed.

Surely God had forgiven Joe's sins – that is, if he'd repented and asked forgiveness. So who was she to condemn him now? And no matter how detestable his ungodliness, he didn't deserve to die like that.

An hour later she checked the A-Z of Wigton and set off for Cumberland Place. But the visit proved fruitless. Thomas Parker was not at home. Or was he? She had the distinct feeling that the house was occupied, but no-one answered her insistent ringing and she came away with the depressing feeling that, three weeks after Joe's death, she had almost come to the end of the line.

As she rounded the bend above Kildale, shafts of sunlight broke through the gathering clouds, casting a yellowish glow over the fells. The storm wasn't far off now and the thought of returning alone to an empty house suddenly filled her with dread. But if she constantly gave in to self-pity, where would that leave her? She wound down the window and warm air rushed into the car.

A sudden urge to do something impulsive and self-indulgent gripped her. But what, with only herself for company and a storm brewing? She would think of something, she told herself, gently increasing the pressure on the accelerator.

CHAPTER 20

At twenty minutes past eight she stood back and admired her handiwork. Four pink candles flickered brightly in the silver candelabra, illuminating the shadowy patio. The wrought iron table was laid with a pink linen tablecloth, white china and four delicate, long-stemmed wine-glasses. A centre-piece of white carnations and chrysanthemums on a base of laurel leaves was almost exactly the replica of one she had seen in a magazine and vowed to copy one day. But Joe had always turned down her requests to host a dinner party, even for Bob and Susan or Sondra and Derek.

In an explosion of morbid defiance, she now opened one of the six bottles of 1982 Chateauneuf-du-Pape which Joe had been saving, for what she had no idea, ever since their first and last visit to France. Holding up the half-filled glass of chilled white wine, she took in the tantalising bouquet before downing a large refreshing mouthful.

'To absent friends,' she exclaimed, turning to the three empty chairs and trying hard to imagine them filled by her mother, Aunt Cecilia and Joe. But even for this one last time she couldn't imagine Joe joining her.

The evening was unnaturally still as she tucked into a plate of smoked salmon and thin fingers of brown bread, but the next moment a clatter behind her made her leap from her chair sending it crashing to the ground. Her knife and fork clanged onto the table, knocking over the wine-glass which exploded into a thousand pieces. The wine disappeared into the pristine tablecloth.

Letting out a shriek she frantically scanned the blackness beyond the patio. Had Joe's murderer returned three weeks afterwards - almost to the minute? Her heart seemed to stop then began pounding uncontrollably as she scuttled, her flowing skirt flapping round her ankles, towards the safety of the house. But before she had covered even half the distance the shadow of a man appeared from the direction of the vegetable garden.

She stopped in her tracks, too terrified to go forward or back. Her mind too seemed frozen and unable to respond. Then, out of the corner of her eye she spotted a garden rake leaning against the bushes and darted towards it just as the figure stepped into the beam of light from the kitchen window.

She recognised him immediately but it took several seconds to regain her composure and control the thumping in her chest. Suddenly Bob Brock lurched towards her, his eyes wide and bright, his mouth twisted in a grin of nervous anticipation.

'Sorry, I bumped into the wheelbarrow,' he said uncertainly. 'I did knock but you . . .you wouldn't have heard. I didn't mean to frighten you.'

Liberty took a deep breath but she was still too winded to speak. What on earth was Bob doing here on a Saturday evening? Perhaps there was a problem at work. But she didn't think so. She saw now that he was looking at the table, a hint of expectant pleasure flickering across his face.

He smiled. 'Are you expecting someone?'

'No. I was just enjoying a quiet meal,' she panted, not caring to explain why there were four place settings and not bothering to conceal the irritation in her voice as she added, 'Alone.'

'Sorry. I wouldn't have disturbed you if I'd known.' His head dropped and, in his familiar little-boy-lost pose, he seemed to be studying a spot on the patio somewhere between them. Then with a jolt he straightened, as if he were standing to attention. 'I've left Susan,' he said.

Liberty's first thought was that he was playing some sort of practical joke and that he would burst out laughing at any moment and shout, 'That got you going.' But the high-jutting chin and stiffly erect body told her that he was struggling to maintain his self-control. Something had obviously happened.

Liberty sighed. Not another broken-hearted male. 'You'd better come and sit down,' she said reluctantly, hoping that he wouldn't misinterpret her offer. 'Would you like a drink?'

He nodded and, picking up her chair from where it lay sprawled across the patio, sank into the one next to it. Liberty took the bottle from the stainless steel ice-bucket and poured two glassfuls of the pale-gold liquid. Her hand still shaking she handed one to him, wondering who else might turn up before the end of this awful day.

He took it rather mechanically, his eyes not leaving her face and it was then that she smelled the whisky on his breath. Suddenly regretting her generosity, she averted her gaze, walked round the table and sat down opposite him with a sigh.

'Do you want to tell me about it?' she asked, gripping the cool glass. But she resisted the temptation to take a sip. She dreaded what she was letting herself in for.

He tossed his head back and took a long gulp of wine. Then, meeting her eyes, he let the words tumble out. 'It's Susan. She's driving me mad. I just couldn't stand it any more. Nag, nag, nag, she never stops. She never gives me any peace. And now she wants to move abroad.' He paused and took another gulp of wine. 'She's got it into her head that it's not safe round here anymore. 'I fancy Spain,' she says. Just like that. 'What about the business?' I ask. Now listen to this. 'Sod the business,' she says. How the hell does she expect me to go swanning off to Spain or some other godforsaken place? I tell you, Liberty, I just can't take any more.' He drained his glass then held it tight as if he were trying to crush it.

What did he want her to say? Liberty decided to re-fill his glass but thought better of sympathising. There was no room for any misunderstandings or ambiguity. He hadn't come to her just for a shoulder to cry on. There were others, like his two daughters, who could fill that role more satisfactorily. No, he wanted more than that. She picked her words carefully.

'I'm sure if you explain to Susan that it's not possible to move abroad she'll understand.'

'Understand? Understand?' he snarled, his face distorted in the candle-light. 'She understands nothing except spending money and driving me mad with her infernal nagging. And if she's not nagging she never shuts up talking. She's like a machine. On and on and on she goes. I'm glad to get back to work.'

He paused and drained his glass again.

Liberty looked at her own almost-full glass and longed to do the same. But something told her that she needed to keep her wits about her.

Suddenly his face brightened, as if a light had been switched on and he continued, 'Well, I've had enough. There's no way I'm going to live in some Mediterranean backwater, I can tell you. I'd go mad. Can you imagine me hanging round all day, dividing my time between a walk to the shop for the morning paper and a dip in the pool? God . . . I'd just go mad.' He helped himself to more wine. 'Or maybe she thinks I'll get a job as a waiter down at the local tapas bar.'

Liberty shrugged. At this moment the thought of Bob a couple of thousand miles away was not unwelcome. He was watching her now, eyeing her up and down in that way she'd seen him ogle young girls calling in at the depot. It was then that she noticed his hair, looking as if it was still wet from the shower. Suddenly recognising his recently-cultivated wet-look style, she wondered how much preparation had gone into this supposedly impromptu visit.

A rumble of thunder in the distance broke the awkward silence. Liberty experienced an over-whelming desire to be rid of him.

'Bob, I understand what you're saying. But I don't see what I can do about it.'

He put his glass on the table and leaned forward, his eyes twinkling in the glow of the candle.

'No?' he asked.

She pretended not to hear and pushed back her chair. 'The storm's not far away. I'd better get this lot inside.'

He thrust out a hand as if to stop her. 'I'm sorry. I didn't mean to bore you with my problems. It's just that . . . well, if I'm honest, this has been coming for years. This Spain thing is just the straw that broke the camel's back. I can't take any more. It's as simple as that.'

'I really think you should talk to Susan,' she said, scooping up the plate of smoked salmon and the almost-empty bottle. But as she turned towards the house he pushed himself to his feet, blocking her way. Her stomach muscles tightened.

'Dammit, Liberty. We've known each other for twenty years. Been good friends, the four of us. But that's over now. Joe's dead and Susan . . . well, that's over too.'

Liberty sidestepped him. 'Bring something with you, will you?' she called, not looking back.

'What?' He glanced at the table before rushing after her. 'Please, Liberty, just hang on. Just hear me out, will you?'

'Bob, I really don't . . .' she began as he caught up.

'Not now. I know it's too soon,' he gasped. 'I'm not totally insensitive, you know.'

'Please, Bob,' she pleaded, walking faster.

'Just say you'll think about it. Please, Liberty. We'd be good together, you and me.'

He was making this very difficult. She reached the kitchen and turned to face him in the yellowing light. 'No, Bob. Now please . . .'

He was leaning against the jamb, panting. 'You're frightened it might make it difficult working together, aren't you?'

She shook her head. 'No,' she answered instinctively. That wasn't the reason. Suddenly she felt very confused. 'Yes. Of course it would make things difficult,' she added. 'But that's not the point.'

'It wouldn't,' he said, leaning over her. 'I wouldn't let it.'

'Go home, Bob,' she said, elbowing the door open. 'You'll feel different in the morning.'

'No. No, I won't. I've felt like this for years. I envied Joe. Did you know that? I really envied him.' He made a move to follow her into the kitchen but she stood in the doorway.

'Please, Bob.' Her voice was low and insistent now. Had the man no sensitivity? 'I don't want to hear any more.'

'He didn't deserve you. Do you know that?'

She'd had enough of pussyfooting around. Suddenly something snapped. 'You just don't get it, do you?' she snarled, thrusting the wine bottle into the soft curve of his stomach. 'Can't you understand? The last thing I want at this moment is a relationship with any man . . . let alone a married man.'

He winced and stepped back. 'Yes, but I've told you. It's over between Susan and me.'

'And I'll tell you what else is over. My days as a dogsbody.' She was furious. Now it was *her* turn to make demands.

His stunned expression told her she was finally getting through.

'We can talk about that on Monday,' he said lamely.

'You won't change my mind. Equal partners, that's what I want.' The words were as much of a surprise to her as to him. 'On a strictly business footing.'

'But you . . .' he stammered.

'Goodnight, Bob,' she said closing the door.

A moment later, the sound of retreating footsteps told her she was alone. She sighed and peered through the window at the green-tinted blackness which every few seconds burst into light. The storm, long-awaited and even yearned for, had arrived at last. But she was no longer relishing it. Her encounters with Bretherton, Tranter and now Bob had drained her. All she wanted to do was crawl into bed and put this day behind her.

As the thunder rolled and crashed, she toyed with the temptation to abandon the table where only half an hour before she had anticipated a peaceful if solitary evening. Now it was being battered by the gusting wind, the tablecloth flapping like a spectre in the dark, the candles snuffed out. Her dinner party might be over but she had a nasty feeling that a long night was only just beginning.

A tinkling sound told her that another glass had smashed and she picked up a tray, glancing warily around her before hurrying out to salvage the remaining glassware and crockery. Cooler air was now whipping round in strong gusts and her thin blouse clung to her like a tight-fitting shroud.

She worked quickly, piling the bowl of flowers on top of half-eaten bread and conscious that an eerie silence had momentarily replaced the sound of the wind. It was as if someone had turned off the volume on a giant television set.

Suddenly an ear-piercing screech filled the night air and she snatched up the over-laden tray, trying desperately to reassure herself that it was only the call of the white peacock that roamed Bagley Hall.

As she hurried across the patio towards the glow of the kitchen light, she didn't see the hand that reached out of the azaleas. But she felt the suffocating pressure of the hot, sweating palm over her mouth. Her hands instinctively shot up to loosen her assailant's grip. But the fingers tightened painfully across her jaw. The sound of shattering china and glass as the tray hit the ground was only half recognised above the buzzing in her eardrums and the gurgling noise at the back of her throat.

Clawing at the hand that blocked her airway, she tried to scream but nothing came. Instead, a searing pain burned into her throat. The thought flashed through her mind that the knife in her back that would surely follow could not be so painful.

But she wasn't finished yet. She struggled and kicked, desperate to wriggle free of the powerful fingers that were throttling her. Summoning all her strength, she jabbed an elbow into her attacker's stomach. For a brief moment the hands round her neck loosened and she dragged them away from her, twisting free. But her release was short-lived. As their bodies locked in a desperate struggle she felt the stranglehold return and the strength ooze out of her limbs. Then, with the icy precision of an executioner, the strong hands systematically squeezed until the last remnants of air had left her lungs.

It seemed like a lifetime, but could only have been a second or two that her body hung in a painful state somewhere between life and death. The nauseous whiff of beer and cigarette smoke wafted close to her nostrils as her eyes flickered upwards to the gathering storm clouds. A flash of lightning lit up the sky at the moment her legs buckled and her body fell limp. The crack of thunder went unheard.

CHAPTER 21

Somewhere in the back of Liberty's consciousness an engine started and her body thudded against a cold, hard object. The suffocating smell of diesel was unmistakeable but it took a moment longer to realise that she was inside the boot of a moving car.

Her mind was racing but her head throbbed so much she had trouble forming any conscious thoughts. The questions were there. But answers were not forthcoming. What was going on? Who had attacked her? And why? All she could think was that somehow she had made contact with Joe's murderer.

The thought sent shivers down her spine and she tried to curl up to protect herself from the buffeting of the car as it sped over bumpy ground. But she couldn't stop the pummelling to her back and shoulders.

Without warning, a sound like gunfire cracked over the noise of the engine.

'God help me,' she gasped. But as she lay petrified she slowly became aware of another sound, more regular and demanding. Of course, the much-needed rain had finally arrived, she realised, listening to the steady pounding of the metal above her head. The drought was over.

A sudden jolt flung her forward, then just as suddenly dragged her back. She let out a yell as first her elbow, then her shoulder caught the full force against the hard shell. The stench of oil and fumes was by now making her gag and she closed her eyes, willing the nausea to go away.

At that moment the engine stopped. She strained to listen above the deafening noise of her thudding heart and the pelting rain. What would happen to her now? Was this the end of the road? She braced herself. First a car door banged and she rocked with the impact. Then footsteps, quick and muffled, were coming towards her.

She held her breath, hoping they would pass. But before she had time to gather her wits together the boot-lid was flung open and a torch shone in her eyes. Instinctively she blinked and covered her face with her hand.

The rain, heavy and cold hit her like the jet from a hosepipe. A flash of lightning, like a neon-light, illuminated the night and she saw clearly the two eyes staring out of a balaclava. Paralysed now with fear she could only make a sound somewhere between a whimper and a scream.

'Get out.' The order was sharp but quickly followed by a breathless rasp which rattled through congested lungs. 'Get out. And no tricks.'

The words were few but there was no mistaking the thick Irish brogue. Something else was familiar but she couldn't say what. Was this the elusive Michael O'Connor, she wondered, as she half crawled, half fell out of the boot onto the sodden earth?

Thunder rolled menacingly and she pulled herself upright against the car's bumper, conscious of the wet mud clinging to her skirt and the rain running in rivulets down her face.

He was beside her now, pushing something hard and cold into her side. The sound of the rain, bouncing off the car, had drowned out his wheezing. So this is it, she thought. This was how she would meet her end. Inexplicably the thought seemed to have lost some of its terror. But then it struck her. How would Ben and Ruth cope with the violent death of another parent? The thought was as sudden as it was distressing. She longed to hold them both for one last time. But it was too late now.

Her eyes cast around in the darkness for a means of escape but all she could see was the thin beam from a torch shining onto the ground in front of her. She felt a push from behind and reluctantly moved forward along the muddy path.

Her thoughts flew back to her last conversation with Ruth on the eve of her departure for Belfast. Her daughter's advice, to stop meddling in affairs she didn't understand, had proved to be prophetic, the criticism justified. Why hadn't she heeded it? A proud conceit that mother knows best? Or was it a newly-discovered resolve to prove herself and not be easily put off? Whatever the reason, it was too late now to call a halt. Too late to whisper a last good-bye. She trudged blindly on, stumbling through water-logged pot-holes, hot tears mingling with the cold rain.

'Get a move on.' She heard the order at the same moment she felt another cold, hard prod in the small of her back. Thunder crashed and simultaneously the sky lit up. It was then that she saw the shadowy outline of a boathouse.

'Right, stop there. And don't move or I'll shoot,' he commanded, pushing past her and dragging back one of the wooden doors. She wanted to run as fast as her legs would carry her but her feet were rooted to the spot. Her skirt, like a sail, billowed and flapped helplessly in the wind.

Then she felt another push in her back. But the fear that she was entering her tomb made her shrink back. The pushing intensified until, at last, she fell headlong over the threshold. Angry frothing waves lashed the inside of the structure, tossing a battered rowing boat against the steps where it was moored. A second later she glimpsed a flash of metal and felt a sharp pain across her knuckles.

'Hurry along there. Make it quick,' came the breathless order. Liberty sucked her throbbing hand and shuffled further into the boathouse, shaking strands of wet hair from her face.

What next? she wondered. Was he about to set her adrift to sink beneath the churning lake? Or would he kill her here?

The gun pressed between her shoulder blades. 'Kneel down. Hands behind your back.'

'Please, no,' she screamed, closing her eyes and dropping to her knees. 'Why are you doing this to me?'

But there was no reply, only the sound of waves crashing against the moorings.

Frantically she tried to think of something to say that might change his mind. But her head still spun dizzily and her limbs were weak and sluggish. She could thrust out her elbow and catch him in the soft of his belly, as she'd done before. But if she tried to make a break for it and failed, what then? She had little doubt he would shoot her.

The odds were that he'd killed before, but if she did as he wanted there might be a chance, a slim chance, that he would spare her. Otherwise, why would he have taken such care to conceal his identity? The thought comforted her and she decided to wait for a better opportunity, hoping against hope that she'd not made her last and fatal mistake.

A noise, distant at first and barely audible above the din of the storm, imposed itself on her consciousness. A car was stopping close by. Had someone arrived to rescue her? Even DCI Leatheringham would have seemed like a guardian angel at this moment. But her hopes were soon dashed. She heard the boathouse door slam shut, followed almost immediately by her captor's gruff voice. Her heart thudded as though it might leap from her chest and her knees shook and swayed on the hard floor.

'By God, you took your time. Where the hell've you been? Oh, forget it. Just fetch me a rope and help me tie her up.'

Suddenly she knew what was familiar about the voice, where she'd heard it before. There was little doubt in her mind now that this was the barman at the Fox and Ferret in Manchester.

The next minute they were dragging her to the ground and binding her. The prickly twine dug into her neck, wrists and ankles and she wanted to cry out. But in a last defiant refusal to reveal her weakness, she bit her lip, keeping her concentration fixed on the thin beam of the torch which dipped and rose. All she could hear was the sound of panting close to her ear as they tethered her, like a dog, to an iron ring on the wall.

Moments later the torch-light disappeared and she heard the clank of the doors. An engine started up and revved away, the hum fading into the distance.

Until that moment she had only fleetingly been aware of the drenched blouse and flimsy skirt which clung to her skin. But now she struggled to suppress the shivering which rattled her aching body. An inhospitable blast of air whipped round the boat-house chilling her even more and a sudden surge of water sprayed her from below.

When Ben and Ruth had complained of being cold as they'd slipped between cotton sheets on chilly nights, her response had been to wrap her arms round them and tell them not to move a muscle. Within seconds they'd been warm and smiling. She tried to imagine comforting arms round her now, willing the heat back into her body. But whose arms? In spite of everything she'd learned about Joe in the past few days, she wished more than anything that they were *his* arms holding her and loving her. She longed to be able to lie once more 'like two-spoons' as he'd called it on their honeymoon, their bodies bending and curving in unison.

But he wasn't there. And never would be. She was alone now, totally. And in this dark, cavernous prison she must confront the demons which constantly assailed her, trying to convince her that, without Joe, she had no future.

She took a deep breath and held it, stiffening her body and subduing the shivers. Then, careful not to tighten the twine around her neck, she hunched her body forward, burying her head between her knees. If she closed her eyes, she could try to imagine what it would be like in the safety of her mother's womb, the warm, throbbing darkness where everything was controlled and harmonious, where nothing sinister could invade.

But the moment she conjured up the familiar picture of a foetus, pink and plump and sucking its thumb, an image as vivid and abhorrent as it was unexpected flashed through her mind. Now she could see it being dragged by a metal instrument attached to one leg. The child opened its mouth to scream but no sound came out as its leg, fully-formed but fragile like a chicken's, broke away from the convulsed body.

Liberty let out a terrified gasp and shook her head violently as the twine ripped into her flesh and thunder and lightning exploded overhead. The picture was gone as quickly as it had arrived but the memory of it was vivid and raw. She uncurled herself and struggled to adjust her eyes to the darkness, desperate to concentrate her thoughts on her escape.

But the numbness in her feet and hands was gradually spreading to the rest of her body. Even if she could find something sharp she doubted she'd be able to saw through her bonds. And if she did, one of the men would probably still be keeping guard outside. Compared to these obstacles, the fact that she had no idea where she was seemed unimportant.

Sheet lightning lit up the night in successive flashes and she switched her gaze to the water that boiled and frothed only inches below her. Till this moment, storms had always fascinated her with their power, a power which she'd always seen as a demonstration of the awesomeness of God's authority over the earth. But not any more. She saw it clearly now for what it was, a clashing of air currents, the inevitable and long-awaited end to the drought. Her God wasn't in the storm, lashing her and torturing her saturated body. She must look for him elsewhere. But when she tried to pray the words wouldn't come.

After a few minutes she gave up, realising that her mind, along with the rest of her body was becoming numb. How long would it be before hypothermia claimed her? she wondered, suddenly wishing it would be quick. She gave in to the exhaustion then, letting it wash over her, feeling her body sag.

But some spark, somewhere deep inside, refused to die. It nagged at her, urging her on, chastising her. Eventually she forced herself into an upright position. Her mission was not yet complete, she could see that now. She knew she mustn't give up. At least not yet.

She gritted her chattering teeth, struggling to work out who might notice her missing, before it was too late. Perhaps Ruth? But then her daughter had become accustomed to her unexplained absences. Possibly Jacob? Or Millie? Or Sondra? Sooner or later, she knew someone would alert the police. But when? She tried to convince herself it wouldn't be long, that she could keep going till then. But she mustn't go to pieces.

She sucked in the cold air and licked at the faintly salty drops of water on her lips, savouring their passage down her parched and bruised throat. Then, painfully and laboriously, she began the task of rubbing the twine that tied her wrists against the rough edges of the stone wall.

It seemed like hours had passed before eventually the bonds loosened and unravelled. Almost immediately the numbness in her fingers turned to a tingling sensation which worked its way painfully up her arms. Her hands felt raw and sticky with blood as she rubbed them together

It was then that she heard a faint creaking sound, in the silence between the claps of thunder. Someone was parting the heavy doors. She stopped and swung round, her heart racing out of control. Had her captor returned to finish her off? She braced herself. But the face she saw, framed in the doorway and illuminated in the stark brightness of the lightning, was not masked and threatening but deathly pale and anxious.

But what on earth was Anthony Simon doing here? She opened her mouth to speak but he pressed a finger to his lips. And then he was next to her, hacking through the twine on her neck with what looked like a small pen-knife. She hugged herself, squeezing the blood round her body, while he swiftly and silently released her ankles.

But when she tried to push herself up, her knees buckled and she lunged forward towards the edge of the landing. The water loomed closer and the memory of her stumble at Joe's graveside flashed through her mind. But this time it was not an iron grip that stopped her fall but an arm, soft yet firm, which slid round her waist and pulled her gently back.

She sank, with a mixture of relief and exhaustion, against his chest and savoured his warmth through her wet blouse. The next moment, with his arm supporting her in the gusting wind he was guiding her carefully down the concrete steps. She yearned to ask him how he'd managed to find her but knew instinctively that questions were best left till later. Whether that time would ever come she couldn't be sure but, for now, all she could do was trust him.

The old rowing boat bobbed precariously, its bow crashing into a tyre which, she could now see, hung from the steps. Surely he didn't think they could escape in that? The lake would be far too rough and the boat was in obvious need of attention. Water, she could see, was already sloshing about in the bottom. But before she could protest, he had withdrawn his arm and was ushering her forward, holding the boat steady against the bottom step with one hand and reaching out for her to take the other.

She froze and shook her head. She'd always had an aversion to sailing, in any form. Not even when Joe had taken off on his many fishing trips, leaving her alone, had she ever been tempted. Her fear had been irrational, she knew, but that didn't make it any less real. Now, peering through the green-tinged darkness at the foaming water she couldn't dispel the thought that she was leaving one tomb for another.

But what choice did she have? Surely Anthony wouldn't risk his own life if there was any alternative? She gripped his hand and half staggered, half fell into the boat, landing heavily against the wooden seat at the back.

Within seconds he had released the mooring rope and was sitting opposite her, pushing against the steps with an oar. The narrow boat rocked uncertainly out onto the lake while Liberty clung, dazed and aching, to its sides. But her fingers were already weak and shaky and the spray was numbing them now. As the boat lurched and tossed, she wondered how long it would be before they were both thrown into the deep, inky blackness.

Suddenly the sky lit up again and a scream filled the air. For a second she thought it had come from Anthony but then she saw his face, puffed and straining and realised it had been some kind of bird, an owl, probably. There was an icy coldness in the air now as it whipped round her, flapping her sodden clothes. Was it only an hour or two ago that her skin had been wet with perspiration as she'd sipped chilled wine on the patio? She could hardly believe it. Her hands, rigid against the violently rocking craft, were so cold and stiff now that she could barely feel them. But as the boat dipped violently she forced herself to cling on, digging the heel of her shoes into the wooden slats on the bottom of the boat.

In front of her, Anthony's darkened outline heaved and lunged as the boathouse, now to her right, disappeared behind a curtain of rain and she could hear his rasping breath above her own. She knew she should help him but saw that the splash of the oars in the angry water was regular and even. He knew what he was doing and she would only be a hindrance. But the thought of being totally dependent on him was not a welcome one.

A wave of nausea now washed over her and she closed her eyes, trying to ignore the rolling and shifting and not daring to look behind. But when she opened them she saw that the water in the bottom of the boat had been rising steadily. At first it had slopped round her feet with the motion of the boat, but quite suddenly the level had risen and now covered her ankles. At that moment a sudden gushing noise startled her and a white-crested wave crashed over her shoulders.

'Anthony! Anthony!' she screamed. 'The boat's sinking.' But she knew that even if he'd heard, he could do no more than keep rowing in the hope that they would reach dry land before it sank. It was up to her to keep them afloat.

The boat was low in the water now and she knew she must act quickly. Almost without thinking she threw off her shoes and dropped to her knees. Hardly noticing the icy chill of the water, she sat back and wedged herself firmly between her ankles, picking up the water-logged shoes to begin the impossible task of bailing out.

Lightning zig-zagged above the fells and for the first time she had a clear view of the lake. It was Bassenthwaite. She was sure of that. But they were still a long way from the shore and the safety of Lowthwaite. They'd never be able to make it.

'Faster, Anthony. Pull faster,' she screamed, watching the dark shadows of the oars loom over her as she frantically scooped up derisory amounts of water. But even before she heard the exhausted groan rise above the howling wind she knew that both of them would need to summon every ounce of strength from their exhausted bodies. She must try harder.

Her arms felt like lead weights and the rain lashed her face almost blinding her. But with a quickening of her rhythm, she began to move with a dexterity and energy unimaginable only seconds before. How long she ladled the water over the side she had no idea. Her hands throbbed and her breath caught in her throat, but she knew she had to keep going if they were to have a chance.

Then she saw it. Not sure at first whether she'd imagined it, she held her breath and peered through the rain. Yes, there it was again. A faint glow twinkled through buffeted trees.

'Anthony, it's Lowthwaite. I can see Lowthwaite House.'

She pointed and shrieked, determined that he should see it too. An oar skimmed the surface of the water as he turned and let out a long, desperate noise like a wounded animal released from a trap. Seconds later she felt the boat glide more easily, washed on the waves which lashed against the shore.

Gravel crunched under them and Liberty realised with a thankful groan that they were safe. The storm was passing, its worst ravages over and Anthony had already jumped into the shallow water and was steadying the boat.

'Take my hand,' he called, reaching out to her.

She grasped his surprisingly warm hand, stepping unsteadily onto the wet shale. Transferring his hand to her waist he held her to him and she sank, her legs trembling, into his arms. Rain ran down his face and onto hers and relief, like the rain, washed over her.

But a moment later she felt his arms tighten round her shoulders and the muscles in his body tense. His hot, sweet breath lingered over her face as his mouth sought hers.

Suddenly alert, she pulled away. The last thing she needed at this moment was the amorous attention of Anthony - or any man - even if he *had* just saved her life. Besides, she had a lot of questions that needed answering.

She looked up at him, wanting to explain but knowing she could never find the right words. In the semi-darkness, as the moon edged from behind the thick clouds, she caught only a glimpse of the wounded expression before he turned away and picked up the boat's mooring rope.

She sighed, wondering if her life as a single woman was destined to be punctuated by unwelcome propositions. Watching the hunched figure dragging the boat to the raised bank where Joe's smaller boat had lain untouched since the day of his death, she made up her mind to get to the house before him.

But, as she took a last look at the two boats side by side, a memory struggled to emerge. What was it? And why did it seem so important?

Her teeth chattering now and her body feeling as though it had been through a pulping machine, she couldn't begin to imagine. Her mind would take in nothing more tonight.

Pebbles were digging into the soles of her feet but there was no way she was going back for her shoes. With the pale rectangle of light from the kitchen in her sights, she ploughed on, groaning and cursing, hoping her ordeal would be over soon.

And then at last she felt the soft wet grass of the sloping lawn between her toes. She gasped with relief and paused to get her breath. It was then that she saw Anthony's dark shadow disappear behind one of the oak trees which formed a guard of honour between the lawn and the meadow. He was obviously avoiding her too, she decided, noticing that the light in the kitchen was blazing brighter now through the fine rain.

But when she finally reached the patio, breathless and near collapse, she stopped, unable to believe the devastation before her. The wrought-iron table was still standing but it was bare, and the heavy chairs lay scattered, one embedded deep in the cottage garden. Fragments of glass and china - part of the irreplaceable dinner set her mother had left her - littered the patio. There was no sign of the candlestick or the pink linen table-cloth. Wondering how long it would be before a piece of glass ripped into her foot, she picked her way through leaves and petals which swirled round in a mesmerising dance.

With a vague sense of elation that she'd made it without further injury she reached the yellow glow which lay like a welcome mat on the flags in front of her. She raised her eyes in relief, but the next moment, she gazed in horror at the French windows which swung precariously on broken hinges, the small square panes in a million pieces among the sodden debris on the tiled floor of the kitchen. It looked as if a whirlwind had ripped through it. Stunned, she shook her head in disbelief. Then, not caring if she cut her feet, she padded in a daze through the wreckage.

She felt as if she'd been violated, her inner sanctum trashed. The old clothes-rack from which she'd lovingly hung bunches of dried flowers and copper pans had fallen across the work tops, spanning the gap between them like a rope bridge over a ravine. Underneath, the stainless-steel toaster and kettle lay dented and her favourite blue pasta jars had smashed beyond recognition. Everything was covered with leaves and flower heads, either dried or from the garden.

Her mind whirled. What had happened? Had she been burgled? Then she realised what she'd done. When she'd rushed out to clear the table on the patio she'd left the French windows open. But then she hadn't expected to be suddenly whisked away in the boot of a car.

Helpless and exhausted, she closed her eyes, unable to decide what to do first. But there was no panic or even fear, just a numbing resignation. She had no energy left to expend on pointless rantings, or even tears. And, to her relief, there was no yearning for a calming brandy. She sighed, aware of a desperate urge to take off her cold, wet clothes and lay her head on a pillow. But she knew she must at least secure the house first.

At that moment a figure appeared in the doorway. Her heart lurched and she let out a stifled cry before she recognised Anthony, his face gaunt and his eyes more sunken than she remembered. He opened his mouth as if to speak, but nothing came out.

The thought occurred to her that he might be struggling to put into words some sentiment they both might regret in the cold light of day. But at this moment she was past caring.

'You'd better come in,' she said, hearing the weariness in her tone. But he deserved more than that. 'I . . . I want you to know how grateful I am . . . for saving my life,' she added.

He nodded and she half expected him to smile but instead he pressed his lips together in a jaded acknowledgement.

'Look, I'm not happy leaving you here alone,' he said at last, 'especially with the door being . . . well . . .' He gazed at the shattered glass as if for inspiration.

Liberty was in no mood to protest. Every part of her body ached and she could no longer control the shivering.

'Look, Anthony . . .' she began, just before she felt a nausea rising from the pit of her stomach.

He held up a hand. 'No. Sorry. I just meant I think I should stay... down here... and make sure you don't have any more unwanted guests.' Then he added, 'I'll ring the police if you like. They'll probably send somebody round but I'll tell them you're too shocked to talk to them before morning.'

She nodded, struggling to control the churning in her stomach and hurried out of the kitchen. She must get to the bathroom, and quick.

Gulping back the bile in her throat, she gripped the banister and, with an almost manic will, dragged herself upstairs. But as she stepped onto the landing she felt the urge to wretch and, with a groan, almost dived into the bathroom, coming to a sudden halt as her head cracked against the toilet seat.

Next morning, as she opened her eyes, the front of her head was throbbing and she found it difficult to think. The sun through the window was shining full in her face. Dazzled and disoriented, she squeezed her eyes shut again. How had she had got into bed? She couldn't remember. Colourful snapshots of her kidnap and escape the previous evening were imprinted on her memory. But it was what had happened to her after her return home that concerned her most.

She remembered Anthony and his offer to call the police, but after that . . .? She put a hand to her head and felt the lump. Had she suffered concussion and if so, who had put her to bed?

With a growing sense of unease she fingered the towelling robe wrapped loosely over the bra and panties she had been wearing the previous evening. But where were the rest of her clothes? She tried to sit up but it was as though her body were being sucked back into quicksand.

Half an hour later, when she finally managed to drag herself downstairs, she found Anthony, the top half of his body naked, slumped across the kitchen table. His face, resting on crossed arms, had lost its pallid, drawn look. But it was the kitchen which had undergone the biggest transformation. She stopped in her tracks and gazed round.

The door had been boarded up, the floor cleared of every bit of debris and the clothes-rack back in its place across the middle of the ceiling. But, instead of dried flowers and copper utensils, Anthony's crumpled grey shirt and her wet skirt and blouse hung like disembodied rag dolls.

He must have been working most of the night, she realised, her gratitude swiftly replaced by a growing awareness that Anthony had overstepped the mark. This was more than just taking care of a dead friend's wife. Suddenly she had an overwhelming urge to get rid of him. But first she needed the answers to a few important questions.

He stirred, his taut body shivering into consciousness. Then, with a sudden jolt of awareness, his head and chest shot up simultaneously. The chair legs grated on the floor before wobbling precariously and coming to rest.

'I'm . . . I'm sorry. I didn't hear you come down,' he said, flinging an arm across his chest as if to cover his nakedness. 'Are you all right?'

Liberty made an effort to give him a reassuring smile but her lips were dry and she felt decidedly unsteady. 'I'm OK. Don't worry,' she said. 'You've done a wonderful job here.' He glanced at her uncertainly and nodded before reaching up and pulling his shirt from the rack.

'Would you like a drink?' he asked. She hesitated. Surely she should be asking *him*.

'I'll get it,' she said firmly, taking hold of the kettle and noticing that the dent wasn't as bad as she'd remembered. 'Want one?'

'Yes, please. Coffee. Black,' he replied. 'I don't know about you but I feel like I need a kick-start.'

She knew exactly what he meant. Her hands shook as she filled the kettle and spooned coffee into two mugs. The jelly-feeling in her legs and stomach was very similar to the sea-sickness she'd suffered on her one Channel crossing to France. She thought about going back to bed but her curiosity was too strong. There were so many questions she needed answering.

It was almost as if he'd read her thoughts. 'By the way, I called the police,' he said, buttoning his shirt. 'But Dr Firth told them you wouldn't be fit enough to make a statement until today.'

'Just a minute,' she said, 'Where does Dr Firth come into this?'

'Don't you remember?' His fingers froze round a button and he screwed up his face. 'You fell and banged your head. You were out cold for about ten minutes. I was really worried about you and rang Dr Firth. He came over straight away, just after you'd come round. He said you had concussion. Don't you remember telling him you felt as though you'd been kicked by a mule? He gave you a sedative.'

Liberty shook her head slowly to minimise the ache that was now like a tightening band.

'So who put me to bed?'

'Nobody. You put yourself to bed.'

'So how . . . ?' She glanced up at the clothes hanging over her.

'Oh!' he exclaimed, concentrating once again on fastening his shirt buttons. 'You left them in the bathroom.'

'So what did the police have to say?'

'Chief Inspector Leatheringham was a bit put-out to say the least but he couldn't go against the doctor's instructions. Anyway, he said he'd expect you at the police station at 12 noon. To be honest, I think he was annoyed he'd have to turn in on a Sunday as well as coming out here on a Saturday night.'

'Sunday?' Liberty's eyes shot towards the clock on the wall behind his head. Twenty minutes to ten. Mass was at half past.

She poured the boiling water and wondered whether she would be able to get to Holy Cross in time. In the circumstances it would hardly be a mortal sin if she didn't. She still felt decidedly shaky and every muscle in her body ached.

In the past she'd missed Mass for far more trivial reasons. Yet something deep within her was yearning to communicate with the God she had blamed for letting Joe die. Did she now feel a sense of obligation perhaps, even gratitude, for sparing her last night? But it was more than that. She couldn't explain it, but more than anything else at this moment, she wanted to make this sacrifice.

'Look, Anthony. I don't wish to be rude but I'll have to get dressed. I'd like to get to Mass if I can.' She put a mug of steaming coffee in front of him and noticed the disappointment on his face. 'I'll never be able to thank you enough for what you did last night. You do know that, don't you?' But without waiting for a reply she hurried on, 'There's just one thing I'd like to know before I go. How on earth did you find me?'

He smiled, a boyish, almost brash smile which made her wonder if he'd seen the whole escapade as a rip-roaring adventure. 'By pure chance actually. I'd been visiting my mother in York and decided to call on you on my way back. It's hardly out of the way and I thought we could go for a drink or something.' He paused as if waiting for a sign that his suggestion would have been welcomed but she gave none. He took a sip of coffee and continued. 'Well, as I was about to turn into your drive, this car shot out. I had to slam my brakes on to avoid him. I knew something was wrong straightaway but I didn't know what. I nearly came to the house to check if you were OK but then I remembered the police had been looking for a light-coloured car and this one fit the bill. I reckoned that if it was Joe's murderer I couldn't let him get away.'

'No. Quite,' said Liberty, blowing on her coffee and glancing again at the clock.

'I was lucky it was raining so hard. He'd no idea I was following him. But when he turned down a dirt track towards the lake, I daren't risk him spotting me so I waited on the main road. I calculated he couldn't get far. There was nowhere to go except into the water. So I left the car and set off walking.'

'Well, thank goodness you found me in the end,' she interrupted, taking a sip of coffee.

'It wasn't as simple as that,' he said obviously put out at being cut short. 'It was pitch black out there and bucketing down. I couldn't see two inches in front of me, except for the lightning. I nearly got run over twice by another car. It passed me first going to the lake. Then, five minutes later it came tearing back. I think there must have been two of them.'

Liberty nodded, remembering the accomplice's roughness in tying her up.

'Then I found the first car,' he went on with a rush. 'I thought there must be something - or someone - in the boathouse but I didn't know what, or who. My first thought was that it might be stolen property. Anyway, the guy in the car couldn't see much. His windows were all steamed up. So I decided to take a look. I nearly died when I saw you in there.' He sat on the edge of the table gripping his mug and looking pleased with himself.

Liberty smiled weakly. 'And the rest is history, as they say. I don't suppose you got a good look at the man in the car?'

His eyes rolled and he shook his head. 'Not really. All I could see was a fuzzy outline. Sorry.' He gulped his coffee.

'What about the car's number?'

He shrugged. 'It was very dark. That's why it was relatively easy for me to get into the boathouse. Neither of us could see anything.'

'The make of the car?'

He shrugged. 'All I can say is it was a lightish saloon. Possibly grey or blue. That's all. I'm sorry it's not much. It's all I could tell the police.'

She couldn't resist a smile. So DCI Leatheringham would probably have concluded by now that it was the car seen outside Bagley Hall around the time Joe was murdered. She'd enjoy sticking a pin in his over-inflated ego when they met later. But first she must get to Holy Cross.

'If I get my skates on I'll have time to drop you off wherever you left your car,' she said hurrying to get dressed.

CHAPTER 22

Broken branches littered the road and everywhere great pools of water submerged the land. A brisk wind still whipped the lake, washing flotsam through the low branches of immature trees that clustered round the water's edge. But the rain had revived the parched landscape. And the sun was beginning to break through the thick cloud. Now the brown-edged grass seemed to sparkle with renewed life as Liberty hurried down the churchyard path at exactly half past ten.

Father O'Malley was just coming onto the altar as she slipped into her favourite pew half way down the central aisle. The familiar smells of musty stone, candle wax and stale incense combined to soothe and reassure her.

The congregation rose, but instead of the priest's usual 'Let's begin our Mass,' followed by the Sign of the Cross he turned, solemn-faced, towards them. The two girl altar-servers, immaculate in red and white, stood either side of him.

'Of your charity, remember in your prayers Ellen Newington who died last night.'

The shock was sudden and intense. Why, she couldn't say, since she'd known for months that Jacob's wife was dying. Liberty bowed her head and blinked back hot stinging tears.

The death was no less a tragedy just because it had been expected, especially for Jacob and their four sons. Poor Jacob. He and Ellen had been inseparable even throughout her long illness. He would be lost without her.

The community too would mourn the passing of this selfless woman who had borne her suffering with patience and courage. Liberty mouthed the words of the prayer, Eternal Rest, confident that Ellen had received her reward and was already safe in the Lord's arms.

Fr O'Malley began the Mass but the words drifted over her in a meaningless haze. She had no recollection of the brief sermon but rose afterwards with the congregation, the Mass sheet shaking between her fingers, and mumbled the next prayer. 'I believe in one God . . .'

The gaping wound within her where grief and self-pity wallowed in abundance threatened to spew out its contents once more. She closed her eyes. The combined shock of Ellen's death and her experiences the night before might have taken their toll, but breaking down in public was not an option.

She opened her eyes and bent down to pick up the hymn book from the bench in front. It didn't matter which page she opened it at, she would concentrate on the words in front of her and try to calm herself. But the hymn her eyes fell on seemed to have been written especially for her.

I lift up my eyes to the mountain,
Is anyone there to help me?
Yes, my God comes to help me,
The Lord who made both heaven and earth.

She closed the book, a speck of hope spreading within her like the ripples on a lake.

Mary Monkton walked to the ornate wooden lectern to begin the bidding prayers and placed the hand-written sheet in front of her. Without warning the spectre of Joe, his small eyes glazed under bushy brows, superimposed itself on the grey-haired, bespectacled woman.

Liberty stared, more in amazement than fear. Joe had always taken great pride in leading the congregation in these personal prayers at the Saturday evening vigil Mass. It was only natural she should think of him at this time. But the hallucination had no power now to disturb her and it faded as quickly as if it had been a light being switched off. Liberty listened with renewed interest to the first request for Divine assistance, to comfort those who have lost a loved one.

'Lord, graciously hear us.' The response came from her heart.

But she was totally unprepared for the second prayer. 'Lord, help all those who were injured by the bomb which went off in a Carlisle hotel last night. Grant that they may recover completely from their injuries and come to forgive those who have caused their suffering. Lord hear us.'

This time she heard the congregation respond but she could make no attempt to join in. She covered her mouth with her hand, the full horror of the words hitting her with an almost physical force.

The newspaper clipping she'd found in Joe's study had reported a similar incident. A breakaway group intent on sabotaging the peace process in Northern Ireland had been responsible then. And her kidnapper had spoken with an Irish accent. The pieces were all beginning to fall into place.

Was Michael O'Connor behind both bombings? And how far was Joe implicated? But she could only guess at the answers to those questions and to the question she craved an answer to more than any other: Did Michael O'Connor kill Joe?

She thought back to her visit to Belfast on Friday and wondered whether she had been wise to leave the Irishman a note. If he'd been planning a bomb attack her message could have panicked him into thinking she knew more than she did. Is that what had happened? She could only guess. Her questions must wait 'til later.

A sudden burst of sunlight broke through the stained glass windows behind the altar, throwing a speckled cloak over the whole church. Her thoughts drifted back to two other services, memorable for different reasons, which had been conducted with this backdrop.

The memory of Joe's Requiem Mass was still fresh and painful in her mind, and the other, although dimmed by the passage of almost thirty years, evoked feelings nonetheless intense and emotional. On that April day the church had been filled not only with family and friends but with flowers. Daffodils and pansies, strung together with gold ribbon, had decorated the ends of pews, and even the permanent musty smell had been stifled by the delicate fragrance of spring flowers.

But she was no longer a naive 19 year old with a full life in front of her. And Joe was dead - along with most of the wedding guests, including her mother and old Father Collins. She wondered what had become of the rest and whether, like herself, her two bridesmaids - friends from her school days in the West Pennines - still derived strength from Sister Monica's lessons for life.

The words now came to her as if conjured up from nowhere: 'There is no greater grief than, in misery, to recall happier times.'

For once she couldn't agree with the spouting of the moon-faced nun in her black and white habit. The fond memory made her smile. But conscious that someone might be looking, she squeezed her lips together almost immediately. Joe would have been scandalised at her irreverence. But then she remembered that Joe's opinion didn't matter any more. Like so many holier-than-thou people before him, he had been a hypocrite. But worse than that, his whole life had been a sham, a pretence, an elaborate cover for his ungodly way of life.

Father O'Malley lifted the Host and she bowed her head, as much in shame as in veneration. Was she not just as guilty of hypocrisy? Here she was, privately passing judgement and condemning Joe while publicly professing her Christian faith. But was it any wonder Joe's legacy of deceit had made her bitter? God knew she was no saint, but perhaps in time she would learn to hate the sin rather than the sinner.

The congregation stood up to recite the Our father. '. . . Forgive us our trespasses as we forgive those who trespass against us . . .' The words slipped out easily and at that moment she knew that her love for Joe would never completely die.

She couldn't deny he'd had a difficult childhood. That must have had some bearing on his outlook on life. Perhaps he really did believe in what he preached, but for some reason related to his upbringing, chose to practise a different code of ethics. Perhaps he believed that what he was doing was justified, was even acceptable to God, although she could hardly take in that someone so indoctrinated in the Ten Commandments would not see adultery as sinful. Or was he so arrogant that he assumed all his transgressions would be forgiven by a merciful God on the last day? Who could say now what was in his mind? His life, like his death, continued to remain a mystery to her.

A line of people filed past to receive Communion. She remained kneeling unable to reconcile the deep feeling of unworthiness and put her head in her hands. But she couldn't bring herself to believe that God's infinite forgiveness wouldn't extend to her and, quickly reciting a silent Act of Contrition she tagged onto the end of the queue.

The Mass was almost over and Liberty was becoming impatient to know more about the bombing in Carlisle. If she hurried she could call home and find the details on Ceefax before meeting Chief Inspector Leatheringham.

The moment Father O'Malley turned to leave the altar she hastily genuflected and hurried towards the door, her eyes fixed on the stone aisle worn smooth by the constant tramp of feet. No-one stopped her as she fled through the graveyard and across the grass in a line almost identical to that taken by Maria Rosa less than two weeks earlier.

The Detective was surprisingly animated when Liberty, tense and with a throbbing headache, arrived at the police station just over half an hour later. He summoned her into the interview room with an uncharacteristic sweep of his long, rather feminine hand.

'Good morning, Mrs Westerman. Or should I say good afternoon,' he said in a salesman-like tone. 'What a beautiful day. So refreshing after the heat-wave, don't you think?'

'Yes, definitely,' she said, grappling with the familiar surge of distaste as the heavily-lined face broke into a repulsive parody of a smile. Insincerity oozed out like the thick, foaming spittle which now made its way between yellowed teeth and the corners of his mouth. He motioned to her to sit down.

The small room seemed just as airless as the last time she'd sat here opposite this charmless individual and she longed to throw open the window. The Chief Inspector rubbed his hands together as if he were cold.

'Good news,' he announced, the grotesque smile widening. 'We've found your kidnappers.'

The news was as unexpected as it was welcome. 'Where? How did you . . .? That's marvellous,' she said, allowing herself to relax a little. She smiled. 'But who are they? And what on earth did they hope to gain? Have you found that out?'

His mood was sombre now and he leaned forward, his hands flat on the table. 'We've found out a great deal, I'm pleased to say. But first I'd like you to tell me what you know about Michael O'Connor.'

Liberty frowned, wondering whether the Chief Inspector was still looking for proof of her conspiracy in Joe's murder. But surely even he wasn't so stupid as to think she'd arrange her own kidnapping. Or her escape in a boat that was almost certain to sink. She shrugged. She'd nothing to hide.

'Very little, actually,' she replied more confidently. 'Except that he was a friend of my husband's from school. They kept in touch afterwards as far as I can make out, although I've never met him. I found his address in my husband's diary and thought he may be able to shed some light on his death. And on Friday I went to Belfast to speak to him but he wasn't there. A neighbour gave me the name of the Ship and Shamrock in Littleport where he could be contacted and I left him a note asking him to get in touch. That's it. That's all I can tell you.'

Chief Inspector Leatheringham nodded slowly. 'You certainly went to a lot of trouble.' He eyed her suspiciously then brightened. 'Well I suppose that clears up one mystery. He must have thought you knew more than you did and wanted you out of the way for a while. Have you heard about the bombing last night in Carlisle?'

'Yes. But I didn't know anything about it beforehand.'

'I'm not saying you did. But that's the reason Michael O'Connor was so jumpy. There he was, he and his co-conspirator, ready to plant a 500 pound bomb. Then you arrive on the scene asking questions and he panicked. We picked up his accomplice last night, soon after your friend, Mr Simon, telephoned us. Silly sod was still outside the boathouse asleep in his car. Hadn't noticed you'd gone.' He laughed, the long, cackle-like sound even more hideous than his smile. 'But the whole operation was a shambles from start to finish. Very amateurish I can tell you. Your note to Michael O'Connor was in his pocket. I don't suppose you know him? His name's Martin Flaherty.'

For a moment Liberty wondered whether to mention that she may have met him at the Fox and Ferret in Manchester. But she thought better of it and shook her head. 'No, sorry,' she said. 'Never heard of him.'

'His job was to make sure you didn't talk to the police while O'Connor carried out the bomb attack then disappeared back to Belfast.'

'This Martin Flaherty, has he confessed?'

'Sang like a canary. There was no way he was going to take the rap on his own after we found bomb-making equipment in his pub. Then there was also a large quantity of fertilizer in aluminium casks in the cellar. I reckon forensics will confirm it was used to make this bomb. Anyway, we have enough now to put Flaherty and O'Connor away for a very long time. The Royal Ulster Constabulary picked O'Connor up this morning, but unfortunately the bomb had already gone off.'

'Was anyone injured?' she asked, remembering the horrific details of the bombing four years ago.

'A night porter and a couple of late-night revellers had a few cuts but that was all. There was nobody else about. From what we can gather it wasn't supposed to go off till ten o'clock this morning when the hotel lobby was at its busiest. But in their typical bungling fashion they'd put a faulty timer in the thing and it went off at two am instead.'

'But why? Why would anyone want to do such a thing? Especially now when the IRA seems to be going along with the peace process.'

The Chief Inspector laughed, his gaping mouth emitting the familiar cackle. 'These clowns are nothing to do with the IRA. They might have thought they'd something in common years ago but now . . .

they'd just like to wreck any peaceful agreement, that's all. And play silly games.'

'So you think they've been doing this sort of thing for a long time?' Liberty scarcely dared ask.

'I'd stake my life on it. But I could do with some more proof. Have you ever seen one of these?' He pulled a red piece of card from his pocket and Liberty recognised immediately the badge of the Irish Rebellion Force.

She hesitated, gazing at the childish inscription. But even after all Joe had put her through, she couldn't bring herself to betray him. 'No, no I haven't,' she lied.

'It was in O'Connor's wallet. Pretty basic, eh? A kid's badge. I reckon he started with this rebellion thing when he was a lad. Now you said your husband was at school with O'Connor.'

'Yes, but Joe wouldn't have had anything to do with bombing people. He was far too scrupulous.' The lies slipped out easily but to divulge Joe's connection with these terrorists seemed like treachery. And to this odious man . . . She would burn Joe's badge when she got home. *And* his address book.

He gave her a withering look. 'Hmm. Obviously we will make enquiries.' It sounded like a threat but she was no longer worried by his constant suspicions.

'Do you think Michael O'Connor killed my husband?' she asked.

'It's possible. But I keep asking myself if he's killed once - and possibly more than once - why didn't he kill you when he had the chance? Why risk everything when he knew you could point the finger at him?' He glared at her, his heavy brows pulled together in a frown.

Liberty gazed back at him. She suspected that the answer to his question lay in this misguided little group's comradeship and deep-seated loyalty to a dead friend.

'I haven't the faintest idea,' she said and smiled. 'Perhaps they intended killing me after they'd planted the bomb.'

'Perhaps. But all in all, I'd say you've had a lucky escape. And that boat was the biggest stroke of luck. Still, with this bunch's record of incompetence . . .'

Bells started to ring in the back of Liberty's head. What was it she had to remember? Something about a rowing boat. 'Yes,' she interrupted. 'It was a godsend. Although the weather wasn't exactly ideal.' Her thoughts were clarifying slowly. She looked at her watch.

'Good heavens. Is that the time? If you're finished, Chief Inspector, I'd like to get going. I have a few calls to make.'

He pushed his chair back and she noted with amusement that his face resembled that of a startled bull dog.

'Of course.'

A fresh breeze was blowing off the lake as she drove back to Lowthwaite House. The scene to her left, for so long obscured by a haze, now dazzled with its clarity. Tiny white clouds hovered in a deep blue sky like smoke signals rising from the mountain tops. The water, no longer grey and foreboding shimmered contentedly.

It was coming back to her now. The boat. The lake. Yes, of course. But why hadn't it occurred to her before? She cast her mind back to the afternoon of Joe's murder.

Ruth and Crispin had popped round for a quick visit at about 5 o'clock. It had been a hot, still day and she remembered quite clearly strolling with them down to the lakeside in search of some cooler air. It was then she'd noticed Joe's rowing boat was gone from its mooring by the edge of the lake. Joe had left for Holy Cross, so she knew he wasn't out on the lake in it.

Remembering that she'd seen it earlier that morning when she'd ridden Merry along the shore, she'd commented that Joe, or Jacob, must have taken it to be repaired. But then the moment had passed, overtaken by Ruth's angry complaints about her father's criticism of Crispin.

The subsequent events of that evening had ensured that the memory was firmly locked in her subconscious. Until now. Now she knew that the boatyard hadn't had the boat. It had mysteriously returned. But when? She trawled back through her memory of those hazy, grief-stricken days after Joe's death. Then it came to her. Chief Inspector Leatheringham had asked her, on the morning after Joe's death, whether he owned the small rowing boat moored by the lake. It must have been there when the police searched the grounds after Joe's murder.

With growing conviction she now saw that it would have been quite possible for someone to have stolen the boat - taken it out onto the lake, or less likely, put it onto a trailer - with the intention of returning in it later that night. As she'd just inadvertently said to the Chief Inspector, it would have been an ideal means of escape on a calm evening.

She parked the car by the stable and walked round the house to the patio. The debris which had swirled round the stone flags had been swept away and a clean tablecloth, held down with plastic pegs, now fluttered on the heavy iron table. But the extent of Anthony's inroads into her privacy held little interest for her at this moment. She must concentrate her thoughts totally on the events of that fateful day.

She flopped onto the rickety bench which nestled among tall rose bushes and sucked in the perfumed scent of the battered blooms, struggling to make sense of what she'd discovered. If the murderer really had used Joe's boat that night to enter Lowthwaite's grounds unseen, that would explain the mystery of why Gregor had seen no-one enter from the road. He'd been watching from his car since about 8:15, an hour before Joe was killed.

It also seemed to bear out Maria Rosa's assertion that Joe's murder had been pre-meditated, committed by someone who knew him. A person on such good terms that they might possibly have asked to borrow his boat? In fact, the more she thought about it the more it seemed likely that Joe must have known who'd taken it since, if he'd noticed it missing there was a chance he might have called the police and foiled the plot on his life.

But why had the murderer not used the boat for his escape? Surely that had been the intention? But perhaps he'd heard Gregor snooping about and panicked, making his escape by the quicker route, on foot. That's what must have happened, she concluded. There was no other explanation she could think of.

She hunched forward, wrapping her arms tightly round her. The thought that Joe's killer had been at Lowthwaite on that afternoon made a shiver run down her spine. But what chilled her to the core was the realisation that, since she could remember no strangers calling, this person must be well-known to her - either an acquaintance or - dare she think it - a friend?

Suddenly the energy drained out of her and she leaned back while the sun warmed her face. The solution to the mystery of Joe's death lay within her grasp, she could sense it. So why did she hesitate to press on? The answer was staring her in the face. Because the prospect of questioning - and possibly accusing friends - appalled her. But if she didn't, this illusory smell of success, like a gust of wind, might suddenly escape.

Clenching her fists and gritting her teeth she closed her eyes in a determined bid to bring to mind every visitor to Lowthwaite House on that Saturday, the 7th August. Whatever it might take she knew she must grasp the nettle.

Half an hour later she jumped up, overtaken by an inexplicable desire to test her theory on someone brighter than herself. But who?

Sondra was the obvious choice and she almost ran to the phone. Sondra would give her an honest opinion about whether her conclusions would hold water. But she soon discovered that her friend was out, organising a golf club charity event, or so Derek said. Could he help? Liberty decided against confiding in him, mainly because he would be likely to give her a lecture on withholding evidence from the police, rather than advising her.

Without waiting to consider the pros and cons, she picked up the telephone and dialled again.

'Anthony? Hi. Can I see you? I've got something I'd like to discuss with you. It won't take long. Shall I come over there or do you want to come here? I can make a sandwich if you've not eaten.'

His stuttering confusion made her smile. 'What? Yes. Of course I'll come. Is everything OK?'

'Yes. Yes. I'll explain when I see you,' she said. 'As soon as you can make it. I'll be waiting.' She put the receiver down with a decisiveness that both surprised and animated her.

Even before the Audi had come to a standstill on the path she was racing, almost childlike, towards it, her long-sleeved blouse flapping in the breeze.

'I've worked it out,' she panted. 'Or at least I think I have. I want you to tell me I'm right.' She turned and led the way to the patio.

Anthony followed, his expression a mixture of bewilderment and apprehension.

'I am right, aren't I?' she asked later, pushing a plate of smoked salmon and cucumber sandwiches towards him. 'That's how it must've been done?'

Anthony took a sandwich and nodded, his dark brows deeply furrowed. 'But what makes you so sure Joe hadn't moved the boat himself?'

'I can't be one hundred per cent certain he didn't. But I do know he didn't put it back. He'd already left for Holy Cross by then. And when he came home he didn't have time. He was killed almost immediately.'

'OK. So who do you think borrowed it?'

'My money's on Giles Tranter. He lives over the road at Bagley Hall. He turned up at about 11 o'clock or just after and said he had some business with Joe. I'd just got back from my ride and Joe was at work so I asked him to come back later. It was about half past one when he came the second time. On foot.' She picked up the tea-pot. 'Tea?'

'Please.' She poured the tea as he bit into his sandwich. 'And Joe was here then?'

'He was cleaning his car. Anyway I don't know what Tranter wanted and I didn't see him leave. He could easily have taken the boat out onto the lake, or he and Joe could have carried it over to his place. He's a dodgy character and I wouldn't be surprised at anything he does.' She shrugged, watching Anthony push the rest of the sandwich into his mouth. 'The only other visitor was Joe's partner, Bob Brock. He came about a quarter past two. Something to do with work I presumed. But I didn't ask. Joe was in the stable, putting his tools away, I think, so I told Bob to go round. I didn't see him again but the car had gone about ten minutes later when I looked out of the window. And as far as I remember, he hadn't got a trailer on it.'

Anthony pursed his lips and frowned. 'But if you didn't see either him or the other fellow, Tranter, leave, how can you be so sure that someone else didn't slip past unseen? Or didn't even come past the house at all? Perhaps they used the lakeside footpath?'

Liberty sighed. 'Yes, I know that's a possibility. But why would this person, whoever he is, risk being seen in broad daylight stealing an old rowing boat just so that he could return in it later? Why not just come in the dark along the footpath? It doesn't make sense does it?'

'Well it wouldn't be as easy - or quick. A footpath would be quite hazardous without a torch. And any light would be too risky. Besides, there'd be a chance of snagging his clothes on bushes and brambles. And if his motive was robbery he might need the boat to carry his haul.'

'Hmm. I suppose so.' She had to admit he had a point. 'But I still think the most probable explanation is that the person who murdered Joe knew him and couldn't risk being seen and recognised. So he borrowed the boat, probably with Joe's permission, and left it somewhere convenient so he could come back later under the shadow of darkness. It was all part of an elaborate plot to avoid detection. As it happened, the evening was overcast and it would have been difficult for anyone to spot a boat on the water. But even if it had been clear, who's going to bat an eyelid round here at someone out for a sail or fishing on a warm summer's evening? And there wouldn't be much chance of being recognised. All very clever, don't you think?'

Anthony stirred sugar into his tea and sat back sipping it thoughtfully. 'It sounds as though you've worked all this out very thoroughly,' he said at last.

Liberty smiled at the compliment. 'I hope so. I know I've not the best brain for this sort of thing but I've tried to think of everything. All I know for certain is that the boat was missing on Saturday afternoon and back again on Sunday morning. As far as I'm concerned, the only person who could have returned it was the murderer. Now if you agree that I'm on the right track then I think it's time to ask Jacob if he saw anyone near the boat.'

'Jacob. Who the hell's Jacob?' Anthony's voice was high-pitched and accusing as he slammed the cup into the saucer.

'Our gardener.' She bit her lip. '*My* gardener,' she corrected. 'He was here for part of that afternoon, working in the garden.' She felt the colour rising in her cheeks and was conscious of being on the defensive.

'Why on earth didn't you mention him before?' Anthony snapped.

Liberty glared at him. 'Because I hardly think that a man whose wife had only days to live - a man who has been totally loyal to the family for over thirty years - is going to suddenly murder his employer. Don't be so ridiculous.'

Anthony spoke slowly. 'I know it sounds unlikely but don't be too hasty. He had the best opportunity. He would be familiar with Joe's movements so he would be able to plan the best time to find him alone. But he couldn't afford to be seen anywhere near here at night. He'd be too easily recognised. Him and his car, probably.'

'Jacob travels everywhere by bike,' she said coldly.

He laughed. 'Even better. On a bike he'd have no chance of making his getaway without being seen. Don't you see? The boat was a brilliant idea.'

Liberty slumped back in her chair. Anything was possible in this crazy world. But not that, surely? It had to be Giles Tranter.

'We've got to get some proof,' she said. 'We could start with Bob. I'm pretty sure he didn't have time to start loading the rowing boat onto a trailer, even if he had one. With a bit of luck he might be able to remember something significant.'

'Good idea,' said Anthony. 'But be careful not to give too much away. Keep it casual.'

'I'll get on the phone right now. Hopefully he'll be at home but, if not, Susan will know where he is.' Deciding not to tell him about Bob's claim to have left Susan the previous evening, she hurried towards the kitchen phone.

Susan answered, launching immediately into a tirade on the aftermath of the storm.

Liberty broke in, 'Susan, I'm sorry but I must speak to Bob urgently. Is he there?'

'Oh, yes. I'll just get him.'

Obviously the wanderer had returned. And, by the sound of it, hadn't even been missed. She could hear Susan's monotonous tones in the background.

Liberty realised then that he might presume she was having second thoughts about his amorous, whisky-fuelled offer. She decided not to put him straight if he did. He'd be more willing to talk if he felt there was still a chance of them getting together. Her ruthlessness surprised her, but she dismissed any qualms by telling herself he would realise his mistake soon enough.

'What can I do for you, Liberty?' He sounded cool and business-like. Obviously her rejection had hit home where it hurt - his pride.

'I'd like you to cast your mind back to the day of Joe's death. You remember coming to see him earlier that afternoon?'

He grunted, seemingly apprehensive about the next question.

She continued: 'Can you recall seeing Joe's rowing boat? The one he kept moored at the bottom of the garden. I need to know if it was there or not. Do you remember?'

'What? Oh, the rowing boat. Well, no.' He hesitated. 'Look, Liberty...'

'No, you don't remember? Or no, it wasn't there?' Liberty waited patiently for his answer, but it was not one she'd expected.

'No, I didn't see it. I didn't go down near the lake. But I did ask Joe if he was going fishing later on. He said he couldn't. That man of yours, what's his name . . .?'

'Jacob?' she offered.

'Yes, that's it. Jacob had taken it to the boatyard to be repainted - or repaired - I can't remember which.'

It was as if someone had walked over her grave. Her heart seemed to stand still then without warning leap against the wall of her chest. She closed her eyes and leaned against the wall, the cold stone sending shivers through her body.

When she put down the receiver, it was several minutes before she felt able to move. It was as if Bob's words had slotted together a multitude of missing pieces.

Atkinson's boatyard was only a few hundred yards along the shore. So, instead of calling out Dave Atkinson to pick the boat up on his trailer, Jacob had often rowed it there for repainting or minor repairs. But Atkinson had always insisted on bringing it back on his trailer.

She had little doubt that she'd finally discovered the truth but the knowledge had erased any enthusiasm for pursuing Joe's killer. How could she accuse a good friend and loyal employee who had been widowed only hours ago? Even if he did kill Joe - and the evidence now seemed damning - he was entitled to some time to mourn in peace.

But when she relayed her fears to Anthony, he had other ideas.

'You can't let him off the hook. Take advantage of the fact that he'll be off his guard. The police will easily break someone like that. A confession would be easy.'

'You sound just like Joe,' she said. "Strike while the iron's hot' and 'don't let the so-and-so get away with it'. That's what he'd have said. But I can't do it. I can't inform the police without hearing what Jacob has to say first. He might have a perfectly logical explanation as to why the boat wasn't returned by the boatyard in the usual way. And why there was no bill. Perhaps I should have a talk to Dave Atkinson when the boatyard opens tomorrow?' She trotted out the excuses. But she knew she was clutching at straws.

She hardly heard Anthony's protests, about the need to notify the police, about the dangers involved in confronting someone who - it seemed - had already murdered once. But she didn't care. All that concerned her at this moment was to discover why? What possible motive could Jacob have had for murdering Joe?

Only Jacob could answer that. And she would give him the chance to explain his version of events before Chief Inspector Leatheringham trampled in and distorted it. But she knew it was unlikely she would extract a confession from the old man.

She needed time to think and, making an excuse about being exhausted after such a traumatic weekend, showed Anthony to his car.

But after he'd driven off, still protesting, she found that rest for her troubled mind evaded her like the mist now gathering over the fells. She wandered down to the lakeside and sat on a hollow tree stump washed up in the storm. The weak, late-afternoon sun gave little warmth.

Why? Why? she asked herself over and over, but the question seemed unanswerable. Such a cold, calculating murder must have a strong motive. Such a mild-mannered man as Jacob must have been pushed to the limit. Had it happened in a moment of madness when he had been out of his mind with grief? But no possible motive suggested itself. Liberty threw pebbles into the water, watching the ripples spread and fade and clinging desperately to the tiny hope that Jacob was innocent.

She spent the evening slumped in front of the television staring blankly at the images flashing across the screen in a desperate bid to dispel the mental picture of Jacob wielding the crow bar which had smashed her husband's skull. Just after eight, Jacob's eldest son rang to inform her of his mother's death. Liberty's stomach churned and for a moment she didn't know what to say. Then, conscious that her voice was unnaturally high and aloof, she said that she already knew and would he pass on her condolences.

When at last she drifted into a fitful sleep, the nightmares were worse than any she'd ever had before. Faceless figures shrouded in flowing black cloaks roamed the room dispensing incense, while Maria Rosa, naked under a fine silk veil, reclined at the foot of the bed. Behind her, nailed to a wooden cross, was Joe, his eyes wide and terrified as if they had witnessed the horrors of hell, his mouth pulled back in a silent scream. His arms, stretched and sinewy, pleaded for mercy. But from whom? Was he asking forgiveness from her? Or from a God who had judged this sinner according to his deeds?

CHAPTER 23

Next morning Liberty awoke with a jolt, thrusting her damp body upright in the darkness, the terrors of the night still vivid. A glance at the luminous figures on the bedside clock showed that it was only twenty minutes past six but she had had enough of sleep and dragged herself out of bed, throwing on her dressing gown and groping her way to the window.

Sometimes the view would inspire her with hope for the day, but now, as she pulled back the heavy curtains, she saw that the soft glow of the sun behind the fells had not reached the lake that, as yet, lay dark and menacing. A brisk breeze blew through the ivy round the window, scattering huge drops of rain from its leaves onto the patio below.

A glance in the mirror confirmed that she had indeed had a rough night. Her fine hair was tangled, its strands knotted and twisted into spirals. But the unmistakable worry lines that had formed across her forehead depressed her the most.

She decided to visit Jacob as soon as she was dressed. He was an early riser and if she delayed he might be out on a job. Even today, the day after his wife's death, he wouldn't take time off, she was almost sure. It wasn't in his nature to let a personal crisis keep him from his work. But, until yesterday, she would never have believed that murder was in his nature either.

The eight am news was just finishing on her car radio as she pulled up in the narrow lane outside the 18th century farm-labourer's cottage where Jacob, and his father before him, had lived their lives. Would it soon be occupied by one of Jacob's sons? she wondered as she climbed the narrow steps which led to the side door.

On the rare occasions she'd called previously, this had been the door she'd used, and she saw no reason now to change her approach. Terracotta pots, bulging with every conceivable bedding-plant, vied for space, but the brown-edged leaves and weary blossoms seemed to be crying out for attention.

The heavily-knotted door was ajar but she decided against going in. Instead she knocked gently and waited, silently rehearsing the story she'd devised. When no-one came, she knocked again more loudly and stepped inside.

'Jacob,' she called. 'Hello. Jacob? Are you there?'

It took a moment for her eyes to adjust to the dimly-lit kitchen but as she did so they focused on the wall facing her. Immediately she recognised the two cases containing huge stuffed fish with lifeless, staring eyes. She remembered that Joe had given them to Jacob only last year but their presence here at this moment unnerved her.

She called out again, glancing round the cluttered kitchen which had seen little change over the past twenty or thirty years. A green-painted dresser was the only concession to brightness, the rest a hotch-potch of discoloured walls and dismal cupboards. She wondered how she could ever have thought of this as cosy.

A noise behind her made her jump and she swivelled round. Framed in the open doorway like a sentry stood Jacob, a spade in his hand.

She gasped, momentarily startled, but not afraid. Nothing about this insignificant, self-effacing man had ever caused her to feel uneasy or threatened. Yet here she was, ready to accuse him of murder. Was she making another of her stupid blunders?

'Mrs Westerman?' He sounded surprised and puzzled, not suspicious as she'd expected. 'I was round at the back seeing to some bushes as was damaged in the storm.'

It was as though, in his plodding, matter-of-fact tone, he were apologising for not being there to greet her. The situation was becoming farcical. They'd be talking about the weather next. She must take control.

She nodded and waited for him to deposit his muddy wellingtons by the door. As he bent down, the pale sunshine streaming through the doorway caught his face and she could see clearly the leathery skin drawn across hollowed cheeks.

'Jacob. I'm so sorry about Ellen.'

He shrugged and padded in thick woolly socks towards the sink. 'She's in God's arms now. Nothing and nobody can harm her any more.' He turned his back towards her as he ran muddy fingers under the tap. 'Would you like a cup of tea?' he asked, reaching for a frayed towel. 'The kettle's not long boiled.'

Was he deliberately trying to be evasive? She couldn't be sure but she suspected he'd guessed the purpose of her visit. When he turned to face her she knew she was right. His eyes shifted from one side of the room to the other but they could no longer meet her own.

'No, thank you, Jacob. But I would like to talk to you.'

He nodded. 'You'd better come through.'

He led the way into a conservatory which had seen better days and now resembled a neglected greenhouse. Shelves piled with plant-pots and assorted bric-a-brac lined one wall and a spindly wooden cart in the far corner held half a dozen huge pots, from which red and pink geraniums fell lifeless over the rims. The air had a stale yet faintly perfumed smell.

Jacob dragged two wicker chairs round a matching table whose surface still bore the signs of the boisterous family which had long flown the nest. He beckoned to her to sit down and she chose the nearest chair, fully expecting him to take the other. But, disconcertingly, he remained standing, gazing out at the modest garden surrounded by sheep-grazed common land. Was this his way of taking control?

'Jacob,' she began, her carefully rehearsed words leaving her. She'd thought of playing him along, asking if he'd seen anyone near the boat on the day Joe was killed. If she pretended to enlist his help there was a chance she could trip him up. But now it all seemed ridiculous. She'd never been any good at telling lies, or playing games with people. Now was too important a time to start. She took a deep breath. 'Jacob, I've found out the truth about Joe's death. I know about the boat.'

She waited, watching the hunched shoulders stiffen, then turn slowly towards her.

His reaction was not the one she'd anticipated. His dark eyes glistened with a sudden rush of tears and he flopped onto a low stool in an almost theatrical gesture of anguish and despair. The words, distorted by gasps and sobs, tumbled out.

'I wanted to tell you. I did. I really did. But Ellen . . . I had to protect her. It would've killed her. Oh, God help me. I don't know what came over me.' He clasped his rough hands tightly as if in prayer and gazed vacantly at them for a moment before continuing: 'I must 'ave been mad . . . even to think about it. I was out of my mind.'

He pulled off his glasses and squeezed the bridge of his nose. Liberty could see the dark circles under sunken eyes which had once been the windows into an untroubled soul. Now they seemed forever dimmed and lifeless.

'What with Ellen being sick . . . An' him goading me like that. He shouldn't 'ave done it.' He paused and his eyes fleetingly met hers.

But Liberty looked away, unable to find the words either to comfort or condemn him.

'It's been tearing me apart, it has.' His voice was calmer now, his breath more even. 'Seeing you suffer an' that . . . and me to blame. Ay, I wanted to tell you but I . . . God forgive me.' His head slumped forward and he hid his face in his hands as the tears began to flow.

Almost in a daze, Liberty watched them dribble through his fingers and soak into his faded pants, making two uneven wet patches.

So her search had ended here, in this tragic house, with this frail and pathetic man. She sighed and shook her head in disbelief. Pity vied with revulsion but she felt not even the briefest satisfaction.

'Why, Jacob? Why did you do it? Just tell me. What made you do such a terrible thing?'

He didn't look up and his voice was muffled.

'I don't know. I've tried to understand. But I just don't know.' He shook his head slowly and rubbed his face on a grubby sleeve. 'I know I shouldn't 'ave taken on so. But I was half out of my mind. And he wouldn't listen. Just kept on and on. He laughed at me, he did. Called me a stupid little man.'

'He . . .?' Liberty gasped. But words failed her. Her fingers gripped the arms of the chair as she fought to control her mounting anger.

As if sensing her sudden hostility, he pushed himself to his feet, shuffling towards a row of seed trays on a work-bench. He had his back to her but she could see he was stroking the seedlings.

'What I did I did,' he continued. 'I'll 'ave to live with that to my dying day.' Then he crossed himself unselfconsciously. 'May God 'ave mercy on my soul.'

But Liberty was incensed. A few platitudes weren't enough to appease her.

She jumped to her feet sending her chair screeching across the floor. The contempt in her voice was unmistakeable. 'You can't mean to tell me that you killed Joe because he laughed at you and called you names.'

Suddenly he twisted round, his eyes wide in amazement and horror. 'Killed Mr Westerman? Me, killed Mr Westerman?' He repeated the words in disbelief, locking his gaze onto hers. 'You thought I killed Mr Westerman?'

Liberty stared at the uncomprehending face. Surely she hadn't got it wrong? 'But I thought you said . . .' What *had* he said? She could recall no confession as such.

'You said you knew what had happened,' he said accusingly. 'I thought you knew I didn't kill him.'

Liberty shook her head, despair and foreboding growing from the pit of her stomach. He waved his arms with a dismissive gesture.

'No. I didn't kill him. I wanted to. By God, I wanted to and I planned it all. Yes, I admit that. I planned it in a fit of madness but I didn't do it.'

His eyes were pleading now and she had no doubt that he was telling the truth. But anger, of an intensity she had never experienced before, gripped her. She lurched towards him wagging a finger.

'So who did kill him? And don't tell me you don't know. Somebody used that boat to get to Lowthwaite House and you know who it was, don't you?'

Jacob shook his head uncertainly. 'I've wished a thousand times I could undo what's done,' he pleaded. 'But it's no use wishing. I'm to blame. I don't deny it. But I didn't kill Mr Westerman.'

She felt like shaking him but instead she clenched her fists. 'Just tell me who did. Who was it, Jacob? Who murdered Joe? And I want the truth.'

He winced and she was left feeling that her insinuation that he might lie to her was almost as hurtful as her accusation of murder.

'As God's my judge I'm telling you the truth. I don't know for sure who killed Mr Westerman. I have no proof.'

'Get on with it, Jacob. The name? Tell me his name.' She moved closer to him now, her finger jabbing in his face.

His voice was low but perfectly audible.

'May God forgive me. I know you have a right to know an' all.'

'The name, Jacob.' She was almost shouting.

He bit his lip. 'Doctor Firth. It must 'ave been Dr Firth. He's the only one who knew.'

The silence seemed to last a lifetime. Liberty gazed, open-mouthed at the trembling figure but her mind was blank. The room seemed suddenly airless and she could hear herself panting.

'But I don't understand . . . Dr Firth couldn't have . . . Not Dr Firth.' It didn't make any sense and she could hear her voice rising.

'You must be wrong. You must be. How could he . . .? Why would Dr Firth want to kill Joe?'

Jacob spoke quietly, a look of desperation in his eyes. 'I don't know. I don't know what was in his mind. But it must 'ave been him.'

Liberty turned away. Had she really the strength to pursue any more suspects? She sank back into the chair feeling the old familiar doubts wash over her and closed her eyes. But if she gave up now all that hard work would be wasted. She pulled herself up and faced the gardener.

'You'd better sit down and tell me everything you know,' she said, in an effort to regain the upper-hand once more.

Keeping his gaze fixed on the floor, Jacob perched on the edge of the other chair and gripped his hands between his knees. After a moment's hesitation he began:

'It was Ellen. She told him. She told Dr Firth about the boat an' that. She'd been bad all day. In a lot of pain she was. I was out of my mind . . .' He squeezed his hands together so tightly she could see the whites of his knuckles.

'Go on,' she urged, reminding herself that Ellen had died in this very house only the day before.

He looked up and fixed her with a defiant glare.

'She'd never so much as hurt a fly. Not Ellen. It wasn't fair. She was dying and he . . . 'An eye for an eye,' that's what the Bible says.'

What was he talking about? Liberty waved her hand impatiently. 'But Joe never did Ellen any harm.'

Jacob shook his head, lifting his eyes slowly to meet hers. 'No. He didn't kill Ellen, thank God. It was poor Miss Cecilia he killed. She brought him up like her own, she did, an' that's the thanks she got.'

Liberty blinked at him in disbelief. Ellen's death must have tipped him over the edge. 'Don't be ridiculous. Joe didn't kill Cecilia. You've got it all wrong.' But then her anger resurfaced. 'And if you think that by making up this cock and bull story you can wriggle out of . . .'

His eyes, 'til then downcast, opened wide and his body seemed to twitch into life. 'No, no,' he interrupted. 'Believe me, it's no story. It's God's truth. Just hear me out. Please, Mrs Westerman.'

'I'll give you five minutes but if I'm not satisfied then I'm going straight to the police.' She wondered whether it had been wise to threaten him but she could see that his drained face held no menace.

'He told me himself, Mrs Westerman. He told me. Told me bold as brass. Said he'd 'finished her off'. Those were his words - 'finished her off. I couldn't believe it either. He could see I was shocked, like, but I think he wanted to upset me, to get back at me. You see, I'd tackled him about his . . . his woman-friend.' He paused, a wariness crossing his face. 'Did you know about her?'

Liberty gave an almost imperceptible nod and he continued.

'I'd seen them, you see. Ay, on my way to a job near Holme End. There they were, large as life, coming out of a house. All cuddling an' kissing. It made my blood boil, I can tell you. To think of 'im deceiving you like that. And 'im a pillar of the church, an' all.'

'But what has this to do with . . .?' Liberty fell silent, trying to shake off the feeling that she was sinking into a quagmire of treachery and hypocrisy.

Jacob too seemed locked in his own world, staring at the hands that twisted between his knees. 'I tackled 'im. Told 'im I knew about his ungodly ways. But he said God had given him opportunities and he couldn't waste them. Said small-minded people like me would never understand. Then he said he was planning something bigger than I could ever dream of.' He looked up at her then. 'It made my blood run cold just listening to 'im bragging. I thought you might be in . . . well, some danger.'

He stood up and pushed open the glass door.

Liberty breathed in the cool air with mounting unease, but decided not to interrupt him.

A moment later he turned and continued: 'It was then he told me about Miss Cecilia. Said she was dying anyway so all he did was 'finish her off'. He made it sound like he'd done 'er a favour.'

'But that doesn't make sense,' Liberty protested. 'Why would he do that? She wasn't suffering. Besides, Joe would never condone mercy killing.'

'No, it wasn't mercy killing. He said Miss Cecilia threatened to cross him out of her will. He said she'd found out about his connection with some Irish group. Something to do with the IRA, he said. He would've lost everything, like. So he killed her.'

He picked up a plastic watering can and began to pour water onto the withered leaves of a variegated ivy plant.

'But why . . .?' The question was only half-formed in Liberty's mind. There were so many why's. 'Why would Joe tell you something like that? If, and it's only an if . . . if it were true, you might have gone to the police.'

Jacob swung round and faced her. 'Oh, no. Mr Westerman was no fool. He knew I'd never do that. How could I? How could I bring scandal on the Church? Him being Fr O'Malley's right hand man an' all. Besides, where was the proof? No, he knew what he was doing all right. He did it deliberate, like. Knowing it would eat at me inside. It was my punishment for criticising him.'

Liberty had heard enough. She'd learned only too well in recent days that Joe had been no saint. But a murderer? She pushed herself out of the chair.

'I'm not listening to this rubbish a minute longer. Surely you don't expect me to believe that my husband was some sort of monster, do you? I think the police will be better equipped to sort out the truth from the lies.'

He dropped the watering can and held out a hand to stop her. 'No. Don't. Please. Don't go to the police. I'm telling you the truth.'

Liberty stopped and eyed him. A tic had started up in the corner of his mouth.

'You still haven't told me why you think Dr Firth is involved,' she said, deciding to test his accusations.

'No, I will. I will. Only in the garden. Not here. I've got to get out of this house.'

She wondered whether it was some sort of trick but in spite of the discoveries of the past twenty-four hours she still couldn't bring herself to believe that Jacob could ever hurt her. He led her round the back of the house into the mature garden where leaves and broken branches littered the scorched lawn. She leaned against a horse-chestnut tree as he picked up a garden fork and began gathering the debris into a pile.

'Ellen could see there was something wrong,' he continued. 'She was good at getting things out of me. Could read me like a book, she could. So I told her. I told her everything. What Mr Westerman had done, like. And how he was plotting something terrible. I said I'd make sure he never hurt anybody else. I thought she'd understand. But it made her ill.' He stopped raking and leant on his fork, gazing vacantly across the fell. 'When Dr Firth came, she begged him to stop me. Course, by that time I'd already taken the boat. Left it in a clump of trees further up the lake. But the doctor said it was all killing Ellen.'

He paused and turned to her with a desperate look, as if pleading for understanding, but all she could do was shake her head in disbelief.

'It brought me to my senses, I can tell you, and I knew I couldn't do it. So I told the doctor I wouldn't, like. He seemed relieved to start with. But then he asked me why I wanted to kill Mr Westerman in the first place.' His mouth jerked uncontrollably as if he were about to break down, but he continued: 'When I told him, he went . . . well, like a mad man. Turned bright red, he did, and his eyes were flashing. I'd never seen 'im like that afore. Then he wanted to know about the boat, like. Ellen had told 'im a bit but he wanted to know more. So I told 'im where it was an' everything. Wasn't any point being secretive.' He bent down and picked up a pile of debris.

For a moment he stared at it then, with a wide sweep of his arms, scattered it across the lawn. When he spoke his voice was low and expressionless. 'I never thought he'd . . . But when I heard, like . . . about . . . I knew straight away it must be the doctor that done it.'

She gazed at him in horror, afraid to acknowledge that his assertions fit the facts. Or most of them.

'The police will have to be informed,' was all she said as, suddenly desperate to be far away from this man who'd caused her so much grief, she pushed herself away from the tree and ran from the garden.

A quiet place to mull over Jacob's words was what she needed now, she realised as she drove towards Lowthwaite. But if she went home there might be distractions. Millie would be there, flitting round with a duster and asking questions. And Bob would be ringing to find out why she wasn't at Westerman and Brock's.

Ten minutes later she slipped off her shoes on the grassy bank where the River Cocker flows out of Bassenthwaite Lake. Swollen by the storm, its relentless, unstoppable flow was at once fearsome and yet energising. For a few intoxicating moments, she sat and dangled her feet in the surprisingly cold water, throwing back her head and breathing in the delicate scent of freshly dried foliage.

At times like this she imagined that no evil could ever befall her. And while she now knew she was deceiving herself, the wonder of nature still held the power to lift her soul.

She tried to still the turmoil of her mind so that she could think clearly. For once in her life she must outsmart someone cleverer than herself. And it wouldn't be easy. She took a deep breath and watched the shadow of a cloud drift over the water giving it a greenish glow. Then, as the shadow moved away, the sun picked out a dragonfly which zigzagged around her, its golden gossamer wings hardly seeming to move. Even at this most difficult moment in her life she couldn't ignore it and gazed in delight, exhilarated and thrilled at being privileged to witness the spectacle.

Not long afterwards she hurried back to the car, having cut a swathe through her tangled emotions to reveal the path she must take. As far as she could see, there was no flaw in Jacob's account. And for all that it seemed fantastic, it had all the hallmarks of the truth. Besides, it was a complex story, too complex, she decided, for a simple workman to have made up. But if Dr Firth really had killed Joe she needed proof. Jacob's word against a well-respected GP just would not do.

Sondra was getting ready for a golf lesson when Liberty arrived at the sprawling bungalow just outside Keswick where she and Derek had lived since before Timothy was born. Her fawn, checked trousers and scarlet jumper gave the fleeting appearance of a competent and energetic professional, but the wilderness of sandy curls dangling round her shoulders made Liberty wonder whether she had only just got out of bed.

'Can you spare me a few minutes?' Liberty asked, following her friend's instructions to come through to the bedroom and make herself comfortable on the four-poster.

'I've got the rest of the day if you want. I don't have to go. Charlie ... that's my new instructor. . . ' She grinned impishly. 'He won't mind if I postpone it 'til tomorrow.' She turned towards the mirror and scooped up handfuls of hair.

'No, don't do that. It won't take long. I just want to bounce a few ideas off you.' Liberty spoke with a casualness that belied the intensity of her impatience to finish the job.

Sondra swivelled round letting the curls fall over her face.

'What's happened? Have you found something out?'

Liberty hesitated before replying. 'I think I know who did it, who killed Joe.' She waited for the reaction that she knew was inevitable and must be endured.

Sondra's arms made small flapping movements rather like a sea-lion and her mouth seemed to open and close in accompaniment.

'Who? Who is it? Tell me. How did you find out? Have the police arrested him? Come on, Lib, tell me. Don't keep me in suspense.'

She made it sound like a game, a silly quiz-show game, but Liberty had too much on her mind to take offence.

'I will. Just give me a chance. But I warn you. You won't believe it.' She paused as Sondra flopped on to the bed beside her, the green eyes wide in anticipation. 'I think it was Dr Firth. In fact I'm pretty certain it was him.'

'Dr Firth?' exploded Sondra, her nose screwed up as if recoiling from an unpleasant smell. 'You're joking, aren't you?'

Liberty shook her head. 'Afraid not. I'm almost sure it was him. But I've got to get proof. And if I'm right . . . this is one man who's not going to pull the wool over my eyes.'

Sondra curled her legs underneath her and leaned back against the pillows. 'The golf lesson can wait,' she said. 'Just tell me all about it.'

Liberty obliged. But, mindful that valuable time was ticking away, she omitted all mention of the weekend's events and confined herself to the relevant details. She could fill in the story of her kidnap later.

Sondra was remarkably self-controlled while she listened, her freshly-scrubbed face betraying a mixture of incredulity and horror.

'So I need your help,' Liberty continued. 'I need to trap him into making a confession. I've got a tape-recorder I can hide in my bag... yes, I know it sounds corny. But I can't think of any other way of getting evidence to convict him. Only trouble is . . . he's no fool. He's not going to confess just because I accuse him. I've got to convince him that I already have the proof. And that it will stand up in a court of law. Any ideas?'

Sondra lay back, her tousled hair draped against the lace-edged pillows and was silent for a moment before replying. 'Yes. There is a way. And it might just work. It's what we do at the drama group when we're scriptwriting and need to show the audience proof that something has happened. We create some written evidence . . . you know, a letter, a receipt, a cheque . . . something like that. Hmm. Just let me think. How could . . . ?'

Her voice trailed off and for a few moments she tapped her elegant forefinger on her lips. Liberty fiddled with her wedding ring, conscious that her stress level was rising along with her optimism.

'I've got it. A letter written by Jacob's wife, addressed to 'Whoever it may concern'.' Sondra waved her arms theatrically. 'It could explain how she told the doctor about her husband's plans. You could say that the note was only found after her death . . . hidden in a book or something.' Sondra paused, looking pleased with herself. 'Yes, that should do it. You could say she'd probably decided not to send it to anyone because it would implicate her husband. But she'd had to write it in case he came under suspicion after her death. The letter would prove his innocence.'

Liberty marvelled at the ingenuity and imagination which she'd always suspected her friend possessed but which rarely surfaced in their day-to-day contact. Sondra was already talking as if the letter actually existed.

Liberty thought for a moment. 'You know, I think it might just work. But will we need to write the letter? Or just tell him that it exists?'

'Oh, write it, definitely. If he asked to see it and you had to come back to write it, he might decide to do a runner. Or, more likely, he'd have time to come up with a plausible story . . . that Ellen was out of her mind with the effects of the pain-killers and didn't know what she was doing. That sort of thing. But if you zap him while he's off-guard, he's more likely to confess. That way, if he decides to retract it later when he's had time to think, you'll have it all on tape. No, we'll have to write it now.'

Sondra jumped up and half ran out of the room, appearing only seconds later with a pen and a pad of lined paper.

'I bought this last week to jot down notes at the golf club AGM. It's probably the sort of paper Ellen would have used. Right, here goes. It's unlikely that Dr Firth ever saw her handwriting, so all we have to do is make it look shaky and use simple language with a few old-fashioned words thrown in.'

Liberty looked on incredulously as her friend scribbled away, discarding the first draft before presenting her with the final piece. It was a credit to Sondra's dramatic talents, containing just the right mix of fact and sentimental comment which, it seemed to Liberty, might have been written by a dying woman.

'That should fool him,' Sondra said, rubbing her hands and smiling with satisfaction. 'But make sure you're convincing. None of your scruples about not telling lies.' Sondra shot her a warning glance. 'You've got to get him so convinced you have enough evidence to send him away for life that he'll sing like a canary.'

Liberty tucked the note into the inside pocket of her open-topped bag. 'Don't worry. I might be a bit ham-fisted but this time I'll make sure I get it right.'

She laughed, but her mood of elation was tempered with a measure of caution. Could she really carry this off? Or would a confrontation with the man who killed Joe prove too much for her?

She patted the tape recorder which she'd popped into her bag before visiting Jacob and wondered momentarily whether she should now enlist the help of the police. But if she did, there was no doubt

Chief Inspector Leatheringham would take over and interview the doctor himself. Without the note or any other evidence, all that he would achieve would be to put Dr Firth on his guard and possibly give him the chance to plan a fresh start somewhere far away.

'But what if I'm wrong? What if Dr Firth didn't kill Joe?' she asked in a flash of doubt.

'Don't even think about it,' answered Sondra looking unusually grim.

She rang the surgery on the gold and ivory telephone in Sondra's bedroom. Her request for an urgent appointment was met with the instruction to come at eleven o'clock, the time morning surgery usually finished.

'Doctor Firth will see you as soon as he can but you may have to wait,' concluded the receptionist.

Liberty left Sondra's house at half past ten and, after a short detour to make a photocopy of the letter at the post office, pulled up outside Dr Firth's surgery thirty minutes later.

She'd left instructions with Sondra to contact Chief Inspector Leatheringham at ten past eleven and explain the situation. That way, she'd calculated, they'd be there to back her up at about twenty past. Hopefully, that would give her enough time to secure a confession. But there were no guarantees.

CHAPTER 24

Liberty's heart sank as she entered the waiting room and saw that seven people, including a toddler and small baby were still waiting to see Dr Firth. She'd been counting on the room being almost empty by now. She sighed and took a seat, realising that she'd probably miscalculated. The police would be on top of her before she'd had time to speak to the doctor.

For twenty minutes she watched the clock on the opposite wall and fidgeted with the strap on her bag, glancing inside now and again to check that the tape-recorder was upright and ready for switching on. After what seemed like a lifetime, the last patient, a teenage girl who'd chewed gum constantly, had disappeared into the consulting room. Two minutes later she emerged clutching a prescription, and Liberty braced herself.

'Liberty Westerman,' called the receptionist from behind a glass grill. 'You can go in now.'

Liberty jumped to her feet and the waiting room swam in front of her eyes as she made her way to the door bearing the simple inscription, Dr J. Firth. Taking a deep breath she reached into her bag, switched on the tape and knocked on the door. The irony of the social nicety was not lost on her.

'Come in,' came the muffled reply and she pushed the door open. James Firth was keying information into the computer on his desk. He smiled as she entered, his gold-capped teeth flashing in the artificial light. Liberty stifled an urge to shudder and poised herself on the nearest chair.

'Now then, what can I do for you, Mrs Westerman?' His voice sounded, as usual, both concerned and curious, and his shiny, unlined face bore no signs of guilt. Balding and bespectacled, he was the personification of respectability.

Liberty cleared her throat, acknowledging her nervousness but aware too that she was not afraid.

'I'll not play games with you,' she began, hearing the shrill note in her voice. 'You and I both know who killed Joe. I've spoken to Jacob Newington and he's confessed his part in it. He's told me that he planned it in detail but couldn't go through with it. I also have the proof here in my handbag that you are the only other living person who knew about this plan and could have carried it out.'

She paused to give him time to protest. But he just stroked the curled edge of his moustache and peered over his steel-rimmed glasses, his jovial smile fixed and unnerving.

She steeled herself and continued: 'I have a letter, written by Ellen Newington. It states that she informed you of her husband's plans. Jacob will testify that he gave you the rest of the information you needed. There's no point denying it. All I want to know is why? Why did you kill my husband?'

When he spoke, his voice seemed deeper than usual, although just as controlled.

'I'm sorry, Mrs Westerman. I don't understand. You seem to be under some sort of misapprehension. Perhaps you could explain precisely what your problem is?'

There was no doubting his coolness but Liberty sensed he was a little too restrained in the face of such serious accusations. She unzipped the inside pocket of her bag and took out the folded piece of paper. The temptation to glance at the tape, to check it was still running, was almost overpowering but she resisted. Even if he didn't make a full confession, there was always a chance he might be careless, confident that, without evidence, whatever he said could be denied later. After all, he would reason, it would be his word against hers.

She held out the photocopy. His hand, firm and strong, more like a navvy's than a professional man's, reached out and gripped it.

'What's this?' he asked, a sharpness breaking through his authoritative voice.

'Read it,' she said with uncharacteristic confidence.

Liberty studied his face intently as he unfolded the paper and began to read. At first his expression didn't change. All she could detect was a slight twitch in his left ear-lobe which, she noted for the first time, was too long for his rather round face. After almost a minute he looked up. The smile had faded.

'Where did you get this?' he asked, an aggressive edge now to his voice.

'Jacob gave it to me,' she lied. 'He found it tucked in Ellen's Bible.'

'You don't believe this fantastic story, surely?' he asked. But his bluff was unconvincing.

'Every word. And so will the police when I show them the original. Jacob is ready to confess his part. I'm sure it will be obvious that he would hardly come forward with such a confession if he were guilty of murder.' She paused, sensing that the doctor was frantically trying to assess the weight of evidence against him. After a moment she continued: 'The police have already been informed and I suggest you make a full confession. It will probably go in your favour if you do. But first I need to know why you did it. What could possibly have been your motive?' Her voice was rising and she checked herself. 'Please, for my own peace of mind. You've torn my family apart. Now I need to hear it from you. Why?'

Beads of perspiration had formed on the top of his dome-like head. He stared hard at the page in his hand.

'I won't deny it,' he began defiantly. 'And I won't make excuses. The man deserved all he got.' He pushed his swivel chair back and walked over to the window.

Liberty pushed down an urge to challenge his statement, her eyes fixed on the back of the portly figure.

He continued: 'In this profession you see so much of death, it becomes commonplace. And, to a certain extent, I play God over my patients' lives every day. But when they're chronically sick or dying it's my duty to ensure they live the remainder of their lives as fully as possible. Do you understand what I'm saying?' He swung round, his face noticeably grey. 'Cecilia Westerman was my patient -the first of my patients to die. She was also the person who did more for me than anyone - even my own mother.' He paused, tore off his glasses and glared at her. 'People laughed at me when I told them I wanted to be a doctor. But not Cecilia. She made it possible. Did you know that?'

Liberty shook her head, wondering what reason Joe had for keeping this particular piece of information from her.

'And I could have repaid her,' he continued, replacing his glasses. 'With the right treatment, she could have lived for another ten years.'

'But didn't you suspect that she hadn't died of natural causes?' Liberty protested, anxious to ascertain all the facts.

'Of course the suddenness of her death caused me more than a little anxiety,' he snapped. 'But I was young and inexperienced. And I *was* treating her for angina. Besides which, the idea that she could be murdered in her own bed was just so preposterous.' He waved a hand dismissively and strode back towards the desk before continuing: 'As it was, I let my patient down and allowed myself to be fooled by that arrogant . . .' His breathing was laboured and his eyes flashed angrily. Then all of a sudden he gave a mirthless smile. 'I suppose there was a certain amount of hurt to my professional pride when I found out,' he added.

'But I still don't understand. Killing Joe makes you no better than *him*.'

The doctor slapped his hand on the desk. 'By God, woman, I didn't plan to murder him in cold blood. I was incensed, outraged when Jacob Newington told me Joe had killed the one person who had provided me with the opportunity to practise medicine. I would have throttled him there and then if I could. And I'd probably have calmed down later, except that the plan was handed me on a plate.' He shrugged indifferently. 'It seemed like fate.'

Liberty was confused. 'But you said you didn't *intend* to murder him.'

'It was only when I was there, with a crow-bar in my hand, that I realised it was madness. But I decided to stay and confront him. To frighten him.' He snarled. 'I should have known he'd be as arrogant and cock-sure of himself as ever. He even had the nerve to gloat over what he called my incompetence at not being able to distinguish between a heart-attack and asphyxiation. Can you believe the gaul of the man?'

'So you killed him.' She tried to keep her voice calm and detached, realising the enormity of his next few words.

'I saw red, I can tell you. Before I realised it I'd struck out.' He sank back into his chair, staring blankly at the wall of books opposite him.

'Then you panicked and ran?' Liberty asked, slotting in the last piece of the jigsaw.

'I knew he was dead.'

For a moment, Liberty couldn't speak as she grappled with a torrent of emotions that threatened to overwhelm her. She felt drained yet somehow determined to savour the moment of her success. Dr Firth remained motionless, his face set and his eyes glazed as if he were in a trance. But what if he suddenly decided to make a run for it? She wouldn't be strong enough to stop him.

'You have your answer, what good it will do you,' he said at last. 'Now, if you're not in need of my professional expertise, I . . .'

She swallowed hard. All she could do was keep him talking until the police arrived. *If* the police arrived, that is.

'I . . .' she began hesitantly. 'I still don't understand how Cecilia helped you to become a doctor.'

He turned slowly towards her and raised an eyebrow, making an odd grimace. 'I thought it would be common knowledge in a close-knit community like this. How the snotty little kid who became a GP was dragged out of the gutter by the woman from the big house.' He gave a short, hollow laugh.

'Cecilia wasn't the sort to broadcast her good deeds,' she objected.

'No, she was worth a million of Joe and his hypocritical posturing,' he said thoughtfully. 'I may not be a believer myself but I know what Christianity is supposed to be about. Which is more than can be said for that . . . that . . .'

He reached out and jabbed at a sequence of keys on his computer keyboard. The screen went dead.

Liberty tried to ignore the little voice in her head that told her Chief Inspector Leatheringham wasn't coming.

'Cecilia took you in for a short time during the war. Joe told me that much,' she began warily.

'Ah!' He gave a throaty laugh. 'He'd enjoy telling you that. But did he tell you how my father died a hero?'

Liberty shook her head. 'I don't think so,' she said lamely.

'No, he wouldn't.' He turned and walked back to the window. 'You know, this view never ceases to amaze me. It's the only thing that keeps me sane sometimes.' Then he twisted his head round. 'Look, I really . . .'

'But you and Joe were never close.'

He stared at her, shaking his head. 'Joe was always a difficult child. Whinging one minute and screaming the next. But Cecilia loved him unconditionally. And how did he repay her? With a pillow over her face.' He rubbed his forehead as if the memory was painful. 'What sort of a person would do a thing like that?'

Only Joe knew the answer to that. Liberty bowed her head and gripped the edge of her chair, struggling to think of something to say. Surely Chief Inspector Leatheringham should be here by now.

'And did you stay close later on, you and Cecilia, when you went to Medical School?' She fixed him with an intense gaze.

He looked as if he were about to turn away again.

'Please,' she pleaded. 'I need to know.'

He nodded and walked back towards the desk. 'She insisted on helping financially. Otherwise there was no way I could have gone.' He shrugged and sank into his chair. 'But more importantly, she instilled in me a sense of my own worth and ability. So you can see why I felt cheated when I was deprived of the opportunity to repay her.' He took a blue-checked handkerchief from his pocket and wiped the sweat from his brow. When he spoke again his voice was slow and measured. 'For thirty years I blamed myself for her death. Thirty years. Then I find out it wasn't my fault at all. Joe must have been laughing his socks off.'

She could think of no more questions and frantically tried to conjure up other ways to detain him. But then, to her relief, she realised he hadn't finished yet.

His eyes were glazed and staring at a point somewhere behind her as he added: 'You know, she was the only person who's ever come close to convincing me there's a benevolent God up there.'

Liberty couldn't resist sneaking a glance at her watch. It was almost twenty to twelve. The police weren't coming, that was clear.

'She was a remarkable woman. Made people feel good about themselves,' she said, suddenly aware of a tremor in her voice. 'But that's what gave her the greatest happiness.'

'Happiness?' His eyes widened and he flashed a warning glance at her.

She shrank back, at that moment glimpsing the intensity of feeling that had driven him to kill Joe and wondering if she'd made one last fatal miscalculation.

'Happiness?' he growled, his voice rising. 'What's happiness, for goodness sake? I can't say I've had much experience of happiness in this god-forsaken world.' He banged a fist on the desk and pushed himself up. 'Now, if you've finished, I've got a few things I need to attend to.'

She had her evidence. If she left now she could alert the police on her mobile phone. Dr. Firth wouldn't escape.

She started to stand up, but he was towering over her now. She gripped the edges of her bag together but too late. He had seen the tape-recorder.

His lips curled in a menacing snarl. 'So that's your little game,' he hissed. 'You had me for a fool there. Just like your murdering husband.'

He made a grab for the bag as Liberty slid between the desk and chair. But he had her cornered, her back up against the bookcase, his body blocking her escape. He thrust out a hand.

'Give it to me,' he demanded.

Liberty's eyes flicked from side to side. Her heart was pounding and her breath was coming in harsh gasps. He was glaring now, inching closer.

'OK,' she said hesitantly, reaching into the bag and pulling out the recorder. Then, in one smooth movement, she flung the bag at his head and kicked out, catching him in the groin with the pointed toe of her shoe.

As he yelped and doubled up, she leaped past him, elbowing him in the face and running for the door. But as she yanked it open, DCI Leatheringham's ungainly frame toppled in.

She gasped and braced herself as, in a kind of parody of some second-rate television drama, he launched himself at the doctor, almost knocking the precious tape-recorder out of her hand. But there was no resistance.

Liberty sagged against the door, allowing herself a few moments of satisfaction as she watched a uniformed sergeant caution the doctor.

'I'm sorry if we alarmed you, Mrs Westerman,' the Chief Inspector said as Doctor Firth, his eyes unfocused and his head held artificially high, was handcuffed and led away. 'Only we thought you might be in some danger.'

'I'm just glad you've accepted that he's guilty,' she said, her voice still trembling.

'There seems little doubt about that. You see, a call came through on the way here . . . an allegation has been made against Doctor Firth.'

'An allegation?' Liberty was confused.

DCI Leatheringham cleared his throat and she knew he was preparing to tell her something she'd rather not hear. 'I believe Jacob Newington worked for you.'

She nodded warily. 'That's right.'

'Then I'm sorry to inform you that the allegation was contained in a note - ostensibly a suicide note - found beside his body. A neighbour discovered him about thirty minutes ago . . . hanging from a tree in his garden.'

Liberty gasped and gripped the door handle. The news was not wholly unexpected if she were honest with herself, but it left her reeling.

It was obvious that he'd been unable to face the scandal - the kind of scandal he'd been so desperate to avoid - which a high-profile court case would bring on his family and the church.

She blamed herself for failing to spot the signs. She should have realised how low he was, that without Ellen to calm his fears and reason with him he would be lost.

But one thought in particular filled her with sadness. That this God-fearing man, who had trusted all his life in the divine mercy of his creator, should commit the ultimate sin of despair. If only she'd offered him some comfort, some hope that one day she might bring herself to forgive him.

But her sense of betrayal had been too deep. And his guilt as keen as if he had wielded the murder weapon himself. She shivered and handed the tape to the detective.

'I think this should explain a lot,' she said, but she felt no sense of achievement, only bitterness and grief.

He took the tape and examined it as Liberty crouched down to retrieve the contents of her bag, tears stinging her eyes. But she instantly checked herself. There was no way this insensitive man was going to witness her distress. Before she straightened up and faced him again, she had blinked the tears away.

'Is it all right if I go now? I'd like to be alone for a while.'

'I may need you to come down to the station later to make a statement,' he said, an uncharacteristic look of concern clouding his unappealing face.

Once outside, Liberty set her gaze on the sunlight playing fitfully on the lake. Beyond, the purple and russet shades of the changing season glowed on the face of Skiddaw. It beckoned her, as it had done so many times before, to revel in its perfect beauty and to take strength from it.

She leaned on the roof of her car and breathed in the invigorating air. If only God were allowed to move in men's hearts as naturally as He did in this landscape.

But this was no time for regrets. This was the beginning of her life after Joe. Thankfully, as Abraham Lincoln - and Sister Monica - had pointed out, the best thing about the future is that it only comes one day at a time.

She jumped in the car, mindful that she still had a mountain of problems to overcome. But first, she would slip into Holy Cross church, light a candle and say a prayer that Jacob's soul would rest in peace. Then she would kneel at the altar and thank God that the burden of bringing Joe's murderer to justice had been lifted from her shoulders.

And afterwards . . . Maybe Anthony might like to join her for dinner at Lowthwaite House.